# SULTAN'S PRIDE

## THE HOUNDS OF ZEUS MC
## BOOK 8

## BY FAITH GIBSON

Copyright © 2024 by Faith Gibson
Published by: Bramblerose Press LLC
Editor: Candice Royer
Proofreader: Kerstin Meier
First edition: April, 2024
Cover design: Jay Aheer, Simply Defined Art
Cover photography: © RLS Model Photography
Cover model: Alfie Gordillo
Back cover photo: Kris Meier – Animal Photography
ISBN: 978-1-7368900-8-0

# DEDICATION

For Nikki.
My Forever friend and sister for life.

# PROLOGUE

THE GUARD PUSHED ON the wall next to where he placed his hand, and a door swung inward. Just inside was a landing with a set of stairs leading down, and beyond that was a long corridor with concrete walls. Tegan was thankful she wasn't claustrophobic. When they reached the end, Victor placed his hand on a visible scanner. Beyond that door was a massive room filled with rows of tables in the middle where women stood filling amber bottles with pills. Stacks of pallets filled the far wall, and men moved between the pallets and the tables. It was eerily quiet save the sounds of scraping pills into bottles and footsteps of the men moving the boxes from the tables to a different area where they taped the boxes, placed labels on them, and added them to their own pallet.

"Over here," Victor said, gesturing to an open spot at the nearest table. "Satu will show you what to do." With that, he turned around and left via the same door they'd entered.

Satu was an older woman with dead eyes. "Thirty pills to a bottle. If the pills aren't perfectly round, they go in the trough." She pointed to a groove in the middle of the table where a few speckled Hive lay. She used a paddle to pull tablets from a pile toward her.

There were markings on the table that counted the pills into two lines of fifteen. Once she had the right amount, she placed a funnel in an empty amber bottle, swept the pills inside, then screwed a lid on. The full bottle went into a box on a stool at her side, filling in the bottom layer. She then added a piece of cardboard to create another layer.

Tegan stepped up to the table next to Satu and picked up the plastic scraper, then pulled a few tablets toward her lines. She examined them to make sure they were all good, then she placed a tiny funnel into a bottle, sliding the pills inside. If her mind wasn't whirling from the thoughts of what the mob boss had threatened, she would have laughed. Tegan wondered what Satu's story was. Had she flushed half a million dollars' worth of drugs down a toilet? Had her boyfriend been a dealer? Was she Bucco's second cousin, twice removed who had begged for a job? Or was she an ex-wife who had looked at another man? Tegan continued working silently, glancing around the room, and making up stories for each of the women, all older than Tegan. Each looking as beaten down as the one next to her.

After about an hour, Victor stepped through a door on the far side of the room and called out, "Table one, break time." The women stopped filling bottles and shuffled single file through that same door. The other women didn't look up. They continued working. After fifteen minutes, table one returned, and Victor called out for table two. Same scenario. Six women filed out for fifteen minutes before returning to work. Tegan had to pee, and by the number of tables times fifteen

2

minutes, she wasn't going to be able to hold it.

When Victor released table three, Tegan yelled, "Mr. Victor? I'm sorry, but I can't hold it any longer." All work stopped, and everyone turned to gape at Tegan.

"Come on then. You can take your break now." Tegan rushed to the far side where he was waiting. There were gasps and a few murmurs of surprise as she passed, but Victor yelled at them to get back to work.

"I'm really sorry," she said when she reached him.

"Don't worry about it. I have three sisters, and none of them can hold it either."

Tegan wanted to ask how a man with three sisters could work for someone who enslaved women, but she kept her mouth shut. He showed her to a large bathroom that looked like something out of a gym with showers on one wall and toilet stalls on the other. The other women using the facilities mostly ignored her. Once she'd finished, he showed her the small breakroom where the others were grabbing snacks and drinking sodas. There weren't any healthy options as far as drinks went, so she grabbed a cup and filled it with water from the tap. When their fifteen minutes were up, Victor escorted them back and called for the next table.

As soon as the door closed behind him, Satu whispered, "You are favored."

Tegan knew it to be true, but the reason wasn't a good one. "And I wish I wasn't."

# CHAPTER ONE

## Tegan

TEGAN GAGGED AS SHE chewed the last bite of burnt toast. Instead of swallowing, she stepped on the garbage can pedal and spit out the blob of bread once the lid was open far enough. She wiped her mouth with the back of one hand while rubbing her belly with the other. Taking breaths through her mouth, the threatening bile retreated. There was little else to eat left in the small house she rented, but she needed sustenance. Just as she reached for the cabinet that housed crackers and other miscellaneous dried foods, someone banged on the door. Tegan wasn't expecting anyone. No one except her neighbor visited. But Brittany knocked, she didn't pound.

Tegan padded barefoot to the front of her small house and threw the door open without asking who it was. It wasn't the first time in her twenty-four years she'd done something stupid. Standing three feet away was an imposing man wearing a scowl, a too-tight T-shirt that looked about five seconds from ripping from his bulging biceps, and a crooked nose. His slicked-back dark hair revealed a high forehead. It was his dead eyes, though, that gave her pause.

"I'm lookin' for Johnny," the man informed her, cracking his knuckles.

Tegan should have been scared. Instead, she was pissed. "That loser's not here."

"His bike is. Johnny, get your thieving ass out here," the thug yelled, pushing past Tegan into the small house she rented.

"I told you he isn't here. He's in jail."

The brute turned on her. "Since when?"

"About two months ago."

"The boss wants his shit."

"What boss and what shit? Johnny doesn't have a job," Tegan asked honestly.

"You don't look that dumb. How can you not know who you're fucking?" he asked as he looked her up and down, stopping on her stomach.

Tegan didn't react by covering her bump. Instead, she notched her chin, her Lion ready to claw this bastard's eyes out. "Yeah, that's me, a dumb woman. But like I said, I don't know what you're talking about. I'll ask Johnny about it the next time he calls."

"You do that," the thug snarled. "And when I come back, if you don't have the goods, let's just say a pretty little thing like you could work it off."

He looked around the sparse living room before leaving without said goods or Tegan. She closed the door on him, cursing the day she'd met John Cashel. Tegan pulled the elastic off her wrist and wrapped her hair in a messy bun, then fanned herself with her T-shirt. The small window air conditioner was already

5

working full time against the July heat. Then again, it could be hormones making her sweat.

"What the fuck have you done, John?" she asked her absent ex-boyfriend. Tegan wasn't the brightest bulb in a pack of sixty watts, but she could deduce by the thug who just left and the term "shit" that he probably referred to drugs. Tegan knew there was nothing unfamiliar in her bedroom, so she went to the spare bedroom where John had stored his meager belongings such as his old six-string and some weights. At first glance the closet was filled with nothing but his clothes, his leather jacket, and four pairs of leather boots. Who the fuck needed that many boots? She pulled out each pair, tossing them behind her. An old blanket was stuffed in the corner, and when she lifted it, Tegan found a duffel. With trembling hands, she unzipped it and just as quickly dropped it. Inside was more money than she'd ever seen in her life as well as dozens of amber bottles. She loosened the cap on one to find green and white tablets.

"You sonofabitch," Tegan hissed. Her fucking ex was a dealer, and he wasn't pushing just any drug. This was Hi-Ve, commonly called Hive, a mixture of meth and coke. Newscasts had been reporting how dangerous the pills were. She plopped down on her ass, staring at the money. Then she counted it. Fifty thousand dollars was spread out before her, and the bastard had been taking her money ever since he moved in.

When Tegan first met John Cashel, a.k.a. Johnny Cash, he was charming. Like the legend whose name he borrowed, Johnny strummed a guitar and fancied himself a singer. Sure, he could carry a tune, but busking at the corner of Conley and Vine didn't a star make. Still, he'd flashed her a smile while singing to her, and like a fool, Tegan hung around until his set was over. Also like the man in black, Johnny had seen the inside of a prison about five years ago, something Tegan found out by accident after he'd charmed her pants off, so when he went back to jail, that hadn't been much of a surprise.

Tegan always had a thing for the bad boy look, and Johnny had that in spades. He rode a motorcycle, was inked from neck to toe, and his attire consisted of ripped jeans and a leather jacket. Within a month of meeting, he convinced Tegan to let him move in with her. Things were good for a while. He doted on her, making her feel like a queen. Little by little, though, the shine wore off as he constantly borrowed money while he looked for steady work, or so he said. He began staying gone more than he was home. Then Tegan ended up pregnant. Even if Johnny had been a good man, she couldn't have hung around. He was human, and as such, couldn't know the truth. She planned on breaking things off and making him move out, but he'd been arrested before she had the chance. She told him they were done over the phone, and he hadn't taken it well, but by the time he got out of jail, she'd be long gone.

Tegan had been planning to leave town ever since she found out she was pregnant, saving money and taking things she and the babies would need to her hideout, but the thug showing up moved up her timetable. Figuring he wasn't likely to wait long on returning, Tegan took the cash and shoved it into a backpack. She then flushed all the pills down the toilet. That took a while. When that was done, she returned the empty bottles to the duffel and hid it in the washing machine under some dirty sheets. Whoever rented the house next would find it, but she hoped they wouldn't figure out what the bottles had been used for since they weren't labeled.

Tegan went to her bedroom and haphazardly tossed clothes into her suitcase, then added her toiletries on top of the clothes. She took the suitcase to the car and put it in the back seat. She didn't have time to worry about packing anything else. She went to the bathroom to pee and had just pulled her shorts down when someone knocked on the front door. Shit. Surely the thug wasn't back already. Tegan stood and pulled her shorts back up and fastened them under her belly while she rushed to her bedroom. Grabbing the backpack, she ran through the house and shoved the bag in the washing machine, making sure it was also covered by the sheets.

The pounding got louder. "Tegan, open the fucking door," Johnny yelled. What the hell? He was supposed to be in jail for several more months. Oh, this was bad. So very fucking bad. Maybe even worse than the thug.

"Hang on!" she yelled back, stopping in her room to grab one of his long-sleeved flannel shirts she wore to work to hide her bump from her co-workers. She finished buttoning it before heading to the door where she flipped the locks, then returned to the bathroom. She really had to pee.

"Where the fuck are you going?" Johnny yelled after her.

"To take a leak, if that's okay with you." Tegan didn't care if it was or not. She just prayed he didn't ask her why she was wearing long sleeves in July.

Johnny followed her and spread his arms against the doorframe. "Are you not happy to see me, Baby?"

Tegan rolled her eyes. "I'm surprised to see you."

"A good surprise, I hope." He bit his bottom lip and gazed at her through hooded eyes. That look had worked once upon a time. It was the reason she was knocked up. It was also the reason she constantly had to pee. The babies were wreaking havoc on her bladder. Not that Johnny knew any of that. He could never know.

"Not really. Some thug came around looking for 'the bosses shit.'" Tegan used air quotes, scowling at him. "What shit is he talking about, Johnny?" Tegan wiped, then stood, and pulled her shorts up. She stepped to the sink to wash her hands when Johnny closed the distance and grabbed her shoulders, turning her toward him.

"Fuck! When was this? What did you tell him?" His normally gorgeous eyes were wild.

"About an hour ago. I told him I'd ask you next time I talked to you, so I'm asking now. What's he talking about?"

Johnny turned loose and ran his hands through his dirty hair. Jail hadn't been good to the man. "Fuck," he repeated. "Where are your keys?"

"Why? You can't take my car, John. I need it for work." *And for getting out of town.* "Take your Harley."

"No. I gotta get the fuck out of here, and they know my bike. Where are your goddamned keys, Tegan?" John didn't wait on her to answer. He rushed through the house to the bedroom where she kept her purse, and Tegan followed. When he found it, he dumped the contents on the bed, grabbing her keys. He then hurried to the spare room and dug around for the duffel.

"What's going on, Johnny?" she asked, already knowing the answer. If she weren't pregnant, she could overpower him if she let her Lion loose, but that would be worse than him knowing she was having his children.

"Where's my fucking bag?"

"What bag? Johnny, what the hell is going on?"

"The duffel bag that was here in this goddamn closet!" Johnny stood and rounded on her. Not once since they met had he lifted a hand to her, but the look on his face was that of a man on the edge. She couldn't let him touch her, or he might hurt the babies.

Someone else knocked on the door. "Tegan? Are you okay? I heard shouting, and I called the cops," Brittany yelled.

"In here with Johnny," Tegan hollered. Johnny took a step back, but his face was mutinous. Instead of hanging around, he rushed out of the house without looking back. Tegan chased after him, but he was already sliding into the driver's seat.

"You son of a bitch!" Tegan yelled as she reached for the door handle, but it was too late. John gunned it, almost running over her toes. Now what was she going to do? With no wheels... Tegan eyed Johnny's motorcycle. It was her only choice. Thankfully, she'd learned to ride when she was younger.

"Tegan, are you okay? I thought he was in jail," Brittany said.

"He was, but somehow got out early." Tegan for once was grateful for her nosy neighbor. She didn't want to think what would have happened if Brittany hadn't interrupted. "Did you really call the cops?"

"Yeah, but you know how they are. If someone isn't dead, they'll take their sweet ass time getting here. You sure you're okay? He didn't hit you or anything, did he?"

"No, he didn't. But I'm thinking I should head out to see my folks and give him time to cool off."

"But he took your car," Brittany stated the obvious.

"I'll call my dad to come get me. No biggie." Tegan wouldn't be calling anyone, especially her parents since they had died a long time ago.

As soon as Tegan assured her neighbor that she'd be fine and the woman left, Tegan returned inside and shoved all her things back in her purse, then changed into jeans that were too snug and her own boots. She didn't have time to worry about the house or to wait on the police. Tegan retrieved the backpack from the washer and slid it over her shoulders. She put her phone in her purse, found the spare bike key, grabbed her helmet, and left through the side door, locking it behind her. Tegan shoved her purse into the saddle bag, bunched her hair under the helmet and strapped it on, then slung her leg over the bike. She shook out her hands, then started the motor. "Please, goddess. Help me remember how to ride."

11

She popped the clutch a couple of times, but she got the bike going and swung a left out of the driveway, heading the opposite direction Johnny had gone. When she planned her getaway, it wasn't on a motorcycle. Johnny was supposed to be in jail another few months, giving her time to get her affairs in order and out of town on her terms. The thug, and now Johnny, had pushed the timeline up.

Tegan's nerves were shot. She thought she had more time to research how to take care of babies. She was only four when her brothers were born, and as such, she wasn't with her mother when she gave birth. Goddess, she missed her family. And she missed Rosie and Marcus. If Tegan weren't different, she would head back to Mining Falls and let her foster parents help her through this ordeal. But Tegan was different, and her parents had drilled the importance of keeping her true nature a secret into her brain. The only thing she knew about birthing babies was what she'd read online, and having to do it on her own was getting to her. What if one of them got sick and needed a doctor? She didn't have insurance. Hell, she barely had any money saved between stocking up for the babies and all the money her boyfriend had borrowed. Until now.

As soon as Tegan figured out that she was pregnant, she began buying the necessities she and her cubs needed, and on her days off, took them a load at a time to a place she used to hide out when she was a kid. She stockpiled non-perishable food for when she couldn't hunt for meat. Her parents had taken them camping in the wilderness often so they could shift and learn about living off the land. With a creek nearby, she wouldn't run out of water, and her body produced the milk her children would need, so she didn't have to buy formula. She had cases of baby wipes and diapers stacked in the corner of the small shack. Tegan made sure the structure was filled with soft blankets and pillows. There was no electricity, so she purchased a propane stove to cook on and heat water for baths as well as battery-powered lanterns. She wasn't looking forward to roughing it, but she would make do until they were old enough to learn to keep their secret. As long as she had privacy to raise her cubs, they would be okay until she figured out a future for them.

The shack was a couple hours away, and after glancing down at the instrument panel, she let out a relieved breath seeing she had enough gas to get there. Tegan stuck to back roads, caught between enjoying the freedom that came with riding a motorcycle and freaking out that she had no cage protecting her or the cubs. Her Lion informed her there were two babies growing in her belly. It also instructed her they would come into the world as humans, not their animal counterparts. She felt bad for her babies, being born to a single mother. She had no one to help her though. Tegan had never met another shifter outside her family, and they were all gone. She might not have a lot to offer, but she did have love, and these babies would be loved like no others.

# CHAPTER TWO

## Tegan

DUSK WAS TEGAN'S FAVORITE time of day. Something about light slowly morphing into dark was magical. The sounds changed too as nocturnal creatures began stirring. In this case, though, it was anything but magical. A deer shot out from the woods in front of her, and Tegan had no choice but to lay the bike down. If she hit the deer, it could send her flying, and she couldn't risk the babies. The bike slid off the pavement into a ditch. It stopped abruptly, and Tegan braced her stomach with one arm while trying to stop her momentum with the other. She landed on her side, her head bouncing off the ground. Fuck, that hurt. Rubbing her stomach, she reached out to her beast.

*The babies?*

*Are shaken but otherwise fine.*

As she gathered her resolve, a strange scent filled her nostrils. It was animal but none she'd ever encountered when her parents took her and her little brothers deep into the woods to shift.

*It's safe. Follow it.*

Tegan trusted her Lion. It had never steered her

wrong. If she had only listened to her beast when it warned her about Johnny, she wouldn't be in her current predicament. Another scent, one more prevalent, was gasoline. She needed to get farther away from the bike. Tegan sat up and scanned her body for injuries. Her hands were scraped and bleeding. Her head throbbed from the impact, and her jeans were torn from sliding across a sharp rock. Her shack was too far away to walk to during the night, so she needed to find some type of shelter.

Climbing to her feet, she removed the helmet and tossed it aside. With the motorcycle out of commission, she didn't need it. After digging her purse out of the saddlebag, Tegan put the strap across her chest, then trudged through the briars and brush, thankful for the flannel shirt. Tegan moved farther away from the road, letting her Lion guide her. It was a slow journey without a clear path, but nearly an hour later, a small cabin came into view.

"Thank you, goddess." Tegan climbed the stairs and knocked on the door. "Hello? Anyone here?" When no one answered, she tried the knob, but it was locked. There was only one window on the front of the cabin, and it was covered on the inside by a thick curtain. If she weren't pregnant, Tegan would shift and begin healing her injuries, but since she was, she had to endure the pain, which was getting worse. Tegan eased her way down the steps and around to the back. There was a small deck, so she climbed the steps and crossed the platform. When she tried the knob, it too was locked. Taking a few steps to the right, Tegan cupped her hands around her eyes and peered through the window. It also had curtains, but these were the sheer kind. Tegan could wait outside on the deck, hoping someone came along, but she needed to get her hands cleaned and bandaged.

Whoever owned the place would have to forgive her for what she was about to do. She studied the door, then the window, deciding the window would be easier to break into. She released her claws and shredded the screen. Then she pulled her purse over her shoulder and shrugged the backpack off so she could remove her shirt and wrap it around her hand. Using her shifter strength, Tegan punched the window, shattering the glass. It sliced her arm, adding to the injuries incurred from wrecking the bike. It took several long minutes, but Tegan removed the remaining shards, dropping them on the deck. She tossed her purse and backpack through the hole, then placed the shirt on the frame and crawled over, thanking the goddess the window hadn't been too high for her to reach.

Once inside, Tegan looked for a light switch, not finding one. Using her Lion's vision, she looked around and noticed several oil lanterns. She would search for matches later. Her priority was getting the blood taken care of. She checked the faucet and thanked the goddess it worked. She cleaned the blood as best she could and grabbed a hand towel that was folded on the counter, pressing it against the wounds to staunch the flow of blood. With her arm against her side, Tegan opened the cabinets until she found a glass and filled it with water, drinking it all down. She refilled the glass, and as she sipped it, Tegan surveyed the interior. One large room housed the living room, kitchen, and dining area. Missing from the kitchen was a refrigerator, which she found odd. In its place was a cabinet used as a pantry. Bright-colored pillows adorned a tan sofa, while a worn quilt rested on the back of a leather recliner. There were two doors other than the one in the kitchen. One of them led to the front porch, and Tegan assumed the other was for the bathroom since there was a ladder leading to a loft bedroom.

"Why couldn't there be a bedroom downstairs?" she asked the empty space. Tegan crossed to the closed door and found the bathroom. She searched the cabinets for a first aid kit or pain relievers, finding neither. Instead, she spotted a single toothbrush, toothpaste, men's deodorant, a razor, and shaving cream. The hand soap was unscented. She opened the shower door and was surprised by the size of the enclosure. A single bar of soap sat on a ledge. There was no shampoo or conditioner. Maybe it was a man's hunting cabin. Since there were no bandages, Tegan grabbed one of the towels from the small closet and took it back to the living area where she used her claws to slice it into strips. She wound the fabric around her hands as well as her forearm.

Tegan sat on the sofa and leaned her head back. The ache was lessening, so she counted that as a win. Cradling her stomach with her cloth-covered hands, she blew out a breath and closed her eyes. What a clusterfuck. She was already nervous about having the babies since she'd never known another shifter who had gone through birth other than her mother. Tegan trusted her beast to help her through the process. Lionesses gave birth in the wild with no help, so shouldn't she be able to do the same? When she thought about shifting and letting nature take its course, her beast let her know it wasn't possible. She was having babies not cubs.

Tegan hated the fact that she was on her own for such a wondrous occasion, but her family had been wiped out in a car wreck when she was fourteen. Tegan had begged to stay home while her parents took her brothers to a movie. Some days, missing them got to be too much, and Tegan wished she had gone with them that day. When the police came to the house, she hadn't understood what was happening. Why they weren't letting her remain in her family's home. She foolishly thought she could stay by herself and go to school until she was old enough to get a job. Even if she'd been old enough, the insurance money her parents had was used to pay for cremation, and the little that was left over went toward the mortgage. Their family home was auctioned after Tegan was allowed to pack a few personal items and sent to a foster home.

Tegan was one of the lucky few who was placed in a loving home with the Thompsons. Her foster mother, Rosie, was patient. Her husband, Marcus, was a gentle giant. It was he who taught Tegan how to ride a motorcycle. The two of them doted on Tegan until they gained her trust. She eventually opened up to her foster parents. Not about her family. Never about them, but about everything else. Rosie taught Tegan to cook. Marcus helped her with homework. They made sure Tegan had everything she needed. If she could be half the mom Rosie was, half the mom her biological mother had been, her cubs would be okay. She just had to get to her shack where all her supplies were. At least she was safe for the time being. She would worry about getting to her place in the woods tomorrow.

Tegan unbuttoned her jeans, giving the babies breathing room, and rested until her stomach rumbled. The toast she had for breakfast was long gone, and she needed to eat. Pushing to her feet, she refastened the jeans, and padded to the kitchen and opened drawers in search of matches. She found them, but she also found a blocky phone in the drawer next to the pantry. Placing it on the counter, Tegan lit several of the lanterns, giving the cabin a soft glow. She then opened cabinets, taking stock of the canned beans and vegetables, about thirty different jars of spices – some she'd never heard of – along with boxes of pasta and jarred sauce. She was lucky Rosie and Marcus had also owned a gas stove, or she wouldn't know how to light the one in front of her. Deciding on spaghetti, Tegan found the pot for the noodles in a lower cabinet and filled it with water. She lit one of the burners and placed the pot over the flame. While waiting on the water to boil, she walked over to the window and picked up her purse to get out her phone. When she tapped the screen, she wasn't surprised to see there was no cell reception. She was deep in the woods after all. Tegan figured the blocky device was a satellite phone, so she felt better about having a way to call for help. Right. Who the hell would she even call?

The heat from the stove added to the stuffiness

from the July weather, so Tegan pushed back the curtains and opened the window at the front of the cabin, creating a small cross breeze with the busted window at the back. She removed her boots and socks, then rolled her jeans up past her calves. She could have taken them off, but if the owner showed up, Tegan didn't want to be caught in her panties.

Her meal of sauce and noodles wasn't gourmet, but it was filling. Tegan rose from the table to take her plate to the sink. Before she could turn on the water, her Lion went on alert.

**Someone's out there.**

*Maybe it's the owner.*

Tegan was searching for a weapon when the back door was kicked in. It wasn't the owner.

"Well, look who we have here," the thug sneered as he pointed a gun her direction.

Tegan raised her hands, praying her claws remained where they were. "John's not here."

"Oh, I know he isn't. He and I had a nice little chat, so I'll ask you one time. What the fuck did you do with the Hive and the money? And why did you have a suitcase in the car? Were you planning to take the money and run? You have no idea who you're dealing with."

"I had a suitcase because I was running from John. H-he didn't know I was pregnant, and I didn't want him anywhere near the baby when he got out of jail. How did you find me?"

"I'm the one asking the questions, Tegan. Where are the pills and the money?"

"The money's over there." She pointed to where

the backpack was still by the window. "But I don't have the drugs."

"Get the bag," the thug demanded, waving the gun its direction. Tegan did as told, and when she got close to the backpack, he said, "Open it." Tegan unzipped it and showed him the cash. "That doesn't look like half a million."

"It's fifty thousand."

"Where are the fucking pills? I won't ask you again." He cocked the gun, and Tegan came really close to peeing herself.

"I-I flushed them," she admitted. "I didn't know what they were."

The thug sneered at her. "You flushed half a million dollars down the shitter?"

"Half a million? But there were only thirty bottles. I'm not very good at math, but that would make each pill worth something like five thousand dollars."

"Did you say thirty bottles?"

"Yeah. That's all I found."

"That lying motherfucker. Regardless, John's not here to pay up, so I guess that means you *do* get to work it off."

"But I'm pregnant," Tegan argued.

"Yes, you are. I'm sure Mr. Bucco will have a use for you anyway." He glanced at her feet. "Get your shoes on. We're going for a walk." He motioned for her to get a move on with the gun, and Tegan didn't have a choice. She couldn't let her Lion out because that would kill her babies. Tegan backed away until she was at the sofa. She sank down and pulled her socks and boots on, rolling her jeans down over them.

"Let's go, Blondie." The man, now holding the backpack, waved the gun again, and Tegan pushed to her feet. She almost turned to get her purse, but eventually, whoever owned the cabin would show up. If they found her purse, they would hopefully tell the cops, and they would know who she was by her driver's license. Not wanting him to notice it, Tegan went to the front door with the thug on her heels.

# CHAPTER THREE

## Sultan

JACKSON'S BELLY WAS FULL of Mexican food that threatened to come back up every time he glanced at Glory holding Tank's son, Patrick, and singing to him. Jax had yet to go visit Ryot and Rhi's new baby, knowing that seeing little Daisy would hurt even worse. It had been fifteen years since he lost the chance to be a father, and it still hit him hard whenever he was around little ones. If he had given in to Crystal's wishes, Coral would be a teenager now. Then again, if he had relented, he wouldn't be sitting with his fellow Hounds because his female wanted him to park his bike and get a "real job" as she called it. Not that she'd known what Jackson did for a living. Nor had she known he was a Gryphon. If he had given in, his heart would have been shredded for a different reason. Being a Hound of Zeus of the biker variety was embedded in his soul.

He was ready to call it a night and get away from the pain. It wasn't long before the others were standing to leave. Ryan "Judge" Jansen, Jackson's best friend, squeezed his shoulder as he followed Jax outside. The group was saying their goodbyes when the alarm to his cabin went off on his phone. He opened the app showing the camera feed, and all he could do was stare in amazement as he watched the trespasser. In all the years the cabin had been in the Lynch family, this was the first time it had been breached. If he had anything to say about it, it would also be the last. Jax called out to whoever was listening that his cabin was being broken into and hustled to his bike.

"I'm going with Sultan," Judge told the group. Sultan didn't tell his best friend not to follow. The intruder didn't look like much, but he didn't know if she was alone. Sultan had a house on Beecher Street close to some of the other Hounds, but his cabin in the woods was his home. His sanctuary. And now it was being intruded upon. No matter the reason, Sultan wasn't going to let her get away with it.

The ride from New Troy to the woods surrounding his home took three hours on a good day, but with it being a holiday weekend, traffic fucking sucked. He explained to Judge as they rode what he'd seen when the alarm sounded. Being shifters, they could hear each other easily, even over the road noise. When they arrived, he and Judge parked in the clearing, and as soon as they shut their motors off, they began undressing. The sun had set several hours earlier, but they had no trouble seeing without it. Past the dense brush, there was a path through the woods, but it was quicker to fly, so after stuffing their clothes into the carrying packs, they shifted to their Eagles and took to the sky. He and Judge landed in the woods behind the cabin and returned to their human forms.

24

Judge sniffed the air. "Someone made supper," he whispered.

The smell of pasta sauce wafted over the air. Jax dressed quickly, and Ryan followed suit. Jackson opened his senses, listening for the female he'd seen on the security feed. There were no sounds of anyone moving inside the cabin, nor were there any heartbeats. Where the fuck was the female? Jax made his way onto the deck and paused as he caught a whiff of something that smelled like animal. When he walked through the kicked-in back door, Ryan followed him inside, and they looked around the small interior. A pot of spaghetti was on the stove. A dirty plate and fork were in the sink. A half-full glass of water sat on the small table. A purse was on the counter next to his satellite phone. Jax rifled through the purse and pulled out a wallet.

He found her driver's license. "Tegan Rowe," he muttered, staring at the photo of the same woman who'd broken out the back window. His Gryphon rumbled, but Jax ignored him. "Where are you, Tegan?"

Ryan looked over Jackson's shoulder. "So this Tegan breaks in, and what? Cooks supper, then just leaves?"

"And she left without her purse."

"How the hell did she find your cabin in the first place? I've been here before and still have to get my bearings when coming through the woods."

"Good question." Jax picked up the satellite phone and called Bishop.

"Hello, Sultan. What can I do for you?"

Jax explained the situation. "I need you to run a check on the female." He relayed the information from her license to Bishop.

Jax stared at Tegan's photo while waiting. Something about the female had his Gryphon itching for a fight.

*Calm the fuck down.*

**You need to find her.**

*What do you think I'm trying to do?*

The sound of keys being tapped came over the phone. "Tegan Chelsea Rowe, twenty-four. The 729 Furman Road address in Coopersville is current." More tapping, then, "Went into the system at age fourteen when her parents and younger brothers were killed in a car wreck. She was then raised by foster parents Marcus and Rosie Thompson in Mining Falls until she was eighteen. Miss Rowe worked at two... no three restaurants as a waitress and rented an apartment close to her foster parents. She now rents the house in Coopersville and works for Onyx Ink. There's another name listed for her address. John William Cashel, age twenty-seven. Originally from New Queens where he did 11/29 for drug possession. Moved to Coopersville in 2046. Was in the local jail for assault. He was..." More typing... "Supposed to be in for six more months but got paroled because of overcrowding. Maybe she was running from him?"

"If she was, then why isn't she here, and where did she go and without her purse?" Ryan asked.

"She was wearing a backpack when she broke in. Maybe it had a different ID in it." Jackson searched the cabin. He didn't find a backpack, but he did find a towel that had been shredded into strips. "She must have cut herself breaking in and used the towel as bandages," he muttered more to himself than the others.

"Yeah, there's a bloody hand towel over here," Ryan added.

"Do you want me to call the police?" Bishop asked.

Jackson hesitated. What if Tegan was running from her... John? That didn't matter. Well, it shouldn't. But for some reason, it did. Why had a photo of this female gotten his Gryphon – and now him – all upside down? "Let us look for a vehicle first. There wasn't one near where Judge and I parked, but there's another road that runs parallel to the property. Sit tight." After disconnecting the call, Jax suggested, "Let's fly so we can search the area, just in case."

He and Ryan stepped outside, removed their clothes, and shifted to their Eagles. It didn't take long to find a downed motorcycle. Jax made sure no other cars were coming and shifted to his human form. He waited for Ryan to do the same, and after they were dressed, they searched the area. "Here's a helmet," Ryan said, pointing to the ground. Using the hem of his tee to pick it up, Jax sniffed it. "Unless Cashel uses floral shampoo, Tegan was wearing this." Under the scent of shampoo was something different. Something not quite Gryphon but close. They scanned the surrounding woods, not finding another helmet.

"If she was riding the bike, that means she wrecked. When I checked the feed before we left, she didn't appear to be injured badly. I want to look at the security feed again." Jackson opened the app on his phone and this time looked at the hours between when Tegan broke in and when he and Ryan arrived. With Ryan looking on, they had some of their answers. Tegan arrived first, then approximately two hours later, a man with a gun showed up, kicking the door in. He and Tegan were in the cabin less than fifteen minutes, where they argued about money and drugs.

*"Well, look who we have here," the thug snarled.*

*Tegan muttered, "John's not here."*

*"Oh, I know he isn't. He and I had a nice little chat, so I'll ask you one time. What the fuck did you do with the Hive and the money? And why did you have a suitcase in the car? Were you planning to take the money and run? You have no idea who you're dealing with."*

*"I had a suitcase because I was running from John. H-he didn't know I was pregnant, and I didn't want him anywhere near the baby when he got out of jail. How did you find me?"*

*"I'm the one asking the questions, Tegan. Where are the pills and the money?"*

*"The money's over there."* There was a brief pause, then she said, *"But I don't have the drugs."*

*"Get the bag,"* the thug demanded. After a few seconds, he said, *"Open it. That doesn't look like half a million."*

*"It's fifty thousand."*

*"Where are the fucking pills? I won't ask you again."* The thug then cocked the gun.

*"I-I flushed them,"* she admitted. *"I didn't know what they were."*

*"You flushed half a million dollars down the shitter."*

*"Half a million? But there were only thirty bottles. I'm not very good at math, but that would make each pill worth*

28

*something like five thousand dollars."*

*"Did you say thirty bottles?"*

*"Yeah. That's all I found."*

*"That lying motherfucker. Regardless, John's not here to pay up, so I guess that means you do get to work it off."*

*"But I'm pregnant,"* Tegan argued.

*"Yes, you are. I'm sure Mr. Bucco will have a use for you anyway. Get your shoes on. We're going for a walk."* A few minutes later, they left via the front door. Jax didn't have cameras inside, but now he wished he did so he could have seen the female instead of only hearing her scared voice.

"Shit, she's pregnant."

"Then why was she riding a bike?" Judge asked.

"She was running for her life, Brother. And from what that fucker said about her getting to work it off, it sounds as though this wasn't their first conversation. Fuck, I need to find her. The man mentioned Bucco, and with that much Hive, I would bet my last dollar he's talking about Phil Bucco."

"Fuck, Sultan. Are you going to call the cops?"

Jax ran a hand over his scalp. "No. I don't trust them to find her before something bad happens. Henderson is an unincorporated community, so the nearest cops would be coming from Oglethorpe, and it's not much bigger. Besides that, my Gryphon is going apeshit."

"Is that because she's pregnant?"

"No. It started when I looked at her driver's license, and when I sniffed her helmet? Game over."

Judge tilted his head. "Does your beast think she could be your mate?"

29

"Yes, but that doesn't make sense. Not from barely scenting her. No, I want to find her because it's the right thing to do." Jax knew he was lying to himself and his best friend. His beast wasn't the only one mesmerized by her photo. It didn't matter that she was pregnant with someone else's kid. More than likely that someone was John Cashel, the man responsible for Tegan being in trouble.

"What do you want to do about the bike?" Judge asked.

"Let's take it back to the cabin. If it belongs to this John fucker, I say we give it to Havyk to fix, then sell it and give Tegan the money."

It was slow going since there was no clear path through the woods. When they made it to the cabin, they leaned the bike against the side of the house. Ryan rubbed his chin. "We'll need your truck or my trailer to haul it. Plus you need a new door and replacement pane for the window. Do you want me to head back home, or would you rather go so you can get the door you want?"

Jax knew better than to say it wasn't Ryan's problem. Their friendship was solid, and there was no way the male would let Jax deal with everything alone. "I'm going to send the video to Bishop and ask him to try and scan the satellites to find whatever vehicle they left in. Then we might as well get a little shuteye. If you don't mind tackling the kitchen, I'll go get a new door and pack a cooler."

"Sounds good. I'm going to sleep out here tonight. My beast is restless, so I'll shift into my Lion and stay by the fire." That sounded nice. Ryan kicked off his boots and undressed. He folded his clothes neatly and placed them inside the cabin so the dew wouldn't get to them. He shifted into his Lion and padded down the steps, stopping a few feet away from the firepit before flopping down on his side. It wasn't often they got to shift into their larger forms. Eagles were easy and something they didn't have to hide from humans. Their Lion and Gryphon forms didn't get to come out nearly as often. It was one reason Jackson loved his cabin in the woods; he could shift freely without worry. They were far enough from the road that anyone trespassing would easily be heard in time for him to shift back.

Jax levered off the ground and went inside to remove his clothes. He hated dirty dishes, but he didn't have the energy to clean up the mess. It had already sat there for hours. A few more wouldn't hurt. His mind went to Tegan and what she could be going through. He didn't trust the local police to find her or to go up against someone like Phil Bucco, so while he got undressed, he made a plan. He wouldn't call Bishop this early, but as soon as the sun was up, he would get the hacker to start searching, and when Jax found her – because he *would* find her – he would make the man who took her pay.

# Chapter Four

## Tegan

TEGAN KNEW THINGS WOULD get worse, but so far, the man had treated her somewhat decently for a mafia don's murderous lackey. If Mr. Bucco was Phil Bucco, he was one of the biggest names on the East Coast and had been in the news on more than one occasion. They were in her car, and even though her hands were wrapped, he made her drive. After half an hour of nothing but the radio for background noise, she asked, "What's your name?"

"Why?"

"Because I'd prefer not to keep calling you thug or lackey in my head."

The man chuckled instead of being offended. "Frederick, or Freddie, if you prefer."

"Thanks, Freddie."

He didn't respond. Nor did he complain about the radio station she listened to. He only spoke to give her directions. When they had to stop for gas, Tegan pulled in at the pump and didn't move to get out. Freddie shoved the gun in a shoulder holster beneath his suit coat, then removed the keys from the ignition. Tegan let out a yawn that cracked her jaw. She couldn't drive much farther without falling asleep at the wheel, so when Freddie got back in, she told him as much.

"My eyes are crossing, and I'd rather not wreck from exhaustion."

"Can you make it half an hour?"

Raising her chin, she challenged, "I can try, but if I wreck, it's on you."

"Fine, swap places." Freddie kept his eye on her as they rounded the car. She wasn't stupid enough to try anything. As soon as she was buckled, Tegan wadded up the long sleeve shirt and used it for a pillow against the door. She was out before they left the parking lot.

The car bumping over something woke Tegan. She sat up, rubbing her eyes as she took in their surroundings. When she considered where a mafia boss might live, she never imagined a tree-lined driveway that went on forever. When the house came into view, Tegan gasped. It was a sprawling, three-story brick monstrosity that would be fitting for a spy movie. Even though it was early morning, the front of the house was lit up with spotlights.

"What is this place?" she muttered.

"Your home for now," Freddie responded. "Let's go." He got out, then opened the back door and removed her suitcase. Thank the goddess for small favors.

As Tegan followed, she clocked four men in suits patrolling the grounds. When they reached the front door, Freddie didn't knock. Neither did he use a key. Instead, he placed his hand on a sensor, and when the light turned green, the door clicked open. Freddie went first, then held the door open for Tegan. When she was inside, he gestured for her to follow. The floor was a patterned gray tile, and the walls were dark wood decorated with paintings of people from another era. A massive chandelier hung over the foyer, and a carpeted staircase split the room, branching off on both sides. Tegan had only ever seen anything like it in movies.

"The kitchen is through that door." Freddie gestured to the right of the staircase. Did that mean she would have the freedom to walk around? He continued up the stairs, and when they reached the first platform, he turned left. On the second level, he strode down the hallway where more paintings lined the walls. Tegan wondered if they were the boss's relatives. At the last door on the left, Freddie motioned for Tegan to precede him. The bedroom held antique furniture, a four-poster bed covered in red and gold linens and pillows, a bench at the foot of the bed in the same gold color, and matching curtains that covered the windows. It wasn't her style, not that she had one, but it was better than the alternative.

Freddie placed her suitcase on the bench. "The bathroom is across the hall. Feel free to use it as no one else is on this wing except you and me. There should be a first aid kit in the cabinet under the sink. Don't go wandering around. I will call on you in a few hours for breakfast, where the boss will speak with you regarding the drugs you flushed. Until then..." Freddie inclined his head before striding out of the room and closing the door behind him. What the ever-loving hell was that? Where was the murderous thug who threatened her earlier, not once but twice? Who made her go first through the woods, keeping the gun trained on her back?

Maybe she was still asleep and this was a weird dream. When one of the babies twisted in her belly, pushing on her bladder, she said, "Nope. Just a fucked-up situation." Tegan tiptoed to the door, opened it, and peeked out. When she didn't see Freddie or anyone else, she eased across the hall. The bathroom was larger than her living room at home. The familiar gold and red theme was present in there as well. Ignoring it, Tegan took care of her bladder. When she felt how soft the toilet paper was, Tegan brushed it against her cheek. It had been a long time since she'd not used the cheap, one-ply brands. After washing her hands, Tegan searched for the first aid kit. Finding it where he said, she unwrapped her hands and the towel around her arm, cleaned the cuts, then covered them with sterile bandages.

Once back in her room, Tegan unzipped her suitcase and removed her few clothes, save the ones she would sleep in, and swapped them over to the tall armoire on the wall opposite the bed. She placed the toiletries on a side table after removing a hair band, wrapping her long waves into a messy knot. After stowing her suitcase in the empty closet, Tegan swapped her dirty clothes for her sweats and a tee, keeping her bra on. She then turned off the overhead light, flipped on a bedside lamp, and slid beneath the covers, leaning against the headboard. She wanted to slide down and sleep, but she didn't trust her host not to come calling.

Tegan opened her senses, listening for any sounds

in the huge house. Someone, she assumed was Freddie, was in the shower. Farther away, a door opened, then closed, and whoever it was strode across the tile floor and up the staircase. Instead of getting closer, the footsteps trailed off across the carpet. Another door opened and closed. The soft water spraying down the hall was soothing, and she fought to keep her eyes open. If either Freddie or the boss entered her room with less than noble intentions, she would use her claws to rip them apart. She couldn't shift fully, but she could call on her fangs and claws without going full-on Lion.

A knock on the door woke Tegan, and it took a few seconds for her to remember where she was. She had a crick in her neck from sleeping sitting up, so she twisted it while pushing the covers back. The door opened, and Freddie entered the room.

"The boss would like you to join him for breakfast."

"Yeah, all right. Let me change." A bone-tired Tegan waited until Freddie was in the hallway to swap her sweats and tee for a pair of shorts and a different T-shirt. The only shoes she'd tossed in the suitcase were slip-on sneakers, so she shoved her feet in them and took a deep breath. When she opened the door, Freddie was standing on the other side of the hallway with his hands clasped in front of him, once again wearing a suit. He walked in front of her instead of letting her lead the way. When they reached the first floor, Freddie turned left and strode to a closed door. He opened it, then gestured for her to enter. Tegan paused just inside the dining room and took in the man sitting at the head of a long table. Like Freddie, he too wore a suit, but that's where their likenesses ended. This man looked up from a tablet and studied her appearance. As best Tegan could tell, he was in his early forties with gray hair at his temples that did nothing to detract from his looks. He bore into her with icy blue eyes. When he finished his assessment, he pointed to the seat next to him.

"Miss Rowe, please join me."

Freddie put his hand on her shoulder to get her moving. She wanted to rip the appendage off, but she needed to behave. At least for the time being, until she knew what the boss man expected of her. She took the seat and placed her hands in her lap, studying the place setting. Who needed so much cutlery for one meal unless they were at a fancy shindig?

"Coffee?" Mr. Bucco offered.

"No, thank you." Tegan reached for the glass of water that had already been poured, and when the goblet touched her lips, she set it back down.

"I assure you the water is safe to drink. If I wanted you dead, Frederick would have killed you at the cabin."

Tegan once again reached for the glass and drank it all down. She jumped when an arm reached past her holding a pitcher of water. Tegan glanced over her shoulder to find an older woman dressed in a black and white uniform with her white hair pulled back in a severe bun. Tegan held the glass out, and once it was full again, she placed it on the table.

The woman touched Tegan's shoulder to get her attention. "Do you have any allergies, Miss Rowe?"

"No, ma'am."

The woman's eyebrows rose briefly, then settled back to normal. She inclined her head before shuffling out of the room.

Mr. Bucco stared at Tegan while sipping his coffee out of a delicate cup. Instead of returning his gaze, she took in the room. Like the rest of the house, the walls were dark wood, which was probably expensive, but Tegan found it depressing. All the windows were covered with heavy curtains as though the man was afraid of sunlight. Maybe he was a vampire. His skin was on the pale side.

The housekeeper, or whatever her title, returned pushing a cart filled with plates and saucers. She served Mr. Bucco first, then she placed a plate filled with scrambled eggs and cream-filled crepes covered with raspberries in front of Tegan. A smaller plate held both sausages and bacon. Tegan noticed Mr. Bucco was given the same meal.

"Thank you, Alice. That'll be all." Alice bowed slightly before leaving them alone. Tegan decided to call the man Phil mentally because Mr. Bucco was ridiculous. Phil chose the innermost fork and waved it at Tegan. "Eat before it gets cold." He cut into his own crepe, so Tegan followed suit after pushing the raspberries off to the side. She loved fruit but not the tangy types.

"Do you not like coffee, or do you not partake because of the baby?" Mr. Bucco – Phil – asked.

"The second one. Caffeine isn't good for them."

"Them, as in more than one?" he asked, his fork suspended in front of his mouth.

"Them, as in I don't know the gender. No insurance, so no doctor," Tegan hedged. She wasn't sure why it mattered if the man knew she was having two babies. The fact that she was pregnant at all should keep her from having to spread her legs for strangers, if that was where he was headed with her recompense.

"With as much money as Johnny was bringing in, why didn't you have insurance? I know private insurance isn't cheap, but he could afford it."

"Because he was a piece of shit who lived off my meager wages, ate my food, drove my car when he didn't want to ride his bike, and basically took advantage of me in every way. I didn't know he sold drugs until yesterday."

Phil narrowed his eyes. "No wonder you aren't more distraught."

Tegan stared right back. "Oh, I'm plenty distraught because he put me in this situation."

"You had to have known that flushing my drugs would come at a price."

"A price for John. I thought I could get out of town and be done with his ass for good."

"You got part of your wish," he said cryptically.

Averting her gaze, she took a bite of the perfectly crispy bacon and hummed at the flavor. It was both sweet and spicy. She then crumbled the rest of it over her eggs before taking a bite of the combo. If she ever met the cook, she would thank them for frying it perfectly. She couldn't stand slimy bacon. Phil allowed her to finish her meal in silence, although she wasn't sure that was a good idea. However he expected her to make up for the lost money would probably make her nauseated more than being pregnant did.

Once she was finished, Phil asked, "Did Onyx know you were running?"

It didn't surprise her Phil knew who her boss was. In all the excitement, Tegan completely forgot to call Onyx. "No, he didn't. I thought I had more time."

Phil placed his elbows on the arms of his chair and steepled his fingers under his chin. "What do you mean?"

Tegan downed her water before responding. "I broke up with John when he went to jail. I didn't tell him I was pregnant because I didn't want him to have anything to do with the child, and I was planning to move out of town and start over somewhere far away from him."

"If what you said about him using you is true, I can't imagine you saved much money for the move."

"No, but I'd saved enough to get started. My rental was a shit hole, my car has almost two hundred thousand miles on it, and" — Tegan tugged on the sleeve of her T-shirt — "I'm not wearing designer clothes. I shop at thrift stores. I eat a lot of beans and rice and ramen noodles. I've learned to be frugal, and the small amount I had saved was enough to get me through until I found another job."

"And fifty thousand stolen dollars would have set you up for a long time. Did you feel guilty at all about taking the money?"

"Nope. I figured John owed me at least that much."

Phil lowered his hands to his lap. "No, he owed *me* that much. Why didn't you take the money and go? Why flush the drugs?"

Tegan toyed with the cloth napkin on her lap. "Because these weren't just any drugs. I've seen the news reports and the death toll of people who take Hive."

"Do you go into houses and pour out folks' liquor or toss out their cigarettes to save them from those addictions that cause more deaths than drugs?" he asked with a smarmy smile.

Tegan imagined slashing through his smile with her claws. "No, because those aren't illegal. One drink or one cigarette isn't going to kill someone."

"Neither is one tablet of Hive, which is no more addictive than nicotine."

"How many pills cause an overdose? I'd say it's many fewer than how many cigarettes cause cancer or how many drinks cause alcohol poisoning."

"That may be true, but it's up to the individual to know how much they can handle. And maybe those who do OD on the drug want to. Maybe it's an easier, less messy way to end their shitty life than a bullet."

Tegan massaged her temples. There was no argument that would make the man realize what he was doing was wrong. "You're absolutely right." Could he hear the sarcasm?

"Excellent. Then you'll have no problem taking John's place in my organization."

# CHAPTER FIVE

## Sultan

WITH THE NEW GLASS in place and the replacement door hung, Jax grabbed a beer and sat on the steps of the deck. When he returned to New Troy for his truck, he filled a cooler with drinks, ice, and sandwiches. The cabin had an icebox in the cellar, but he never bothered with it. While he was gone, Ryan cleaned the kitchen. He offered to hang out with Jackson, but it was the Fourth of July, and Ryan loved the big fireworks display in town, so Jax tried to send him home. His best friend wasn't having it.

"Do you honestly think fucking fireworks are more important to me than supporting you? Fuck you, Sultan. I'm going to chop wood, and you're going to get your head outta your ass." Judge stomped off, picked up the axe, and disappeared into the trees.

Now, alone with his thoughts, Jackson tried to relax. Tried to capture the serenity he usually felt at the cabin, but it was being illusive. Someone kidnapping his ma— Tegan would do that to a place. Maybe he could ask Rhiannon for something to clear out the negativity.

During the three-hour drive back, he called Bishop to discuss next steps in finding Tegan. He also texted Ryot and asked to be passed over for any mercenary jobs in the foreseeable future. He didn't give an explanation, and Ryot didn't ask for one. There were plenty of Hounds to take his place. As for his position as sergeant-at-arms in the MC, someone would step into that roll in his absence. Thinking about Tegan, he wondered where she learned to ride a motorcycle. It bothered him that she was on one while pregnant.

Her being pregnant with another man's baby didn't bother him. Yes, he was getting way ahead of the program in thinking about raising someone else's child, but he felt it to his soul Tegan would be important to him. He pulled up the photo of her driver's license, enlarged the thumbnail size picture of her face, then saved it. The female had wild, wavy blonde hair and amber eyes. He'd never seen a human with eyes that color, and it solidified the notion she was some type of shifter. Other than Gryphons, he personally knew of Gargoyles and wolves, so it wasn't out of the realm of possibilities for her to be something different. He had shared that bit of information with Bishop hoping that every clue about the female would lead them closer to her.

Henderson, where the cabin was located, was closer to Coopersville, so Jax decided to hang out there instead of driving back to New Troy just in case Bishop got a hint she had been taken back to her hometown. He doubted that was the case. Coopersville, one of the small cities that opted out of renaming itself with "New" after the apocalypse, wouldn't be where a major mob boss like Phil Bucco set up shop. Jax wasn't knowledgeable of all the big players, but the two on the East Coast he was aware of were Phil Bucco and Yesu Chen, and both were bad news. Knowing the thug who broke into the cabin was taking Tegan to Bucco didn't bode well for the female, and that had Jax and his beast itching to hit the road. Until he knew which direction to head, he had no choice but to sit on his ass and wait.

Normally when he stayed at the cabin, Jax hunted for his meals, cooking whatever animal he killed over the firepit, but he didn't want to shift and take a chance at missing a call from Bishop. The male was skilled with hacking, but Lucy was better. War's daughter was still in New Atlanta working on some formula that used Gargoyle DNA to prolong human life. Jax wasn't supposed to know about the serum, but he'd overheard a phone call between Lucy and Rory one day when he went to visit his pseudo parents. If Bishop didn't get a lead on where Freddie had taken Tegan, Jax would call Lucy and request her assistance, or that of the Gargoyle computer specialists she spent time with in New Atlanta.

When his satellite phone rang, Jax snatched it up and answered before it could ring twice. "Sultan here."

"Hey, Brother. Sorry it took so long getting back to you. I was able to catch Tegan's car on CCTV heading southeast. I lost it once they got on 87 North. Bucco must have his own hacker, because his shit is locked down tight, but I finally managed to get through their firewalls. I was able to locate a couple of properties where I think he holes up. Both are near Lake Champlain, with one of them in New York and the other in Vermont. I'm working on satellite imagery for both locations, but either one is going to be hell getting into. Someone like Bucco will have heavy security."

Jax ran his free hand over his scalp, exhaling harshly. Havyk and crew had gone up against a drug lord in South Texas, but as far as Jax knew, they'd never encountered the mob in their mercenary gigs. This wasn't something he could do on his own, so he needed to call in reinforcements. "I know this is a holiday, but I would appreciate it if you would keep at it."

"A female's life is on the line. I won't stop until we have her back."

"Thanks, Bishop. In the meantime, I'm going to call Ryot and ask for help. Once I have a crew, we'll head east, and hopefully by then you'll have a bead on which location we should target."

"I'm on it."

Jax disconnected, then dialed his president's number. It took a few rings before Ryot picked up.

"Hello?" Ryot answered. The satellite phone showed up on the other end as unknown caller.

"Ryot, it's Sultan."

"Hey, Brother. Is everything okay? It's been ages since you asked for time off."

Jackson told Ryker everything that happened at the cabin and his most recent conversation with Bishop. "I need a crew to help find Tegan. The guy took Tegan to someone named Bucco, and there's only one man with that name I know of who deals in that much Hive."

Ryot whistled. "You want to go up against the mob to rescue a female you don't know?"

"Yes, I do. War went after Kerrigan, and he didn't know her. I'd rather not do this on my own, but I will if I must. Judge is here with me, but I'd still prefer to have numbers. Tegan's pregnant, Ryot. And even if she weren't, there's no way my conscience would let this go."

"Havyk would be good since he took down Alvarez."

Jax shook his head even though Ryot couldn't see him. "No. Nobody with kids or mates. I'm not saying some of us won't make it out of this alive, but this is the mob we're talking about. They're going to be heavily armed."

"Do you have a plan?"

"No. Until Bishop figures out where they've taken Tegan, I won't know what we're dealing with. Once he pinpoints the location, we'll do recon and go from there."

"I don't like this, Sultan, but I get it. Do you think six of you will be enough? I can send the four horsemen. None of them are on jobs right now. Let me make a few calls, and I'll send them your way. I'll need the coordinates to the cabin since I've only been there once, and we flew most of the way in."

Jackson hated that so many would know where his place was, but fuck it. It no longer felt like a sanctuary, and Tegan's life was on the line. "I'll text you the coordinates since there isn't an address. It'll take a few minutes to walk out of the woods to get a cell signal. Give whoever you have coming this number. It's my satellite phone. Also, tell them to pack a cooler of drinks and ice. We can hunt for food, but if you recall, I don't have a refrigerator."

"I remember it was primitive."

Jax smiled for the first time in days. "It's not that bad. I do have running water and a bathroom. There's a propane tank that fuels the stove and water heater." He didn't add that he also had battery-powered, solar security cameras. It wasn't that primitive.

"I'm teasing." Ryot let out a sigh. "I don't have to tell you to be safe, Sultan. I'm not looking to replace my sergeant-at-arms anytime soon."

"I'll be as safe as I can. Thank you, Ryot."

"No thanks needed. This is what we do. I want to call Pop, but I'll talk to you soon." With that, Ryot disconnected. If he was calling Sutton... Ryot's dad was a former policeman who had been around a couple of centuries, so maybe he'd dealt with the mob before. Anything that would help Jax find Tegan and bring her home safely was welcome.

Jackson stood and headed toward the clearing where his truck was parked. Cell reception was spotty along the way, but once he reached his vehicle, he had enough bars to send his coordinates to Ryot. When he got back to the cabin, Ryan was coming out of the trees carrying an armful of wood.

"Want some help?" he asked, and Ryan arched a brow. Jax held out his hands. "I'm sorry about before. I wasn't thinking. Well, I was, but not clearly."

"I get it, Brother, but you have to know going up against someone like Bucco is going to be a pain in the ass, not to mention dangerous. If our roles were reversed, would you leave me alone to tackle a mobster without backup? No, you wouldn't."

47

"You're right. I called Ryot and asked for more help. I told him I didn't want anyone with a mate or kids because of how dangerous this will be."

"Let me guess; he's sending the four horsemen?"

Jax grinned. "Yes. We know they're all single, plus none of them are out on assignments." Maximus, Storm, Shadow, and Legend, a.k.a. the four horsemen of the apocalypse, were some of the oldest, yet best Hounds Jackson knew. They were also the most violent when it came to mercenary work. The four of them came to New York via California right before the apocalypse caused by The Ministry some thirty years ago, and now they lived together in a huge house out in the middle of nowhere. There were rumors the males were in a poly relationship, but Jax had never noticed any of them being affectionate. Maybe they kept their personal lives private. No one knew how old they were, only that they were around when the United States gained ownership of California, and that was two hundred years ago. Individually, they were tough as nails, but put them together? They were a force unlike any other, and Jax was grateful to have them backing his play. He couldn't give two shits less about their sexual proclivities. They were honorable, and that's all that mattered to him.

"We might get out of this alive after all," Ryan muttered, and Jackson had to agree. "I've got the wood, but why don't you head out to get some groceries and more ice? We don't know how long we'll be here, plus..." Ryan looked around as though someone might be listening.

"Plus, Max is a food snob?" Jax finished.

"Oh, Zeus, is he! Never again will I go to a restaurant with him. Never. Again."

Jax laughed remembering Ryan telling him how Maximus went into the kitchen of a fancy restaurant to give the chef pointers on his Beef Bourguignon, saying he used the wrong wine. The chef, who also owned the restaurant, kicked him out of not only the kitchen but the restaurant as well.

"Let's hope he's not as picky about campfire potatoes and rabbit," Jax joked.

"Yeah, no. Maybe add steaks to the grocery list."

Jax chuckled as he held out the satellite phone. "I'll leave this with you. If Bishop calls, have him reach me on my cell."

"You got it."

## *Tegan*

NEEDING TIME TO THINK, Tegan tossed the napkin on the table and asked, "May I be excused?"

"We haven't finished our conversation," Phil stated.

She pointed to her stomach. "Yes, well, little Shania isn't up on societal etiquette, and I need to use the bathroom."

He leaned forward, his eyes narrowed. "I thought

you didn't know the gender."

"I don't, but I'm trying out different names instead of calling them him or her," Tegan lied. Her Lion had assured her both babies were male.

Phil leaned back and lifted his coffee, which had to be cold. "Very well, but you are to come straight back. We have much to discuss. Frederick, escort Miss Rowe to the restroom."

Tegan pushed her chair away from the table, and when she turned, Freddie was waiting for her only a few feet away. She smiled at the killer, and he did his best to remain stoic in front of the boss, but one side of his lip rose minutely. Tegan would take the win. Freddie directed her to a small powder room on the first floor, and as Tegan relieved her bladder, she chewed on her bottom lip while pulling off a small amount of toilet paper. Tegan contemplated her dilemma. She couldn't overpower either man without shifting, and she couldn't shift without harming the babies. Nor could she get past the guards outside, so she didn't see an option other than playing along for the moment. She had no idea how long it would take the owner of the cabin to find her purse.

Tegan knew nothing about selling drugs, but if John could do it, Tegan felt she could as well, if that's what it took to stay alive. Then again, would they let her out into the world alone where she could go directly to the cops? She doubted it. Her only choice was to return to the dining room and hear Phil out. After washing her hands, she pushed open the door to find Freddie tapping away on his phone with one meaty thumb. He finished his text, then put the phone into an inner coat pocket. His tie was a little crooked, so Tegan walked up to him and fixed it. She patted his hard chest, and said, "There you go," before strolling back to the dining room, leaving him stunned.

The plates had been cleared from the table, and Alice lingered close to Tegan's chair. Phil sighed. "Miss Rowe, would you like a cup of tea? I've been informed we have several varieties that do not contain caffeine."

Tegan turned to Alice, smiling. "That would be lovely. A mint flavor or chamomile, if you have it. Just nothing with berries. I'm not a fan."

"I do have a nice peppermint. I will return promptly." Alice bowed slightly before walking away.

Tegan sat and propped her elbow on the arm of the chair, setting her chin on her fist as she gave Phil her attention. "Thank you for your patience, Mr. Bucco. Being pregnant is not without its challenges. Do you have children?"

Before he could answer, Alice was back with a tray. On it was another one of those thin cups with a tea bag in it, a silver pot of water, a few slices of lemon, and a bowl that looked like it contained honey. "There's milk on the table," Alice said after setting the tray down.

"Thank you, Alice. For future reference so you aren't wasting time nor resources, I take it plain."

"Very well." Alice poured the water over the bag, then set the cup in front of Tegan. She then took the tray and excused herself. Tegan only knew the proper way to drink hot tea because her mother hated coffee and drank a cup of herbal tea every morning. Tegan glanced around for a clock. Not seeing one, she began counting in her head.

51

"What are you doing?" Phil asked.

"Waiting for the tea to steep."

"But you're bobbing your head," he groused.

"I apologize. I don't have a clock to watch, so I was counting the seconds in my head."

Phil didn't seem amused, so Tegan made sure to keep her head still. "And how long must you wait?" he asked.

"Three minutes and thirty seconds. That makes for a robust flavor, plus the longer it's steeped, the more antioxidants are released. I take it you don't drink tea?"

"Not without ice and a lot of sugar."

"Hmm." Tegan didn't know anyone who drank sweet tea that wasn't from the South, and his accent was northern. Where in the north, she couldn't pinpoint. Needing something to do with her hands, she removed the bag from the cup and placed it on the saucer. Lifting the cup to her mouth, she blew across the top of the liquid before taking a sip. She'd not let it steep long enough, but she was getting antsy, and that never boded well for her.

"Going forward, Alice will bring your tea already steeped. Now, back to our arrangement. I cannot allow you out into the world to take John's place selling the product, so I've come up with an alternative. You will work packaging the pills for the time being."

"I appreciate that. I'll be the best packager you've ever seen." Tegan did her best to keep the snark out of her tone.

"No time like the present. Victor?"

"Yes, Mr. Bucco?"

"Please escort Miss Rowe to the warehouse."

52

Victor, who Tegan hadn't noticed until that moment, sidled up to her chair. "Let's go, Miss Rowe."

Tegan downed the rest of her tea and set the cup gently on the saucer. "Please thank Alice for me," she said, smiling at Phil. She waved at Freddie as she followed the new man from the room.

Before the door closed, Phil asked Freddie, *"Is she really that stupid?"*

Using her shifter hearing, Tegan listened as she got farther away. *"Probably. She did let herself get knocked up by the likes of John Cashel."*

*"She will continue to sleep upstairs instead of bunking with the others, and she'll have breakfast with me every morning. I want to ensure both she and the baby are healthy."*

*"To what end?"* Freddie asked. *"Packaging product doesn't take much brainpower or strength."*

*"Nor does it pay off half a million of missing Hive. Do you know what is worth that much? A healthy, white baby on the black market. Then, once Tegan has recovered, I'll sell her too."*

# CHAPTER SIX

## Tegan

TEGAN STUMBLED, BUT VICTOR grabbed her arm before she could faceplant on the hard tile. "Careful, Blondie. Wouldn't want you to mar that pretty face."

"Thanks," she muttered, choking back a sob. Bucco was going to sell her baby? And her? He was right; she was stupid. Stupid to think she could smile and be amenable and he would somehow go easy on her. Victor stepped up to the wall immediately past the staircase, pressed his hand to the wood paneling, and an outline of his hand turned green. He pushed on the wall next to where he placed his hand, and a door swung inward. Just inside was a landing with a set of stairs leading down, and beyond that was a long corridor with concrete walls. Tegan was thankful she wasn't claustrophobic. When they reached the end, Victor placed his hand on a visible scanner. Beyond that door was a massive room filled with rows of tables in the middle where women stood filling amber bottles with pills. Stacks of pallets filled the far wall, and men moved between the pallets and the tables. It was eerily quiet save the sounds of scraping pills into bottles and footsteps of the men moving the boxes from the tables to a different area where they taped the boxes, placed labels on them, and added them to their own pallet.

"Over here," Victor said, gesturing to an open spot at the nearest table. "Satu will show you what to do." With that, he turned around and left via the same door they'd entered.

Satu was an older woman with dead eyes. "Thirty pills to a bottle. If the pills aren't perfectly round, they go in the trough." She pointed to a groove in the middle of the table where a few speckled Hive lay. She used a paddle to pull tablets from a pile toward her. There were markings on the table that counted the pills into two lines of fifteen. Once she had the right amount, she placed a funnel in an empty amber bottle, swept the pills inside, then screwed a lid on. The full bottle went into a box on a stool at her side, filling in the bottom layer. She then added a piece of cardboard to create another layer.

Tegan stepped up to the table next to Satu and picked up the plastic scraper, then pulled a few tablets toward her lines. She examined them to make sure they were all good, then she placed a tiny funnel into a bottle, sliding the pills inside. If her mind wasn't whirling from the thoughts of Bucco selling her babies, she would have laughed. Just yesterday, she was flushing these same pills down her toilet, and now she was packaging them to be sold. Tegan wondered what Satu's story was. Had she too flushed half a million dollars' worth of drugs? Had her boyfriend been a dealer? Was she Bucco's second cousin, twice removed who had begged for a job? Or was she an ex-wife who had looked at another man? Tegan continued working silently, glancing around the room, and making up stories for each of the women, all older than Tegan. Each looking as beaten down as the one next to her.

After about an hour, Victor stepped through a door on the far side of the room and called out, "Table one, break time." The women stopped filling bottles and shuffled single file through that same door. The other women didn't look up. They continued working. After fifteen minutes, table one returned, and Victor called out for table two. Same scenario. Six women filed out for fifteen minutes before returning to work. Tegan had to pee, and by the number of tables times fifteen minutes, she wasn't going to be able to hold it.

When Victor released table three, Tegan yelled, "Mr. Victor? I'm sorry, but I can't hold it any longer." All work stopped, and everyone turned to gape at Tegan.

"Come on then. You can take your break now." Tegan rushed to the far side where he was waiting. There were gasps and a few murmurs of surprise as she passed, but Victor yelled at them to get back to work.

"I'm really sorry," she said when she reached him. "As I told Mr. Bucco, the baby makes it rough on my bladder."

"Don't worry about it. I have three sisters, and none of them could hold it either when they were pregnant."

Tegan wanted to ask how a man with three sisters could work for someone who enslaved women, but she kept her mouth shut. He showed her to a large bathroom that looked like something out of a gym with showers on one wall and toilet stalls on the other. The other women using the facilities mostly ignored her. Once she'd finished, he showed her the small breakroom where the others were grabbing snacks and drinking sodas. There weren't any healthy options as far as drinks went, so she grabbed a cup and filled it with water from the tap. When their fifteen minutes were up, Victor escorted them back and called for the next table.

As soon as the door closed behind him, Satu whispered, "You are favored."

Tegan knew it to be true, but the reason wasn't a good one. "And I wish I wasn't," she whispered back. "Satu, is anyone here of their own free will?"

The women on the other side of the table glared at Tegan, and Satu shook her head. "No, but at least all we have to do is this." She pointed at the pills. "Others, not so lucky."

"And the men?"

"They come and go. Work their way up in the organization. Now quiet. We are getting looks."

Tegan put her head down and returned to filling bottles. They got a twenty-minute lunch break where they were fed sandwiches and chips, then another fifteen-minute break. She was wrong in assuming they would stop for the day around dinner time. A small buffet was set up in the break room, and Tegan fell on it like she was starving. The spaghetti wasn't much better than what she'd fixed the night before. Saying the greens were a salad was generous considering it was nothing more than iceberg lettuce with a few scraps of shredded carrots on top. The bread was plain white loaf bread. Tegan internally scoffed at the meager meal. A man like Bucco could afford to feed his workers better, but he was a criminal who sold drugs, women, and babies. She finished eating, then went to pee again before standing in line, waiting to return to the warehouse. It wasn't until eight that night when Victor opened the door and more women filed into the room as those around the tables placed their scrapers down and headed to the door. Tegan made to follow Satu, but Victor stopped her.

"You will come with me." Tegan followed him to the door she'd come through that morning that led back into the house.

"Where are the others going?" she asked once they were in the long concrete hallway.

"They sleep in the bunks. Twelve hours on, twelve off. Mr. Bucco wants you to be more comfortable since you are with child."

If he wanted her to truly be comfortable, he wouldn't have her standing on her feet that long, but she didn't say that aloud. She felt guilty because all the other women were older, and they were sleeping on bunks. When Victor opened the door into the house, Freddie was waiting. Victor didn't follow them. Instead, he returned to what Tegan thought of as the workroom. Freddie escorted Tegan to the same bedroom she slept in the night before.

He opened her door, but paused before letting her in. "How was your first day?"

"Long," she admitted. "If I'm going to stand on my feet for twelve hours, I need better shoes. My back is killing me."

"What size do you wear?"

"Nine."

"I'll see what I can do," he offered, moving out of the way. "I'll escort you to breakfast in the morning."

"Hey, Freddie?"

"Yes?"

"How did you find me at the cabin?"

Freddie stopped in the doorway. "I put a tracker on John's Harley. Goodnight, Tegan."

Tegan muttered, "Night," then closed the door and leaned against it. She needed a shower in the worst way, so she grabbed her toiletries and headed across the hall. She was too tired to wash her hair, so she bathed off the funk of the day, then after drying off, put on her sleep clothes and brushed her teeth. Staring in the mirror, Tegan wondered how her life had turned to shit so quickly. She wasn't a bad person. She hadn't been a bad kid. She'd been a good big sister to Thomas and Terrance. She'd behaved when she lived with Marcus and Rosie. Sure, she made a mistake in trusting John, but was that really her fault? And now she was paying for his sins. Tegan returned to her room, closed the door, and flipped off the light. She slid beneath the covers and tried to sleep, but it eluded her. After tossing and turning for hours, she turned on the lamp and climbed to her feet. Walking to the window, Tegan pushed aside the heavy drape, staring out into the darkness.

*Something is out there.*

Flashing her eyes, so she could see better, Tegan noticed a large eagle sitting in a tree. It looked as though it was staring back. Tegan placed her palm to the glass and prayed to her goddess. *Please get me out of this. My babies don't deserve to be sold. I don't deserve it either. Please have mercy.* With a sigh, she let the curtain fall closed. Tegan turned out the lamp and crawled under the covers again. She was out in seconds.

## *Sultan*

JAX WAS UNLOADING THE groceries when Maximus, the de facto leader of the four horsemen, called and said they were bringing Trenton Shepherd with them. Trenton's daughter, Quinn, a dire wolf shifter, was their mercenary work handler and Kayos Lazlo's mate. Trenton was a regular wolf shifter as well as one of Sutton's oldest friends, having met when they both served in the army. After they retired, Trenton tried to get Sutton to work with him in the mercenary business, but the elder Lazlo preferred to go after The Ministry. Once they took down the cult in the States, who knew what Sutton would get up to?

When the quintet arrived a few minutes before seven, the former soldier came bearing gifts in the form of weapons, including long-range rifles fitted with suppressors, hand grenades, flash bangs, and more ammo than Jax had ever seen. He also brought Jax and

Ryan dark clothing suited for a rescue mission. The inside of the cabin looked like a small armory. All the mercs had started carrying handguns on their jobs, but they weren't familiar with what Trenton had brought, so the wolf spent an hour going over each weapon and how to use it safely.

Trenton then passed out small comm devices. "I know we're all shifters with excellent hearing, but these will allow us to communicate quietly at longer distances should the need arise."

"Where did you get all this stuff, or do I even want to know?" Ryan asked, testing the fit of his comm.

"After we rescued Quinn from her mother's pack, I began stockpiling weapons in case we needed them in the future. I still have a contact from my old army days, and he hooked me up," Trenton explained.

Ryan removed the comm and returned it to the black box it came in. "No questions asked?"

"No, but I did tell him I was helping on rescue missions, and that was all he needed to know. Sikes runs off-the-book ops much like the one we're undertaking. He's good people."

Jax timed it so that the steaks were ready to go on the grate when the others arrived. Ryan had found the perfect downed tree, which he cut into two-foot sections, giving everyone something to sit on as they chowed down on steaks and fire-roasted potatoes. As they ate, Jax filled them in on everything he knew so far. As they were finishing their meal, Bishop finally called. Knowing time was of the essence, the hacker had asked the New Atlanta Gargoyles for help since he couldn't get a positive lock on Bucco. The Goyles had more resources, and with their help, Bishop was able to pinpoint the mobster's whereabouts. He was holed up in a former vineyard this side of Lake Champlain, three hours east of the cabin. Not only had Bucco bought the defunct business, he'd also purchased all the houses in a twenty-mile radius, most of which sat empty. Bishop sent specs of the house and outbuildings. Since there was no reception at the cabin, Jax ran toward the road long enough for the images to download, and when he returned, they discussed the best course of action for getting Tegan safely out of the house, which resembled a Tuscan manor. *If* she was being kept in the house.

With a location, they packed the weapons, Jax locked up the cabin, and the seven men trudged through the woods where they climbed into two large SUVs and headed out. Jax hated leaving his truck behind, but the vehicles had been coated with a new bullet-resistant polymer. The four horsemen rode together, while Jax, Ryan, and Trenton took the other vehicle. It was after midnight when they arrived in the small town, and they opted to scope out one of the empty houses first. The area between the houses and the vineyard was mostly wooded, which helped them immensely. Being able to shift into their Eagles allowed them to do a flyover and determine the guard situation at the manor.

The house they chose was farthest away from the vineyard. Using their shifter senses, they didn't detect anyone inside, so Sean "Shadow" Tapley picked the lock and eased open the back door. He, Legend, and Jax checked the interior while the others stood guard outside. The clock on the stove shone through the dark, which told them the power hadn't been turned off. Jackson pointed up, and the other two Hounds nodded and went different directions downstairs. Jax eased his way up the carpeted stairs to clear each room. The first room to the right was a nursery with three cribs. There was a changing table, and the dusty shelf below it contained a stack of diapers. A tub of baby wipes sat next to the stack. Jax opened the tub and touched the wipes. They were dried out. The closet was empty save a couple of old blankets on the shelf. The room next to it was set up the same. Something about seeing so many baby beds set off alarms in his head. The master bedroom contained two twin beds and a dresser with no mirror. It too was dusty. Either no one had been there in a while, or whoever owned the place wasn't worried about cleanliness. He eased open the drawers to find small sweatpants and T-shirts along with panties and socks. The en suite was void of any toiletries, but there were towels and wash cloths in the small closet. When he met Legend and Shadow downstairs, he told them what he found.

Shadow ran a hand through his beard. "That tracks with all the baby supplies I found in the pantry. The canned formula is out of date by a few months. Let's go outside and tell the others."

Jackson went first, explaining the cribs and twin beds. "It's possible whoever lived here had sextuplets or were foster parents, but the twin beds in the master leads me to believe it's something more nefarious."

"The pantry is full of bottles and powdered formula and very little food items," Shadow said.

Legend and the other horsemen looked at one

another, and if Jax didn't know better, he would say they were having a silent conversation.

Max crossed his arms over his beefy chest. "We've come across this setup in the past. It was before the apocalypse, but it's stuck with us. We took down a trafficking ring where they kidnapped pregnant women, kept them locked up until they gave birth, then sold the babies."

"What happened to the women?" Ryan asked.

"If they were in good health, the fuckers raped them to make more babies. If not, they were sold off," Max seethed. "The four of us worked for fifty years searching for as many of these syndicates as possible, but we never found who was responsible for funding the 'endeavor.' Most often it was trafficking women and children. Only that one time were babies involved. We didn't have someone like Lucy or Bishop to trace the money, so it was slow going. The best we could do was voice the traffickers we found, but there was always someone higher up the food chain. The ones doing the kidnapping and raping were never allowed to know who was in charge."

Storm set his hand on the back of Max's neck and squeezed. "Our search led us from the West Coast to the eastern seaboard, but then the apocalypse happened. As you know, the world came to a halt, and with it the ability for these fuckers to easily move people. The government had bigger things to worry about, and to be honest, we all needed a break from the atrocities we'd seen for half a century, so we stepped back."

Trenton, who'd been quiet up until that point,

asked Jackson, "Did Bishop mention anything about seeing women when he located Bucco?"

"No, but that doesn't mean there aren't any. The man who took Tegan said Mr. Bucco would still have a use for her, and I'm loath to think that this is what he meant by that." Jax swept a hand toward the house.

Max stepped away from Storm's hand. "Then let's find her. Sultan, Shadow, and I will do a flyover of the property. While we're gone, the rest of you search the other houses. If Bucco is selling babies, I doubt this is the only house used for that purpose. If you run into trouble, try to keep as many alive as you can to question them, but don't hesitate to take them out if you're in mortal danger."

Max and Shadow stripped, handing their clothes to Legend and Lock. Jackson made quick work of his own clothes, and Ryan took them from him. "Be safe," his best friend said.

Jackson exhaled and let his Eagle take over. He launched himself into the inky sky, following the two older Hounds.

# Chapter Seven

## Sultan

THE VINEYARD WAS SITUATED on approximately eight acres. The grapevines, or at least where they used to be, took up the majority of the eastern three acres. The main house, a small outbuilding, and a barn made up two acres, with the rest being wooded. The outbuilding and barn were dark, but there were a few lights on in the house. They split up, flying over each building and the surrounding trees. Jax surveyed the barns from the air, then he landed on each building, listening for signs of life inside. He found none. When he flew over the trees at the back of the property, he noticed a path leading toward the river. He followed it to the end, where a dock floated on the water. It appeared to be in good shape, which wasn't surprising. If he were a mafia don and wanted to make a quick escape, the water would be a good way to do so.

He flew back toward the house, having left it for last. Jax landed on a tree near the back of the house where several lights were on. The windows were covered with heavy drapes, so he couldn't see inside. Making his way to the front of the manor, a thrumming energy flowed up from below. It wasn't a machine. Jax hovered, listening, and searching, but he couldn't explain what he felt. There were four guards, just as Bishop said, which meant Jax couldn't fly lower to investigate. The men were armed with illegal rifles, but that didn't surprise him since Bucco was known for trading in all sorts of weaponry.

Jackson once again landed on a tree branch to study the lit room at the front of the house. It was also covered, but the drapes moved, and if Jax had been in his human form, he would have sucked in a breath or punched his fist in the air. Maybe both. Tegan looked out into the dark, barely lit from behind from a small lamp. He studied her closely. Tegan's driver's license picture didn't do her justice. Her long, wavy hair was down around her shoulders, and she had a glow about her he'd seen in other pregnant females. Even when they were nine months along and weary with the aches and pains that came with being with child, females shined from within. Tegan didn't appear to be harmed, but her eyes were despondent. Then those same eyes flashed golden, and he knew his instincts had been right. Tegan was something other than human.

Jax remained still, but Tegan still stared right at him, placing her hand to the window. He wanted to go to her. To let her know she was safe. Tegan stepped away from the window, letting the drapes close, and Jax felt her absence in his soul. He flew to where he was supposed to meet Maximus and Shadow. Landing next to the two Hounds, Jax shifted to his human form. "She's there. In one of the front rooms on the second floor."

Max clapped him on the shoulder. "This is wonderful news. I counted six distinct heartbeats in the house. We don't know if most of them are guards or if some are staff. I want to get inside the outbuilding and barn, but I don't want to bust any doors down, and Legend is the lock picker. Let's head back to the house and see what the others found, if anything. Then we can return to check the buildings."

Jackson didn't want to leave, knowing Tegan was so close, but he assumed with it being so late, she wasn't going anywhere. "Did you feel a strange energy coming from below the ground on the far side of the house?"

"Yes. The vibrations weren't strong enough to be machinery, but there is something below ground. We'll be sure to find out what when we return. Let's head back and make a plan." They shifted and flew back to the house where the others were waiting.

As Jackson, Max, and Shadow pulled on their tactical pants, Max told them everything they'd seen during their flyover. When finished, he asked, "What did you find here?"

Storm filled them in. "There were no people in the houses, but the rooms were set up the same as this one. There's only one reason for this many houses to have nurseries set up in such a way."

Legend set his hand on Storm's shoulder, squeezing. "We need to get Bishop looking further back, if that's possible. I want to know where the babies were taken."

Max's face darkened. "It appears drugs aren't the only thing Bucco is peddling." He leaned against

Shadow, looking up into his friend's face. "We have sat on the sidelines too long. I want to find these children and stop the madness."

Shadow wrapped an arm around Max, pressing their heads together. "I'm in agreement. Legend, Storm, what say you?"

"Aye," the two males agreed in unison.

Jackson caught Ryan's eye, and he lifted one eyebrow. Hearing the four horsemen speak in such a way was both odd and interesting. Ryan's lip twitched, but until they were alone, they couldn't discuss the males.

Max raised his head. "Then we have a new mission. Legend, we want to check the outbuildings, and I didn't want to kick in doors. There were no heartbeats in those buildings, but I'd still like to see what Bucco is hiding out there, if anything. I believe our best course of action is to check the buildings, then we take out the guards. Once inside, Sultan and the wolf can get Tegan out while the rest of us secure the building and find Bucco. We will voice the male and find out everything we can about his operation, most importantly where the babies are."

"Are we killing him?" Trenton asked. "Or turning him over to the police?"

"Neither. The local cops are likely on his payroll, and if we kill him, his underboss will take over. The death of the don is but a speed bump in the mafia world. The Bucco and Chen families have overthrown all the smaller families in power and have only grown since the apocalypse. They have contingencies in place for everything that could go wrong. They're smart as well as evil. We will keep him alive and use him to take down his own empire. It won't be done quickly, but as agreed, this is our new mission. Sultan, can Bishop handle the security cameras inside the house?"

"I'll have to ask. Bucco has his own computer specialist. Let me call him now." As he pulled his phone out, Jax tried not to stare at the four horsemen, but he couldn't figure out their dynamic. Bishop answered, and Jackson told him succinctly what they'd found at both the manor and the empty houses. "We're going to the manor to rescue Tegan, but we don't want to be caught on camera."

"I had to deal with The Ministry earlier, so I called Julian Stone for help with your mission. I'm going to conference him in. Hang on." A few seconds later, Julian came on the line. "I'm here, Jackson. Please repeat what you've found so far for Henry and me." Jackson sighed heavily, then recounted everything. Fingers were flying across keyboards as Julian said, "Bishop had us looking into the camera situation. I can tell you there are two guards inside plus an older couple who keep to the northeastern corner of the first floor. I'm assuming they're servants by the way they're dressed, but whether they're working for Bucco willingly…"

"Got it."

"There's something else. When we finally got through the firewall, Tegan and one of the guards exited a section of wall, like a secret panel, so I doublechecked the schematics for the manor. There are two large rooms on that side of the building. One looks like a parlor and the other appears to be a library slash poker room. The entrances to both are facing the stairs. If you look at the schematics, the rooms butt up to one another with no door between them. I checked the feed, and Tegan wasn't in either of those rooms all day."

"Was it on the west side of the house?"

"Yes. How did you know?"

"I felt a strong energy when I flew over that area of the property."

"That means — Hang on. Henry found something."

"Hey, Jackson. I've been searching the video backward in time, and I managed to go back as far as this morning. Tegan was accompanied downstairs by the guard who kidnapped her. He led her into the dining room where she had breakfast with Bucco. There's no audio, so I can't tell you what was said. At approximately eight-thirty a.m., the same guard who led her from the door to nowhere took her through that door. I scoured the feed, and once Tegan disappeared to that part of the house, she didn't return until a few minutes past eight tonight. Wherever that door leads is where she stayed all day."

Max scowled at the phone. "So we don't know where the secret door leads or if there are other guards beyond."

Henry responded, "That is correct. Also, the secret panel is equipped with a biometric palm scanner. The good news is I can manipulate the cameras for you. With Julian and I working in tandem, he can keep Bucco's hacker busy while I take over the security feed. When you're ready to go after Tegan, I can loop the feed for as long as you need. I can also cut the lights, so you'll have that advantage if you'd like."

Trenton pointed toward the manor. "But we still don't know how many guards we're up against."

"True, but once we're in the house, one of us can stand guard at that panel and take out anyone who comes through from the other side," Legend said.

"What if whoever comes through is an innocent? I don't want to shoot first and ask questions later," the wolf countered.

"If I might make a suggestion," Julian interrupted. "The way the staircase is configured, you can hide behind it while keeping the panel in view. If someone comes through dressed like a mafioso, take the shot. Or voice them. Your call."

Trenton shook his head. "I'm a wolf shifter. I don't have that ability. One of the Gryphons will need to guard the panel."

"We can decide that later," Max said. "Julian, if we go in now, are you and Henry ready?"

"Yes. How long will it take you to get there and ready to breach the property?"

"We need a few minutes to gather our weapons. It took us less than three minutes to fly earlier, so we should be ready in fifteen minutes."

"We'll be waiting." Julian disconnected.

Trenton said, "In case you've forgotten, wolves can't fly."

Jackson clapped him on the shoulder. "Sure, you can. It'll just be on the back of a Gryphon."

"Nikita's going to give me hell," Trenton muttered. His granddaughter rode Kyllian's Gryphon when he rescued her, and from what Jax heard, she begged to go flying when she wasn't begging to ride in her sidecar. The younger dire wolf was something special.

"It'll be easier for me to carry all our gear in my Gryphon form anyway." Jax had never had anyone on his back, but it wouldn't be a hardship. Jackson removed his pants while the other Gryphons also stripped. They stored their clothes in individual pouches, which they would carry in their Eagle claws. Jax shifted to his larger Gryphon form, and Trenton climbed onto his back.

"Hold onto the feathers right above his fur," Ryan instructed. "You'll want to lean forward for takeoff."

Ryan placed the two bags loaded with weapons in Jackson's talons. When he had a good grip, Jax squawked once. Trenton got the message, leaning forward, and Jax lifted off. Ryan's red-feathered Eagle was right behind them. Trenton's grip was sure, but not too tight, which Jax was grateful for. As he flew, he imagined Nikita letting out a whoop as she enjoyed the ride. Trenton was more sedate, but at one point, he did chuckle under his breath, and Jax grinned to himself.

Jax hovered briefly so the other Hounds could take the bags from him. Then he set his talons and paws on the ground and lowered onto his Lion's haunches so Trenton could dismount.

"That was exhilarating," the wolf whispered.

While the Hounds dressed in their tactical gear, Trenton removed weapons from the large duffels. He passed them out, then strapped a rifle across his chest, adding extra magazines to his vest. Jax could imagine the male as an army sniper. His movements were quick and sure.

Jackson opted for a double shoulder rig over his bullet-resistant vest and slid two .357 Magnum Desert Eagle hand canons into the holsters. Max strapped several knives on his person, looking as comfortable with blades as Trenton did with a rifle. Jackson was curious about the four horsemen's backgrounds, but now wasn't the time to ask. Honestly, it might never be the right time. He had a feeling those males had seen some bad shit in their long lives, worse than what Max already recounted.

Trenton handed out the comms. Being shifters, they could easily hear one another, but with the small devices, they could connect to Julian and Henry without needing a phone. Jackson called Julian to let him know they were in place and ready to go.

"I've connected to your comms, so you can hang up," Julian said. Jax disconnected, and then Julian's voice came through the small earpiece. "Checking comms." When everyone affirmed they heard him clearly, the Gargoyle said, "Henry has the cameras looped, and I have Bucco's hacker chasing his tail."

"We're going to check the outbuildings before we breach the manor," Max stated.

"Understood. I'll remain quiet unless there's movement in the house you need to know about."

Armed and ready, they moved stealthily through the woods toward the barn. Legend picked the lock while everyone stood guard.

"Wait," Julian urged. Tapping on the keyboard sounded. "I should have checked this sooner, but both the barn and the smaller building have alarms on them. Give me a second… Okay, they're disabled."

Jax blew out a breath. That had been close. Legend finished the job, and he eased the door open, with Jax, Shadow, and Max following.

"We have multiple crates," Jackson said for Julian's and those standing guard's benefit. Max removed one of the knives from his vest and pried open the lid to the first crate they came to. The container appeared to be filled with wine, but Max lifted the wooden box.

"Fuckin' hell," Shadow muttered. Jax peered over his shoulder to see hundreds of amber bottles filled with pills.

Max picked up one of the bottles and opened it, pouring a few of the tablets into his hand. "Hive."

"The current street value of Hi-Ve is a hundred dollars a pill," Henry commented.

Max pushed around the bottles. "Estimating there's two hundred bottles in this one crate, that's over half a million." He looked around the barn. "There are seventeen crates so roughly ten million dollars just sitting here."

"The guy who took Tegan said John Cashel owed Bucco half a million, but Tegan only found thirty bottles," Jax said.

Shadow opened a crate on the next row. Lifting the layer of wine, he said, "That means either Cashel sold the rest and hid the money or there's a shit ton of Hive out there somewhere unaccounted for." He replaced the wine, then lowered the lid. "For the sake of time, let's assume the rest of these are full of the same and move on. I'm feeling twitchy."

Maximus tensed. "That's not good. Let's go." Max led them out the door, and they hurried to the next structure. "Julian, we're at the smaller building. Still good to go in?"

"Yes."

They rushed from the back of the barn to the smaller building, and Legend once again made quick work of the lock. Unlike the barn, this building was filled with old machinery that didn't appear to have been used in quite a while. Jackson stepped behind a mower to inspect one of the shelves when his toe caught on something. Looking down, he noticed a metal ring.

"I think I found something," he whispered. When the others joined him, he pointed. "I wonder where this leads?"

"And do we investigate now, or wait until we've rescued Tegan?" Ryan whispered.

Max bent over and pulled the ring, lifting the door a couple inches. Someone in the area beneath coughed. Someone else sneezed, but the next sound had the hair on Jackson's arms standing on end.

"Julian?" Jackson prodded the hacker at the sound of a gunshot.

"That was Bucco putting a bullet in one of his men. The guards are converging on the dining room."

Max lowered the trap door. "Legend, you and Trenton stay here and find out how many women are in the hole. The rest of you, let's get this done. Sultan, take the front. Judge and Shadow flank him on either side, and I'll go in through the back."

By the time Jax got to the front of the manor, one of the guards had returned to his post. Jax took him out with a single bullet, then deposited him in the woods.

He felt eyes on him and glanced up to see Tegan looking down at him from her window. He gave her a brief nod, hoping she understood help was coming. There were more guards than they expected, but the Hounds had the element of surprise on their side. They converged on the dining room where Bucco had killed his man, but Julian kept them apprised of the don's movements.

"He's headed upstairs."

Jax stepped past the man on the floor when a shot hit the wall close to his head. Jax swirled, pistol up, ready to fire, but Ryan put one in between the man's eyes. Jax inclined his head to his best friend for having his back.

"All clear?" he asked. When he received an affirmative, he said, "Then I'm going after Tegan."

# CHAPTER EIGHT

## Tegan

TEGAN GRABBED HER STOMACH and groaned. Did her babies not realize it was time to sleep? Obviously not by the way they were kicking. The fact that they were big enough to cause such torment didn't make sense. From everything she'd read, the babies shouldn't be developed enough to play soccer, but here they were. Maybe it was because she was a shifter? Tegan wished she'd paid more attention to when her mother had been pregnant with her brothers.

Rolling to her side, she sat on the side of the bed. She knew better than to sleep on her back, but sometimes it just happened during the night. For whatever reason, her little ones only wanted her lying on her right side. She rubbed her bandaged hands over her stomach until they both settled. Figuring she might as well pee since she was awake, Tegan stood and padded to the door. She slowly twisted the knob, hoping not to wake Freddie. As she eased the door open, angry voices echoed up the stairs. From the sounds of it, Freddie was already awake and getting a verbal smackdown from Phil.

"Do you think a woman ever goes anywhere without her purse? Did you even bother to check and see if her phone was on her before you took her? According to Avery, Tegan hasn't missed a day of work since she started her job, so of course Onyx was going to look for her when she didn't show up or answer her fucking phone. And what do you think he then did when he found Tegan's house trashed? He called the fucking cops. Cops I do not have on my payroll! They'll be looking for her, and by god, they better not find her here."

"I apologize, Mr. Bucco. John said Tegan took the pills with her when she left. I believed him, then I went after her."

"And when you found her, she said she only flushed thirty bottles."

"Which makes more sense, now that I think about it. It would have taken hours to flush as much Hive as John had, and she was gone by the time I trailed John and forced him back to the house, which was less than an hour later."

"Then where's the rest of it? Either John stashed the rest of the crate somewhere, or he sold it and hid the money. Neither works for me, Frederick."

A gunshot sounded, followed by a grunt and a thud. Tegan squeaked, then slapped her hand over her mouth, praying Bucco hadn't heard her. Multiple voices shouted soon after, but Bucco yelled at them to shut the fuck up.

"Get him out of here," he instructed.

She stepped back into her room and closed the door. Her stomach convulsed, but it wasn't from nausea. The pain wasn't unbearable, but it didn't feel good either. Returning to the bed, she climbed on, but instead of lying down, she bunched the pillows behind her and pulled the covers over her legs. If he would shoot one of his men, would Bucco do the same to her?

No, he wanted her babies, and he wouldn't get them if she were dead. Fuck, she needed to find a way out of there, but how?

As Tegan waited for Bucco to storm up the stairs, she prayed. Again. It would take a miracle for her to make it out of the manor with her babies. The alternative was unthinkable. She'd heard of women and kids being abducted for the purpose of being sold to traffickers, but that was something that happened to others in an abstract way. Now that she knew it was a possibility for her... Tegan shivered. The only positive was that the cops knew she was missing. Then again, would they have any clue that John had worked for Bucco? If they searched her house for clues, maybe they'd find the empty bottles in the washer. Tegan had never been in trouble a day in her life, so it wouldn't make sense that she would have drug containers. John was the one who had been in jail recently.

**Something's going on outside.**

Tegan flipped back the covers, but before she could stand, her stomach spasmed again. She rode the wave until it subsided, then she went to the window and pushed back the drape. Scanning the area, she saw one of Bucco's guards fall to the ground. A figure dressed in all black picked the guard up and tossed him over his shoulder as though he weighed nothing and jogged into the trees. When the figure returned, he was alone. As though he knew she was watching, the man looked right at Tegan and nodded. How the hell had he seen her in the darkness? And did his nod mean he was coming after her next, or was he there to help?

**He's safe.**

*How do you know that?*

**I can feel it.**

Tegan had learned long ago to trust her animal, and if it said they could trust the man, then she would. But there were other guards, and Bucco also had a gun. She needed to warn the man, but when she looked down, he was already gone. Footsteps pounded up the stairs, and her door was thrown open by a furious Bucco.

"Let's go," he demanded.

Tegan dropped the curtain as her stomach clenched again. "Ahhh." She clamped her hands over the babies as she hissed through the pain.

"What the fuck is wrong with you? I said let's go."

Tegan clutched the bedpost, biting her bottom lip. "You'll have to give me a second."

"We don't have a—" A woman screamed somewhere in the house. "Fuck!" Bucco took off out the door, leaving Tegan. Instead of heading back the way he came, he turned left out her door. She had no idea where he was going, but in that moment, she didn't care as long as it was away from her. She slid to her butt, hiding behind the massive bed. Tegan opened her shifter senses, listening for any sign of Bucco returning or the man from outside coming after her. A gunshot was followed by a weird, softer *pfft*, then a thud. Tegan had seen enough action movies to figure the second sound was from a gun using a silencer, although that was probably the wrong terminology considering the shot wasn't completely quiet.

"All clear?" a deep voice asked. "Then I'm going after Tegan."

Oh, shit. Tegan had nowhere to hide. Her stomach made it impossible to slide under the bed, so she lowered herself to her side and held her breath. If she hadn't been a shifter, she wouldn't have heard the soft tread sneaking up the staircase. It had to be the same man from outside because he didn't pause at the other rooms. His footsteps stopped at her door.

"Damnit, she's not here. And where the fuck is Bucco?" Another spasm hit, and Tegan couldn't stifle the groan. The man rushed across the room, and Tegan covered her head with her arms. "I'm not going to hurt you, Tegan. My name is Jackson Lynch. I'm here to take you home."

*He's safe.*

Tegan moved her arms and looked up into the greenest eyes she'd ever seen. Her Lion purred, wanting to rub its fur all over the male. *Not now, you hussy.* Tegan held out her hand, and Jackson gently helped her to her feet.

"Bucco ran left out of my room," she cautioned. Jackson turned loose and padded to the door, sticking his head out.

"Max, Bucco is either hiding on the second floor, or there's another secret panel somewhere." Jackson's voice was barely a whisper, but whoever this Max was must have heard him, because within seconds, another man appeared in the door. He gave Tegan a onceover, then retreated down the hall.

"Are you okay?" Jackson asked. "You sounded as though you were in pain earlier."

Tegan subconsciously placed a hand over her stomach. "I'm honestly not sure. I'm not far enough along for it to be contractions."

When she doubled over from another spasm, Jackson asked, "You sure about that?"

## *Sultan*

JAX PADDED QUIETLY UP the stairs, his gun trained in front of him, listening for any sound of Bucco as he made his way down the hall, but there was nothing. He used his shifter hearing as he neared Tegan's room, and there it was. An erratic heartbeat. He pushed open her door, but the space was empty. "Damnit, she's not here. And where the fuck is Bucco?" Was his mind playing tricks on him? Then he heard a groan from the other side of the bed. Jax crossed the room to find Tegan on the floor with her arms over her head.

"I'm not going to hurt you, Tegan. My name is Jackson Lynch. I'm here to take you home."

Tegan moved her arms and looked up at him, fear mixed with something fierce behind her stunning eyes. After a beat, Tegan held out her hand, and Jackson gently took it, easing her to her feet.

"Bucco ran left out of my room," she cautioned. Jackson couldn't admit to her that there were no other heartbeats surrounding them, so he turned loose and made his way to the door, sticking his head out.

"Max, Bucco is either hiding on the second floor, or there's another secret panel somewhere," Jackson whispered into the comm.

Max ran up the stairs, and when he got to the door, he paused to check on Tegan, then he continued down the hall.

"Are you okay?" Jackson asked. "You sounded as though you were in pain earlier."

Tegan set her hand on her protruding belly. "I'm honestly not sure. I'm not far enough along for it to be contractions."

She'd barely gotten the words out before she was doubling over. Jax holstered his weapon. "You sure about that?" He went to her, wanting to alleviate the pain somehow. He didn't know anything about being pregnant other than what he'd learned from being around the mates.

After a few seconds, Tegan straightened. "Pretty sure. I mean, I'm only three months along."

Jax knew better than to mention how round she was. Rhiannon nor any of the human mates he'd met were that large until their sixth or seventh months. If she was some type of shifter, as Jax suspected, could she not know how long her gestation period was?

Tegan walked over to the closet and came out with a suitcase, which she began filling with her clothes. "Did you get all the women from the workroom?"

"Workroom? Where is that?"

"It's through a secret panel on the first floor. I didn't count the women on second shift, but there were fifty-nine on the first."

Max entered the room. "Do you think the butler or

84

housekeeper can access the panel? Because none of the guards had clearance."

"I don't know. Is Alice okay? She's the housekeeper. She was nice to me." Tegan removed the elastic from her hair, then twisted it up once more.

"She and the butler are tied up, but we didn't kill them. We don't kill innocent people, and until we find out if they are working for Bucco willingly..." Max let Tegan assume the rest.

"There's another one of Bucco's men – Victor – he's the one who took me to the workroom and brought me back. I don't know if you killed him or not."

"Max," Legend interrupted through the comm. "There are half a dozen women in the hole, all of them pregnant. But we have a bigger problem. There's a tunnel that runs between the house and here. One of the women said there's also a tunnel that leads to the dock."

Tegan sank against the bed. "That's what he was planning on doing with me. Taking my babies, then selling us to pay for the missing drugs."

The fact that Tegan heard Legend through the comm solidified his assumption she was a shifter. The arch of Max's eyebrow indicated he hadn't missed that tidbit either, but he didn't mention it. Jax stepped closer and took her hand in his. "You're safe now, but we do need to get out of here."

"What about the women?" Tegan asked as she stood.

Max sheathed the knife in his hand. "The rest of us will remain behind until we ensure everyone else is safe."

"Do you have everything?" Jax gestured to her suitcase.

"I need to get my toiletries and put on some shoes." Tegan brushed past him, but as she made it to the door, she grabbed onto the frame.

When Max narrowed his eyes, Jackson sighed. "I'm not sure leaving is a good idea. I think I need to call Rev."

"Rev? Why not take her to the hospital?"

Jax tapped the side of his nose. Max angled his head to the side and sniffed the air. "Gotcha. But maybe take her to the house down the road in case things get messy here? I'd hate for her to be giving birth and Bucco or an unknown guard return."

"Giving birth?" Tegan huffed. "It's not time."

Jax smiled softly. "I'm pretty sure your babies think it is."

"Babies? How do you know I'm having more than one? I'm not that big."

"The same way you heard Legend talking about the women in the hole." Jax arched a brow, daring her to refute the truth.

"Y-you, you're a…" Tegan gulped and took a step back. Fur sprouted along her arms, but she closed her eyes and chanted, "No, no, no. We can't."

"Tegan, look at me," Jackson urged. When her eyes popped open, he continued. "Take a deep breath and hold it." When she did, he also inhaled. After a few seconds, he exhaled, and she did the same. "I swear on all that's holy, you, your little ones, and your secrets are safe with us."

"I thought I was the only lion shifter left," she

whispered, a tear rolling down her cheek.

That answered that question. "I'll get your toiletries and you slip on your shoes so we can go. Max was right that we shouldn't risk you giving birth here." Jax stepped past her and crossed the hall where he grabbed the few items he found. He returned to the bedroom and placed her things in the suitcase, then zipped it.

"Julian, are Tegan and I clear to leave?"

"Yes, but I don't recommend you walking a pregnant woman back to the house, nor do I recommend you flying. Not until you tell her the truth."

Ryan piped in with, "I'll head back and grab one of the SUV's. Give me a few minutes," at the same time Tegan asked, "What truth?"

"Thanks, Brother," he responded to his best friend. To the female, he said, "We're not lion shifters. We're Gryphons. We can also shift to our lion and eagle forms separately."

"That was you in the tree."

"It was. How did you know it wasn't one of the others?"

"I could feel you," Tegan said, tapping her chest. "In here."

His Gryphon preened, but Jackson ignored it, although he admitted softly, "Yeah, I felt it too."

Max cleared his throat. "I hate to interrupt this moment, but we need to get downstairs."

Jackson grabbed her suitcase and held out his hand. Tegan didn't hesitate to take it. Max led the way down the staircase, and Jax kept an eye on the female

87

to make sure she wasn't going to slip if another contraction hit.

"Holy shit," she muttered. Dead bodies were strewn across the floor. "I'm glad you guys are on my side." Tegan released Jackson's hand and headed toward the dining room. When she saw the man who kidnapped her, Tegan pulled her leg back and kicked him upside his bloody head. "That's for taking me, you bastard." She stomped him in the groin. "And that's for trashing my house. How am I supposed to get my deposit back!"

Jax couldn't help himself. He grinned, pulling her to his side. Pressing his lips to her ear, he whispered, "I have money, Sweetheart. You don't have to worry about your deposit."

# CHAPTER NINE

## Tegan

*SWEETHEART?* OH, BOY. HER animal purred, and Tegan swallowed hard. She knew what her beast thought about the tall male with his shaved head and thick beard, but she couldn't trust it to be true. She was pregnant with someone else's babies, so there was no way a male like Jackson would want her as a mate. No, he was being nice because of her situation.

Tegan walked over to where Alice and the butler were tied to a couple of dining room chairs. Tegan knelt beside the older woman. "Alice, were you willingly working for Bucco knowing the kind of man he was?"

"No, Miss Tegan. Like you, I was forced into his employ to work off someone else's debt," Alice whispered.

Tegan inclined her head to the man beside her whose mouth was gagged. "And what about him?"

"Harold is my husband. It's his brother's fault we're here. Much like with you and John, we were in the dark about Gerald's drug dealing. You see, Harold and Gerald were identical twins, and Mr. Bucco's men

89

mistook my Harold for his brother. When the mistake was cleared up, we were already being held here. Mr. Bucco put us to work to pay for Gerald's theft."

Alice looked up as Tegan felt Jackson's presence behind her. "The others will take care of them, but we have to go now." He helped Tegan stand, and Tegan gave the older woman a smile.

Jackson led Tegan from the dining room and out the front door where a large SUV idled. He tossed her suitcase into the back of the vehicle, then helped Tegan into the back seat and slid in next to her.

"Tegan, this is Ryan."

"Hello. Thank you both for getting me out of there."

Ryan inclined his head to her, then turned, put the vehicle in drive, and pulled away from the manor. "I called Rev and gave him a heads up," Ryan said. "He and Bethany are on their way."

"Thanks, Brother."

"Who are Rev and Bethany?" Tegan asked.

"Rev is a doctor, and his mate, Bethany, is a nurse. Since you're a shifter, we can't take you to the hospital, so the next best thing is coming to us. Bucco owns all the houses in the area, and while they aren't where I would choose for you to give birth, they're better than trying to find somewhere nicer and not making it on time."

"But it's not time— aaaah." Tegan gritted her teeth. She couldn't deny she was having contractions.

Jackson grabbed her hand. "Squeeze if you need to." She took him at his word and clamped down on it as she endured the pain. When she blew out a breath, he asked, "How did you find my cabin?"

"*Your* cabin? Oh, goddess. I'm sorry for breaking in. I was riding the bike because my asshole ex-boyfriend stole my car. I was on my way out of town when I wrecked. My place was another thirty or so miles away, and there was no way I could walk that far. I'll pay for the damages."

"I'm not worried about that. I've already set everything back to right."

Tegan sighed. "As for how I found the cabin, a deer ran out in front of me, and I had to lay the bike down to keep from wrecking. My Lion smelled... well, you I guess, and I followed your scent through the woods."

"And your ex-boyfriend, he was the father?"

"He was the sperm donor, nothing more," Tegan hissed. "I never should have gotten involved with John Cashel, but in the beginning, he was charming. That all changed when I let him move in with me. The bastard was making bank selling drugs all while pretending he didn't have a job and taking my money. I'm a receptionist for the goddess' sake and barely able to pay my rent. Even if he hadn't been a loser who got arrested for third degree assault, I still wouldn't have stayed since he was human and had no idea what I am. I've been planning to leave town ever since I found out I was pregnant. With him in jail, I was able to save a little money and store supplies for a couple months at a little hideaway I used to go to when I was younger. I thought I had more time, but for some reason, John was released early. Before he showed up, one of Bucco's men, Freddie, came around looking for John and the drugs. I told him John was in jail and that I didn't know anything about the drugs, which I didn't. Freddie left, and I searched the house. I found fifty thousand dollars and thirty bottles of Hive, which I flushed. I packed a suitcase because I wasn't going to wait around for Freddie to come back. I put my suitcase in the car and went back inside to pee, but before I could leave, John showed up. When I told him about Freddie, he freaked and took my car because he said Freddie would know his bike. Since Freddie had threatened to come back, I took the Harley. I wasn't due yet, so I thought I had time to get to my other place."

"Did you have someone waiting to help you? Maybe a friend we can call?"

"No. I lost my family when I was a teen and was put in foster care. My foster parents don't know I'm a shifter, and I can't tell them. I don't know any other shifters, uh, except for you."

"You were going to do this on your own? That's mighty brave."

"I didn't have a choice. Like I said, I don't know any other shifters. My parents left their pride before I was born because my dad got a job in New York. Both sets of grandparents had already passed away, and my parents weren't close to their siblings. I never met any aunts or uncles, so I had no idea who to call for help."

"The good news is you aren't alone now. It'll take Rev and Bethany a while to get here, but at least we know they're coming to help."

"We're here," Ryan said as he pulled into the driveway of a two-story brick house. It looked nice enough to Tegan, but maybe there was something wrong with the interior.

"Before we go inside, I have to warn you," Jackson started, but another contraction hit. He placed his palm against her nape. It didn't help with the pain, but she appreciated the gesture. Once it eased, he said, "We need to get you inside." Jackson got out of the car and held out a hand for her. Once she was on her feet, Tegan didn't turn loose. Her Lion insisted this male was their mate. Tegan had no reason to doubt her beast, and if this was all the contact she got with him, she would take it.

Once inside, Tegan looked around. The house didn't appear to be lived in. There was furniture, but there were no photos or knickknacks. There were no small appliances on the kitchen counter.

Ryan walked in with her suitcase. "I'll put this in the master bedroom, if that's okay?"

"Thanks, Ryan." Jackson tugged Tegan's hand, and she turned, giving him her attention. He then took her other hand and pressed them both to his chest. His steady heartbeat thumped beneath her palms. "Before your last contraction hit, I was going to give you a heads up about this place. The main bedroom has two twin beds, but the spare rooms are full of baby cribs. The other houses close by are outfitted the same way."

"I wonder why there aren't babies here now. Why are the houses empty?"

"When we were searching for you, we located several pregnant women beneath the floor in the outbuilding. Maybe Bucco only brought them here when it was close to time for them to give birth. We really don't know."

Tegan stepped closer. "Why were you searching for me?"

Jackson brushed a knuckle down her cheek. "I have a security system at the cabin that alerted me to your presence. I only watched the video long enough to see you break in. Ryan and I got on the road immediately. We live in New Troy, so it took over three hours because of holiday traffic. By the time we got there, you were gone, and I looked at the video feed from after you arrived to when we did to see Freddie kick the door in, then usher you out at gunpoint. I also found your purse, so I gave our hacker your information as well as forwarded the video to him. He was able to locate your car using CCTV cameras. Freddie mentioned Bucco's name, and Bishop found two locations Bucco owns close to the last area your car was seen. We got lucky when we found you in the first one. Come on. Let's get you upstairs before another contraction hits."

When they reached the top of the stairs, Ryan was closing one of the doors. "There are a few towels and wash cloths in the bathroom, but we're going to need things for the babies once they get here. I'm going to take the SUV and run to the store. Do you need bottles and formula?" he asked Tegan.

"No, I plan on breastfeeding. I don't have any money on me, but I promise I can pay you back later. Please get diapers and wipes. Maybe a couple of pacifiers, thin blankets, and some sleeping gowns."

Jackson pulled out his wallet and handed Ryan some cash. "Grab food and drinks. We also need two car seats. As soon as Rev clears them to travel, we're getting the hell out of here."

Ryan took the money and added it to his own wallet. "You got it. If you think of anything else, text me."

Jackson went into the attached bathroom and returned with all the towels. "I don't know how clean these are. I also don't know how soon the babies will be here. Hopefully, they'll hang on until Rev and Bethany get here."

Tegan took one of the towels and spread it out on the closest bed. That wouldn't do much good, so she added another on top of it. She shouldn't care that she was going to ruin the bedding. If Bucco used this house for a baby mill, he could afford to buy a new comforter. "Are you sure we're safe here? I assume your friends didn't catch up with Bucco or you'd have mentioned it."

Jackson ran his hand down her arm. "I vow on all that's holy, that man will never get near you again."

"Sultan! We've got incoming!" Ryan yelled. Tegan didn't know who Sultan was, but Jackson cursed a blue streak.

Gunfire erupted outside. "Max, we could use some help here at the house," he said as he unholstered one of the pistols at his side. "Someone is shooting, and Judge is out there alone." He wasn't on a phone or walkie talkie, so he must have some type of device in his ear. Jackson removed the other gun and moved to the door, ready to defend her. Tegan was tempted to look out the bedroom window to see the action, but she didn't want to get her head shot off, so she walked into the bathroom and lowered the toilet seat lid. Right as she started to sit, another contraction hit. Tegan grabbed the vanity and bent over, placing her forehead against the cool surface.

She wasn't ready to have her babies. Were they coming early because of the stress she was under? Or did shifter pregnancies not last as long as humans'? Fuck, she wished she could ask someone. Liquid gushed from between her legs. "No, no, no." Tegan waddled to the bedroom as soon as she could move. She kicked off her shoes, then she pushed her soaked shorts and panties down her legs. After stepping out of them, she grabbed the pillow off the second bed and placed it atop the one where she was going to lie down. Using one of the spare towels, Tegan eased down onto the twin bed, then covered her lap. Another contraction hit, and Tegan gritted her teeth, doing her best to keep from screaming. She didn't want to interrupt Jackson's concentration.

"Tegan, what is it? What's wrong?" he asked anyway.

"My water broke."

"Oh, shit. Let me—" More gunfire cut off his words, this time it sounded like an army was outside.

"Go, Jackson. They want to sell the babies, so if they happen to get past you, they're not going to hurt me." His green eyes were filled with worry, so she added, "Please, go help your friend."

Jackson strode across the room and pressed his lips to her forehead. "I'm sorry."

"Don't be. This is my fault, not yours. Now go."

He was barely out the door when the next

contraction came, this one stealing her breath. With the pain was pressure between her legs.

*It's time.*

Tegan wanted to yell at her Lion for stating the obvious, but her focus was on the stretching between her legs. When she found out she was pregnant, Tegan knew then she would have to do this alone and studied everything she could about home birthing as well as how to care for new infants. She was scared shitless, but she had no other choice. Her little ones were counting on her. She still worried that something would go wrong, and she would have to take one or both to the hospital, but being in the middle of a war zone, she was screwed if that happened.

*Jackson's doctor friend is on his way.*

Tegan rolled over and got to her knees. She placed one hand on the headboard for leverage and held the other below her vagina. With each contraction, Tegan pushed, screaming the room down, and when the pressure between her legs intensified, she turned loose of the bed as the first of her babies – a son – slid into her waiting hands. Tegan placed him on the towel and used a clean one to wipe as much gunk from his tiny body as possible. Her son, Theodore, scrunched his little face and let out a bellow that rivaled his momma's previous ones. She released a claw and sliced through his umbilical cord, leaving it long enough to tie it off since the clamps she'd purchased were at her shack.

Tegan didn't have much time to tend to Theo as his sibling was right behind him. She placed him on the foot of the bed and prepared for the next baby. As the next contraction hit, Tegan braced herself and pushed.

Blood oozed from her body, and dizziness had Tegan swaying.

"Please, goddess, help me," she begged. The second child didn't come as quickly as the first. Tegan had to push several times, and she was certain she would pass out from the pain. Taking shallow breaths like she'd watched in a video, Tegan huffed and puffed, sweat dripping down her face. She leaned her forehead against the headboard and closed her eyes, taking a brief breather. When the next contraction hit, she begged the goddess and her unborn child. She pushed with a yell, startling Theo who began crying. More blood leaked from her vagina, and she pushed harder than before, begging her Lion to help. "Come on, my little love. You can do it. Please, baby..." Tegan screamed as she hunkered over, calling on the goddess, her beast, and all the strength she had left. She barely caught the baby as her hands were slick, and he – another boy – was covered in blood and goo. "You did it, Ollie. Such a good baby." Tegan placed him on a towel and took a few seconds to catch her breath. She took care of his cord, then placed Ollie next to his brother. Two little bodies lay close to her, crying and flailing their arms. Theodore was named after her mother, Thea, and Oliver was named after her father, and both were perfect as far as she could tell. Strong lungs. Ten fingers and toes. Dark swatches of hair on the back of their heads. *Fucking John.*

Tegan needed to pass the afterbirth, but she didn't want to do so on the bed. She grabbed another towel as she got down on the floor and placed it beneath her. It wasn't as painful as pushing out the babies, but it was a hell of a lot messier. Tegan tried to get to her feet. She needed to clean Ollie up. She also needed… Blackness crowded her vision, and Tegan swayed to the side. She barely caught herself as she pitched sideways. No, no, no. Her babies needed her. She had to…

# CHAPTER TEN

## Sultan

JAX WAS TORN BETWEEN leaving Tegan and helping Judge, but he'd never forgive himself if something happened to his best friend. He tore down the steps, but when he got to the first floor, he paused instead of running headfirst outside without a plan. The gunfire was coming from the back of the house, so Jax went out the front.

"Judge, where are you?" Jax asked through the comm, but he didn't get an immediate answer. He eased his way around the house, keeping to the shadows. Using his Eagle's vision, Jax searched the darkness.

"Sultan, I'm pinned down thirty yards in the trees behind the house," Judge finally said. "There are three men, and they all have assault rifles."

"Can't you voice them?"

"I tried, but they're all wearing hearing protection."

"Shit, Judge. They're moving. Spreading out." Jax aimed and fired at the one closest to him, hitting the male dead center of his back. The thug went down, spraying bullets as he did.

"Fucking hell," Judge whispered. "That was too damn close."

One of the men turned and sent a barrage of bullets Jackson's way. He dove to the ground and rolled until he was no longer being shot at. He waited a few seconds before raising his head. Slowly, he got to his knees with both pistols pointed toward the trees. He searched the trees for the shooter, but the male had disappeared.

"Incoming in fifteen seconds," Max said in their ears. Jax prayed it was soon enough.

The whooshing of wings let Jax know someone was in his Gryphon form. He rose to his feet, keeping his hand cannons aimed at the woods while glancing up. Max was riding one of the Hounds while pointing his own rifle toward the ground. The Gryphon hovered above the trees, and Max fired two shots. The assault rifles sprayed wildly as the men went down.

"Ah, fuck!" Judge yelled.

"Ryan!" Jax took off through the woods to where Judge's anguished cry came from. He kept his head on a swivel until he reached his friend. Jax holstered his guns as he dropped to his knees. Blood ran down Ryan's forehead, and his left arm was missing a chunk of flesh.

"Godsdamnit! Max, Judge needs help. Call an ambulance."

"No, Sultan. The bullet barely grazed my head," Judge argued. "It's not that bad."

"The fuck it's not. Part of your arm is missing, Brother."

Ryan looked down where the flesh was ripped. "Huh. Wait, where's Tegan?"

"I left her upstairs. She told me to come help you."

Max dropped to the ground and rushed over. "I've got Judge. You go see about your female."

Shadow shifted from his Gryphon and joined them. "We've got him, Sultan. Go."

Jax hated leaving Ryan, but Tegan's contractions had been close together. He pressed his hand to Ryan's cheek before rushing back to the house. With the comms live, he could still hear what was going on outside. When he entered the house, the sound of babies crying met his ears, but he couldn't hear Tegan talking. He took the stairs two at a time, and when he got to the master bedroom, he froze. Two babies were wrapped in towels on the bed, but Tegan lay on the floor next to… Jax swallowed hard, avoiding looking at the bloody mess.

Jax crossed the room and pressed his fingers to her neck. When he found a strong pulse, Jax blew out a relieved breath. "Come on, Little Momma. Your babies need you." Jackson spread a towel over Tegan's lower body, then he shrugged out of his rigging, placing the guns on the spare bed. He removed his vest, leaving him in a T-shirt. He picked up a fussing infant, the one she hadn't cleaned off. Jax swayed the baby while speaking softly to it… He pulled back the towel. A son. He moved the towel on the other infant to find another boy.

Footsteps sounded on the stairs, but before Jax could reach for one of the guns, Trenton called out, "I'm coming up." The wolf paused in the door, but when he saw Tegan, he asked, "Is she...?" as he strode to the bed and picked up the other crying boy. Trenton rocked the infant in his arms, singing softly to him. The baby's wails lessened as he shoved his tiny fist in his mouth.

"She's passed out." Jax went into the bathroom and found a washcloth. He turned the water on, letting it heat up. Once it was warm, he ran the cloth beneath the stream, then squeezed out the excess. He took the baby back to the bedroom and placed him on the bed. As he cleaned the boy, Jax spoke to Tegan. "Come on, Tegan. Your sons need you." The baby he was wiping down stopped crying and sucked on his thumb, staring up at Jax with big eyes.

"Hello, little one. I'm Jackson, and I'm going to get you someplace safe as soon as possible. Until then, we need to get your momma to wake up." While coaxing Tegan, Max and Shadow brought Judge inside and placed him on the sofa. Jax listened through the comm as his best friend griped about being fine.

*"If you say you're fine one more time, I'm gonna tape your fucking mouth shut,"* Max threatened.

Judge huffed but didn't respond until Shadow mentioned going for medical supplies.

*"I was on my way to get baby stuff before I was attacked. Maybe you can ask Sultan what all they need. My head's pounding, and I can't think straight."*

*"Fine, huh?"* Max grumbled.

A few seconds later, Shadow came upstairs. When he saw the babies, he grinned and walked over to Trenton. Shadow ran a finger along the boy's forehead, then he pulled back the towel and splayed his hand

103

across the infant's chest. "Lungs sound healthy." he said. He covered the baby before doing the same to his brother. "His too."

"That's good to hear because Tegan's not doing so good."

Shadow walked over to Tegan and asked, "May I?"

Jax didn't know how the male was assessing their health, but he nodded anyway. He trusted all the Hounds.

Shadow knelt beside Tegan and spread his hands out, hovering inches above her body. He closed his eyes as he moved his hands from her head down to her thighs. Gasping, his eyes popped open.

"What? What's wrong?" Jax asked.

"She's not human," Shadow whispered.

"No, she's a lion shifter. I figured you all heard our earlier conversation through the comms."

"I missed that, but I did have my hands full with one of the guards." Shadow stood, smiling softly. "She'll be okay once she wakes up. Her body is resting. Now, Judge said you need things for the babies?"

"Yeah, he was headed to the store earlier when Bucco's men showed up. How did we miss them?"

"There are underground tunnels, and we have no idea where the exits are. Max is standing guard downstairs just in case. He called Sutton who is sending some Hounds to help us look for Bucco. He also called the FBI since the local cops are more than likely on Bucco's payroll. We don't have the resources to rescue over a hundred women and get them somewhere safe. Now, what do you need from the store?"

Jackson listed off everything they'd talked about earlier. "I gave Judge money." Shadow waved him off as he left the room.

After thirty minutes of coaxing, Jax used his Gryphon voice on Tegan, more his beast calling to hers than coercion. It worked. Tegan groaned, and Jax squeezed her hand gently while cradling the baby in his other arm. "That's it. You can do this, Tegan. You're strong. I know it. You have two precious boys, and they need you to wake up." Her eyes fluttered, and when they opened, she snarled at Jackson. Her Lion's long fangs slid from her gums, and claws tipped her fingers. Jax stood and took a step back, but he turned the baby carefully toward her. "Look who I have," he said softly, showing the female her child.

Her eyes flickered from Jackson to the baby to Trenton and back. Fangs and claws receded. "Sorry." When she tried to sit up, her arms gave out.

"Do you have the strength to shift? Will that heal you or at least help enough until Rev and Bethany get here?"

Tegan closed her eyes for a few seconds. When she opened them, she shook her head. "Don't have enough strength."

"Let me help you." Jackson handed his baby over to Trenton and pulled down the bedding, then he stacked the pillows against the headboard. He placed one arm behind her shoulders and the other under her knees, easily lifting her onto the bed so she was sitting up. He drew the covers over her legs and praised her, "You did great, Tegan. You're an amazing female. I'm sorry you had to do it alone." Jackson turned to take one of the boys from Trenton.

"I didn't have a choice," she muttered. Tegan's eyes filled with tears as Jackson placed her son in her arms. "Oh, Ollie." She didn't bother wiping her face, letting the wetness slide down her cheeks as she cooed to her baby nestled against her chest. The other one began fussing, probably at hearing his mother's voice. "Bring him to me please." Trenton carefully settled the baby on Tegan's other side, then spread one of the spare towels over the blood on the floor.

"My brave Theo." Tegan nuzzled both their heads. Jax sat next to her thigh and placed a hand on the closest baby's back, relishing the rise and fall of each breath. He took note of which baby was which. Theo's hair was thicker and darker than Ollie's. That would probably change over time, but for now, Jax had a way to discern the brothers. Theo started crying again, bobbing his head against Tegan's chest. That made her cry harder.

Trenton stepped closer to the bed and brushed his hand over Tegan's hair. "Hey now. None of that. You're doing so well. If memory serves me correctly, your babies are probably hungry. I know my Quinn was fired up as soon as she came into this world, and nothing would calm her down until she got her tummy full. Do you think you have the strength to nurse them?"

When Tegan snapped her eyes up to the male, Jax stuck a finger under her chin. "Trenton and I will give you privacy. I'll hold Ollie while you feed Theo since he's the one fussing. I can turn my back, or you can use a blanket to cover up."

Tegan took a few seconds, blinking hard. Jax brushed the tears from her cheek, giving her time to decide. He would give her all the time in the world for anything she needed.

"There's a button-up in my suitcase. Would you get it for me please?"

Jax rummaged through her bag, ignoring the lace panties, until he found the shirt. "Let us hold the boys while you change." Jax placed the garment on her legs, took Ollie and handed him to Trenton, then lifted a crying Theo. He and Trenton turned their backs so she could change. Jax focused on the boy and not the fact that Tegan was undressing behind him. He didn't want to be that male, but her natural scent beneath the tang of blood was intoxicating.

"You can turn around now." Tegan had left her shirt unbuttoned. He handed Theo off, and when Tegan had him cradled in her arms, he took Ollie from Trenton and settled him against his chest, turning his back so Tegan could nurse. "Hello, my little Theo. Are you hungry?" Within seconds, the baby quieted, and Jax took that as a good sign.

Jackson swayed the younger twin in his arms, humming low in hopes it would soothe the boy until it was his turn to eat. He waited until Theo stopped fussing to ask, "Do twins run in your family?"

"The boys aren't twins. They're litter mates. At least that's how my mom explained it when my brothers were born." While Theo continued to nurse, Tegan talked about her parents, her little brothers, their deaths, and how she had been taken from their family home. It broke his heart. Then she spoke of her foster parents, and his heart lightened again.

"Theo's done, I think."

Jackson glanced over his shoulder. Tegan had covered her breasts and was holding out Theo to swap. Jax asked, "Did you burp him?"

Tegan's eyes filled with tears. "I forgot."

Jax gave her a kind smile. "You're doing great, Tegan." When she went to lift Theo, Tegan struggled. "If you don't have the strength to hold him up, place him on your lap. Like this." Jax sat down next to her and demonstrated on Ollie.

"Goddess, I suck at this," Tegan whispered, fat tears rolling down her cheeks.

Jax reached over and ran a fingertip through the wetness. "You listen to me. You gave birth to two babies all on your own with no help. No anesthesia. You're the strongest female I've ever met."

"Do you have kids?" she asked as she patted Theo on his back.

Jax had to clear his throat before he could answer. "No, I don't."

Trenton must have noticed Jax's reticence. He added, "There are a couple of babies and a few younger kids in our lives, so being around little ones isn't new to us."

Jax closed his eyes briefly and swallowed hard. When Theo let out a wet burb, Tegan chuckled. "There you go," she praised.

Jackson grinned, and when he opened his eyes, he sucked in a breath. Tegan's smile was like the sun shining through the clouds. Her hair was plastered to her forehead from sweating, and he had a strong urge to brush it off her face. Instead, he held out his free arm for Theo so they could swap babies. When Ollie was settled in Tegan's arms, he turned his back to give her privacy once more. Jax pressed Theo to his chest, and soon after felt wetness against his shirt. Carefully holding the baby away from him, he burst out laughing. "We definitely need diapers."

"I'll go grab a couple," Trenton offered and walked down the hallway to one of the nurseries. When he returned, he took Theo from Jax and laid the baby on the opposite bed. Jax moved the weapons to the dresser, then watched as the wolf expertly wrapped the disposable around the little one's bottom. When he was done, Trenton handed Theo back to Jax with a knowing smile. "I'm going downstairs to check on Judge."

Jax inclined his head to the male.

"If you feel up to traveling, I would prefer to have Rev and Bethany meet us at the cabin. I want to get you and the boys as far away from here as soon as possible. You mentioned the place you were headed isn't far from the cabin, so we can stop there and pick up all the supplies you bought on the way."

"And after he examines us, are you taking us home?" Tegan asked, her voice quivering.

# CHAPTER ELEVEN

## Tegan

TEGAN DIDN'T WANT TO go back to her rental. She didn't want to raise the babies alone. Not now that she'd met her mate. But Jackson didn't know they were mates. Or if he did, he hadn't mentioned it.

Jackson sat down on the bed with his back to the headboard. His arm was warm against hers, even through the long-sleeve. "I hadn't planned on it. You said you have no one to help you, so I'm offering. Tegan, when you recognized me as the eagle outside your window, you said you felt it in your heart. I'm going to be honest with you. Gryphons don't have fated mates, but my beast has claimed you. I'm not saying this to sway your feelings but to let you know I'm all in, if you'll give me a chance. I have plenty of room for the three of you. If you don't feel comfortable living with me, there's the Providence House. It's a home for those we rescue from cults who need a place to recover and reacclimate to living outside their compounds."

"You rescue people?" Who was he and this group of hounds? He made it sound like the Gryphons were a bunch of saints.

"Not me specifically, although I do help with taking out the leaders if necessary."

"Taking them out as in killing them?"

Jackson didn't look at her when he answered. "Yes, but only as a last resort. We don't go around killing innocent people. Have you heard of The Ministry?"

Who hadn't? They were the most infamous cult in history. "Of course. I might not be the brightest woman in the world, but I did go to high school."

Jackson did look at her then. "I didn't mean to imply you aren't smart. I know you are, or you wouldn't have thought ahead to setting up a place of your own for you and the boys. The Ministry is who the Hounds focus on. If we find other cult-like communities, we leave them in peace if they aren't hurting anyone and the members are there of their own accord. Several of the Hounds' mates have been rescued from The Ministry, and we're doing our best to eradicate the leaders for all the chaos they've caused since the apocalypse. Ryot, our president, his first wife was taken to one of their compounds along with his unborn child. McKenzie, his daughter, was given to someone else to raise, and his wife tried to escape, dying in a car crash in the process. Mac was reunited with Ryot when two of his brothers tracked a missing woman to that same compound."

"Your president? And what kind of name is Ryot?"

"Zeus called his Gryphons 'The Hounds of Zeus' when he created us, and that is also the name of our motorcycle club. Not all Hounds are in the club, but all Gryphons are Hounds, if that makes sense. Ryot is

111

Ryker's biker name, and he's the president of our club. My biker name is Sultan, and I'm the sergeant-at-arms. Ryan's moniker is Judge. When you meet Zareck, he'll use those names instead of our given ones, and we'll call him Rev, short for Reverend, instead of Zareck."

"Is he a preacher? And why do they call you Sultan?"

"No, Zareck isn't a preacher, but he is someone we go to when we need to talk things out. He's the most level-headed Hound I know. As for me, my middle name is King. It was my mother's surname before she married my father. Ryker's father gave me the moniker when I first joined the club. Both my parents passed many years ago, and Sutton became a second father to me. There was already a Hound with the moniker King, so Sutton chose Sultan because it is similar in meaning to king, and I think he liked that it was close to his own name. Sutton was president of the Hounds before he passed the gavel to Ryot so he could focus on The Ministry. He and his mate, Rory, oversee Providence House."

"Why would they take me in at this Providence House? I'm not being rescued from a cult."

Jackson pressed a kiss to her temple. "They would take you in because it's the right thing to do."

"I don't want to be a burden."

"You aren't. Not to me nor to those who run Providence. When I said I had money, I didn't mean Bucco levels of wealthy, but I own my home, I have a sizable savings account, and I can provide for you. Whatever money you saved you can spend on the boys, or you can put it in the bank. One of the Hounds

112

can drive your car back, so you won't have to worry about wheels. Although, I would offer to get you something bigger. Another thing, we found the Harley and moved it to the cabin. It's not in too bad of shape from where you laid it down. Havyk, one of the Hounds, is aces with bikes. He can fix it up, and we can sell it if you'd like."

"But I don't have the title. Isn't that stealing?"

Jax scoffed. "Like that fucker John didn't steal your car?"

"I guess, but I do have it back." Tegan brushed a kiss against her sleeping son's head. "Jax?"

"Yes, Wildcat?"

Tegan looked into his emerald eyes. "Wildcat?"

Jackson grinned at her. "Yeah. You partially shifted when I first came into your room. Scared the shit out of me."

"Right. You're a Gryphon."

"Hey, fangs and claws are fangs and claws. The fiercest Hounds I know are the females. Wait 'til you meet Rory. She's scary. Ryot and his four brothers respect the hell out of Sutton, but their mother?" Jackson shook his head, smiling. "You'll understand once you meet her."

There it was again, his assuredness Tegan would meet this female. Tegan leaned her head against his shoulder and relished the safety. How long had it been since she felt as though she weren't truly alone? Since she left her home with Rosie and Marcus.

"How'd you learn to ride a motorcycle?"

Tegan smiled, thinking of the first time Marcus turned her loose on a bike. "My foster father, Marcus, rode. While Rosie taught me to cook and do laundry, Marcus showed me other things like changing a flat tire. He helped me with my homework too."

"Were you the only kid in their house?"

"Yeah. They weren't in it for the money like a lot of foster parents. I now consider them my parents because of the way they raised me with so much love. They always take in older kids instead of the little ones. They had a few before me, and they've had two since I moved out. A sweet boy named Bobby lives with them now. He wants to open his own bakery one day, and I have no doubt he'll make it happen. That kid is amazing in the kitchen. I'm not close to the other one, but there's something special about Bobby. I think of him as my little brother."

"They sound like wonderful people. Are you going to take the boys to visit them?"

Tegan frowned. "How can I? What would happen if we were there, and the cubs shifted in front of them?"

"Well, I could go with you, and if that happened, I could voice Rosie and Marcus. Gryphons have the ability to make humans forget something they shouldn't see. We can also influence them to do things, but we don't abuse the power."

Tegan leaned away from Jackson so she could really look at him. "That's scary as hell. Have you used your voice on me?"

"I did when I was trying to get you to wake up, but only because I didn't know how long you'd been unconscious, and the boys needed you. I promise I would never voice you in any way that is harmful.

114

Tegan, I know you have no reason to believe me, but I'll ask that you listen to your Lion. What is she telling you?"

"To trust you." Tegan took a deep breath, ready to tell him the truth. "Jax?"

"Yeah, Sweetheart?"

Tegan chickened out. "I need a shower. I stink."

Jackson's body shook with silent laughter, and Tegan grinned. When he got his mirth under control, he tugged her tighter to him. "I think you smell like a miracle. The miracle of childbirth. If you allow it, I'll be the best stepfather to Theo and Ollie. I'll be the best mate to you." He pressed his nose to Ollie's downy hair and inhaled.

"Have you ever thought about having kids?" Tegan asked. Jackson tensed, and she knew in her heart there was a story there.

"I, uh… I had a daughter. Almost." Leaning his head back, he closed his eyes. "I had a female in my life a long time ago, but I never claimed her as my mate. She wanted me to park my motorcycle and give up the club. When I refused, she left me. Soon after, she was in a car wreck. A bad one. When her parents called to tell me she was on life support, that's when I found out she was pregnant. Crystal hadn't told them we were broken up, so they were confused as to why my name was no longer her emergency contact. She wasn't far enough along for the baby to make it without her, but Crystal would never survive off life support. Since the baby was mine, they left it up to me to decide whether to pull the plug."

Tegan's heart broke for him, already knowing how

115

his story ended. "Jackson, I'm so sorry. How long has it been?"

He leaned his head against hers. "Fifteen years. It took a long time to get over the fact that she hadn't told me about the baby. Even longer for the pain of losing my baby girl to recede." Jax exhaled, and said, "We have company."

He rose from the bed and carried Ollie to the door. Tegan studied her mate as he stood in the hallway, waiting for whomever it was. Jax was tall, built, and had quite a bit of ink from what she could tell, adding to his bad boy vibe. Unlike John, Jackson had a home and money. He'd already showed her more kindness than John ever did without wanting anything in return. Still, she couldn't admit to him he was her fated mate. Not yet.

A stranger appeared in the doorway carrying several shopping bags. He dropped them to the floor and held out his hands. "May I?" Jax handed Ollie over, and the male rocked and cooed the baby. "What's his name?"

"Ollie. And Tegan is holding Theo. Tegan, this is Sean Tapley, but we call him Shadow."

"Hey, Tegan. How are you feeling?" Shadow crossed the room and ran a fingertip across Theo's soft scalp.

"Pretty good considering. Thanks for helping rescue me."

"Eh. All in a night's work. I bought some sub sandwiches if you're hungry, or I can make breakfast after I tend to Judge's arm." Shadow handed Ollie back to Jax and retrieved the bags, placing them on the spare bed.

"Are sandwiches okay with you, Tee?"

*Tee.* No one had called her that since she was little, but she liked it. "Yeah, I'm not picky."

"Now that you're here with the car seats, I want to get on the road as quickly as possible. Do you want to eat first or take a shower?"

"Shower, definitely. Will you stay in here with the cubs?"

"Absolutely. Shadow, we'll meet you downstairs in a few." The male gave a mock salute and closed the door on his way out.

"Do you think you could shift now? That might make you feel better too."

Tegan didn't have to think about it. "My Lion is itching to get free."

"Okay, if you'll put Theo down, I'll lay Ollie next to him so I can watch them both."

Tegan kissed her oldest baby and placed him on the bed. She caressed her youngest's head when she passed by to get to her suitcase. After pulling clean clothes out, she took them and her toiletries to the bathroom and started the shower to make sure there was hot water. As the shirt slid down her arms to the floor, she could feel Jackson's eyes on her. Tegan wasn't shy about her body, so she let him look his fill as she padded naked back into the bedroom and stretched her arms over her head before letting her other side loose. It had been months since she could take to her fur, and she'd missed it greatly. Tegan stalked to where Jackson was kneeling beside the bed and bumped his arm with her nose.

117

"Wow. You are one beautiful Wildcat." Jax ran a hand over her head and down her back. Tegan's tail swished with contentment. Her beast wanted to give Jax its belly, but Tegan denied the animal.

*I want a shower, and we need to hit the road. There will be time for belly rubs later.*

After brushing against Jackson's side, her Lion padded over to the cubs, sniffing them. It wanted to climb on the bed and curl up with them, but there wasn't time. The lioness gently licked each boy's foot. Only then did it give control back, shifting to her skin. Jackson's eyes traveled from her feet all the way up to her face. Tegan bent over, cupping his cheeks, and pressed her lips to his. She wouldn't take it further than a chaste kiss. They didn't have the time nor the privacy for anything else, plus she wanted to brush her teeth. Tegan strode to the steam-filled bathroom and stepped under the hot water. She scrubbed her body, shampooed her hair twice, and shaved her legs while the conditioner did its job. Her body was sore, but shifting had taken care of the tearing from her babies exiting her body.

Tegan towel-dried her hair, then twisted it up into a messy bun. She hated leaving it wet, but needs must. She brushed her teeth, put on deodorant, then slipped into shorts, her bra, and a loose T-shirt. She wadded her dirty things up and took them to her suitcase. She returned to the bathroom for her toiletries and added those on top of her clothes. Both boys were asleep with Jax watching over them. While she was in the bathroom, he'd pulled his harness on over his shirt. Jax looked like a badass with the pistols sheathed in their holsters.

*Thank you, goddess.* Not only were her sons here and safe, but Tegan had found her mate amidst the turmoil of the last two days. She would go to New Troy and let him get to know her before she told him the truth.

Jax stood and held open his arms. Tegan walked up to her mate where he wrapped her in a tight embrace. He kissed her temple, but she wanted more. When Tegan turned her face up, Jax pressed their lips together.

"I can't wait to get you home," he whispered against her mouth. "Trenton has the car seats in the SUV. I'd like to hit the road. We can take a sandwich with us and eat while driving."

"What do you want me to do?"

"Stay here with the boys. I'll get everything loaded, then I'll come back for you."

Tegan nodded against his chest, inhaling his scent. Jax pressed his lips to hers once more before zipping her suitcase. He grabbed it and the shopping bags, pausing at the door to wink at her. Tegan took Jackson's place on the floor beside the bed, staring at the wonders that were her sons.

# CHAPTER TWELVE

## Sultan

JUDGE WAS PATCHED UP and ready to go by the time Sultan had Tegan's things in the SUV. Jackson and Max had discussed leaving the four horsemen and Trenton with only one vehicle, but Max assured them Sutton was sending more males.

"Legend brought Tegan's car from the vineyard. I'll follow you and your family."

Jax didn't correct his friend. As far as he was concerned, Tegan and the boys were his. With the comms live, the Hounds had overheard Jax explaining what happened to his baby girl. Instead of focusing on the sad, each one wished Jax and Tegan well after he thanked them for helping rescue his female. Jax removed the comm and handed it over to Trenton. He kept the pistols, but he took off the rigging and stowed it under the front passenger seat. He wouldn't be caught without a way to protect his family or Ryan if the mob were to somehow follow. Jackson pulled up the security feed at the cabin to be sure no one was waiting for them. He went so far as to start from the time he and the other Hounds left, scanning through to the present. Thankfully, no one else had been there.

Getting the boys situated was a learning experience, but Trenton helped, having experience with his daughter although Quinn was now a grown female. They made it out of town without any of Bucco's men tailing, and the drive was filled with Tegan recounting everything that she'd been through, her discussions with Bucco, and the Hive packaging in the workroom. She ate her sandwich and tended to the sleeping babies while Jax explained what happened outside while she was giving birth.

Jax glanced at Tegan in the rearview mirror. His mate was wedged between the car seats. At some point, she'd taken her hair out of the bun, and it was now a wild riot of waves. "If you'd like, we can stop off at your place and grab the supplies you stored on the way to the cabin."

Tegan focused on Ollie instead of meeting his eyes. "Oh, uh, that's okay. I'll just get new things when we get to New Troy."

Jax didn't press the issue. He wouldn't make her feel bad about the lack of supplies or the quality. His female had done the best she could with what she had. He knew that in his heart. He couldn't imagine being in her place, pregnant with no one to turn to. That was behind her now. She had Jax and a host of Hounds and mates to help with the cubs.

"Are you sure going to the cabin is safe? What if Freddie told Bucco how to find it?"

Jax had thought about that, thus the reason he looked at the security feed. "We won't be there long. I have a feeling Bucco is more worried about his compound being infiltrated than coming after you. If he's smart, he'll stay away."

"Did you find the tracker? That's how Freddie found me. What if someone else has access to the signal?"

"Tracker? Fuck. No, we didn't find it because we weren't aware of it. I'll have Ryan take care of that as soon as we get there."

"Okay. I trust you." When they arrived at the clearing, Tegan leaned forward. "How are we doing this?"

"You mean getting through the woods with the boys?"

"Yeah."

"There's a path from this direction. Where you wrecked the Harley is through the woods at the back of the cabin. If you aren't up to walking that far, I can carry you while Ryan carries the boys in their seats."

"I'll walk as far as possible. If I get tired, then you can carry me."

"You got it, Wildcat." Jax got out and opened the back door on his side of the SUV. Ryan had parked Tegan's car and was already pulling Theo's car seat out.

"Hey, Theodore. Did you have a good nap? You like the hum of the tires on the road?" Judge took off through the woods, pointing out the different types of trees and birds.

Jax removed Ollie's carrier, then held out his hand to help Tegan. Once on her feet, she placed her hands on her hips. "Uh..." She gestured toward Ryan's retreating back.

"You might as well get used to it. Before you met me, you had no help. Now you'll have more than you probably want. The night you broke in, a bunch of us were having supper together, and I don't think little Patrick saw his parents more than five minutes the whole time we were at the restaurant."

Jax locked the SUV, pocketed the keys, then took Tegan's hand and led her down the path behind Judge, who never stopped talking to Theo. "Let me know if you need a break."

"I will." Tegan squeezed his hand. Jax was mindful to keep pace with Tegan since her legs were shorter. She made it about halfway to the cabin when she tugged him to a stop. "I can't believe I'm this tired already."

Before Jax could call out, Judge reversed course and held out his hand for Ollie. "Now I get to talk to both my nephews." He took off repeating a lot of what he'd already told Theo, and Tegan giggled. Jackson picked her up bridal-style and followed his best friend.

"I could get used to this." Tegan had one arm around his neck and was running her fingers through his beard with her free hand.

Jax growled. "I could too." He pressed a kiss to her forehead. "I can't wait for you to heal up so I can show you how glad I am you're... in my life."

Tegan leaned her head against his shoulder. "But you don't know me. Not really. What if we aren't compatible?"

"I have a good feeling about that, but we can get back to Troy and take our time getting to know one another."

Judge placed the babies on the porch while he unlocked the door. He took them inside, leaving the door open for Jax. When he carried her over the threshold, he said, "Welcome back." Jax set Tegan on her feet, and she joined the boys in front of the unlit fireplace. When Theo started fussing, she unfastened his harness and pulled him out.

Ryan held out his hands for the keys. "I'll run to the car for their things."

"Before you do that, Tegan said there's a tracker on the Harley. See if you can locate it, then maybe take it the opposite direction and drop it somewhere?"

"Fuck, yeah." Ryan took off out the back door. Once he was outside, Tegan sat down on the sofa and lifted her shirt and bra so Theo could nurse. Jax appreciated the fact that she wasn't shy around him. Then again, a mother feeding her child was the most natural thing in the world. He didn't understand why folks got so bent out of shape about seeing it happen in public. Jax got Ollie out of his seat and showed him around the cabin. Since there wasn't much to see, he took the baby outside for some more fresh air. It was a little before noon, and the sun was already warming things up.

"Found it!" Ryan approached, holding the small black device in his palm. "They already have a lock on this location, but at least now we can take the bike to New Troy without them knowing."

Jax nodded. "Truth, but I still don't plan on hanging around. As soon as Rev gives them all a clean bill of health, we'll head to New Troy."

"Okay. Let me get the tracker away from here, then

I'll grab the babies' things." Judge pressed a kiss to Ollie's head before taking off through the woods.

When Jackson took Ollie inside, Tegan had Theo on her shoulder burping him. "I love your cabin. Do you come here often?"

"Only when I need some down time. It's been in my family for several generations. I remodeled the bathroom, but I've kept most of it original. Thus, no electricity."

Voices in the woods alerted Jax to Ryan approaching with Rev and Bethany. "The others are here. I'll meet them outside while you feed Ollie, then we'll get the three of you checked out so we can get back on the road." They swapped babies, and Jax kissed Tegan before heading outside.

"Rev, Bethany, thank you both for making the trip. Tegan's inside nursing Ollie, and this little one is Theo."

Bethany held out her hands, and Jackson passed the baby over. She fussed over him while Rev clapped Jax on the shoulder.

"A lion, huh? I didn't see that one."

"Neither did I, but there are Gryphons, Gargoyles, and wolves, so why couldn't there be other types of shifters?"

Rev smiled at his mate as she sang to Theo. "You like her."

Jax shoved his hands in his back pockets and looked up at the trees. "I do. My Gryphon insisted she belonged to me the moment I saw her driver's license photo. When I met her, I had to agree. Zeus has blessed me with this second chance." Jackson explained about

125

his past, giving Tegan time to feed Ollie. Bethany had tears in her eyes as she handed Theo back to Jax.

"But enough about that. I'd like to get back to New Troy sooner rather than later in case Bucco sends men here. Let me go see if she's finished." Jax needed a few minutes to rein in his emotions. Talking about his lost baby girl never got easier.

When he entered the cabin, Tegan had Ollie over her legs, patting his back. "We're ready."

## *Tegan*

JAX CALLED FOR HIS friends and held the door open as they entered the cabin. After introductions, Bethany, a stunning brunette, stopped and brushed her hand over Theo's head before crossing the room. She knelt beside Tegan, placing her palm to Tegan's cheek. "Hi, Tegan. How are you feeling?"

"Not bad, all things considered. I was able to shift, and that took care of everything, even the stretching."

Bethany patted Tegan's cheek gently, then turned her attention to Ollie. "We'll check the boys over, then the men can take them outside while I do an exam if that's okay?"

"I thought your mate was the doctor?"

Rev chuckled. "Oh, I am, but Bethany is just as knowledgeable. Probably more so when it comes to the female anatomy. She's delivered more babies than anyone I know. You're in the best hands with her." Tegan would much rather the female check her over anyway, so she agreed.

Rev opened a black bag and pulled out a stethoscope. The adults were quiet while he listened to both cubs' chests. When he leaned back, Rev smiled at Tegan. "I would like to do more extensive testing, but it sounds like both boys are healthy," the doctor assured her. "I was worried about the fluid in their lungs considering you thought they were premature, but I think you being a shifter means the babies' were born right on time considering their size. If you weren't a lion, they would have needed a hospital."

"I was going by a human's gestation period. Like I told Jackson, I don't know any other shifters. My family was killed a long time ago, and I was young when my brothers were born. Three months might be normal for my kind."

"Do you have a pediatrician lined up?"

Tegan tensed. "No. I couldn't trust a human doctor because I don't know when the cubs will take to their fur. I don't remember how old I was when I shifted the first time, but I'm pretty sure my brothers were toddlers when it happened with them, but I couldn't take the chance."

"Oh, you poor dear," Bethany said, brushing a loose strand of hair back from Tegan's face. "Well, you aren't alone now. I'm not sure if Jackson told you, but we have a large family of Hounds who will be more than happy to help you and your boys."

The back door opened, and Ryan entered. "The tracker is miles from here. How are my nephews?"

Rev stood and clapped Ryan on the shoulder. "Your nephews are in good health. Let's take them outside and give the females the room."

Bethany was all business as she examined Tegan. She asked some personal questions about breast tenderness and leakage as she checked her private bits. As Tegan suspected, shifting had taken care of needing stitches. All in all, she was in good shape. Bethany offered to help give the babies a sponge bath.

"Uh, I don't have any baby wash. Will soap hurt them?"

Bethany walked to the table and showed Tegan the contents of a shopping bag. "I stopped and grabbed some along with some baby towels."

"You're too kind."

"Not at all. How about it?"

"Yes, please." Tegan walked to the back door and asked Jax to bring the brothers in for bathtime. He followed the females into the bathroom where Bethany turned on the tap in the sink. He held Ollie, and they paid close attention to how Bethany bathed Theo. She didn't submerge them, explaining their vitals needed time to stabilize. She also told them how to take care of the umbilical cords. The boy fussed and wiggled, but when it was Ollie's turn, he sucked on his fist quietly. Once both boys were clean with new diapers, they returned to the living room. When Jax hovered, Tegan asked if she could speak to Bethany alone.

"Of course. I'll be right outside if you need me."

Jax kissed her forehead, then headed outside.

"Thank you, both you and Zareck, for driving here and checking on us. I, uh, don't have insurance, but I can pay you cash."

"No need to worry about that. Consider it a welcome to the Hounds gift. Have you thought more on Sultan's offer for you to live with him?"

"I would appreciate having the help, but I don't want to be a burden to him. He mentioned some place that catered to those who were rescued from The Ministry?"

Bethany glanced out the back window. "Providence House is run by a wonderful couple, Lynette and Branson Miller. There are only two women staying there at the moment, so Lynette will have plenty of time to help you and your cubs get settled."

Tegan wrapped her arms around her waist. She didn't want to stay anywhere other than with Jackson even though they were mates, but after the story of his past female, Tegan didn't want to force the issue. "I think that'll be best. At least for now."

"Then let's tell the men the plan. Sultan will need to call Rory and give her a heads up."

"Would you tell them? I need to use the restroom."

"Of course. See you in a few."

Once Bethany was outside, Tegan crawled over to the back window so she could gauge Jackson's reaction to Tegan going to Providence instead of to his home. She used her Lion's hearing to eavesdrop.

*Bethany placed her hand on Jax's arm. "Tegan has decided to stay at Providence."*

*Jax clenched his jaw. "Then I need to call Rory. Please*

hold Ollie." He passed the baby to Bethany, then took off running through the woods.

"What the fuck?" Ryan whispered, but Tegan heard him clearly. "After all he's done to rescue her? She won't give him a chance?"

Bethany swayed Ollie back and forth. "She doesn't want to be a burden."

"That's bullshit, and you know it."

"I do, but she doesn't. Think about it from her perspective. She's been through hell these past couple of days, and the man who should have been there for her is the reason for that hell. For months, she thought she would be having these babies and raising them alone. It's going to take a minute to realize she has all of us in her corner. Besides that, she just gave birth, and her hormones are wreaking havoc on her system. We'll get her settled with Lynette, and Jax can court her properly. Show Tegan he's all in."

Jax had already said he was all in, so why was Tegan fighting him?

Jax returned from the woods, his face stoney. "It's all set. Rev, if you and Bethany would drive her back to New Troy, I'm going to stay here and take care of a few things before I drive back."

Shit. He wasn't happy. Tegan ducked down and crawled out of the kitchen, not stopping until she was in the bathroom. As she peed, Tegan wondered if she'd just screwed up.

Everyone was waiting for her in the living room. Jax's mood hadn't improved, and Tegan hated it. With arms crossed over his chest, he said, "If you give me the address of your place, I'll go get all the things you bought for the boys. No need in spending money on supplies you already have."

Tegan didn't want him to see her shack or how little she'd bought, but he wasn't giving in. "It's not easy to find. There isn't a mailbox."

"But you drove to it, so give me basic directions and landmarks." Tegan's shoulders sagged. Once he saw it, he would change his mind about her. He arched a dark eyebrow, waiting.

"I did. It's about thirty minutes northeast on Highway 77." Tegan told her mate all the landmarks to look for and how to navigate through the woods to get to the shack.

Jax pressed kisses to both boy's heads before approaching Tegan. He hesitated a moment, then kissed her lips softly. "I'll meet you in New Troy." With that, he was gone.

# Chapter Thirteen

## Sultan

JACKSON GRABBED THE SATELLITE phone and walked outside with Ryan on his heels. His beast was fighting him, pissed that he didn't demand Tegan go home with them.

**They are ours, dammit. Do not let them go with Rev.**

*It's not what she wants. I'll do as she wishes, but I'll visit her often to show I'm there for her.*

His beast was not happy with those terms, but it was the best Jax could do. With shaking hands, he punched in Rory's number.

"Sultan? Everything okay at the cabin?" Sutton asked, answering his mate's phone.

Jackson explained everything as concisely as possible before stating Tegan wanted to stay at Providence House.

"It's kind of crowded because we rescued some folks from Haven last night, but they'll have a room for Tegan and the boys. I'll have Rory call Lynette."

"Thanks, Sutton."

"No thanks needed, Son. This is what we do." With

that, his friend disconnected.

"You're really good with the boys." Ryan's eyes were soft, and Jax wondered if his best friend wanted kids of his own. Even when talking about Crystal and Coral, Ryan never mentioned wanting a mate or a family. Some males were loners, content with their lot in life.

"Children, especially babies, are precious. They didn't ask to be brought into the world, and the way I see it, they should be cherished. Even if they're as rambunctious as Major."

"That boy is a trip. What amazes me is how different Marshall is. Talk about precious." Ryan shook his head, smiling. He wasn't wrong. Mayhem's twins were like night and day. Major was loud and funny as hell, while Marshall was soft-spoken and loving. Jax wondered if Ollie and Theo would have different personalities like the twins. "You want me to go with you to her place?"

"Nah, Brother. Why don't you head home? I have a feeling there's not much to pack up. I'll get that done, then I'll be on the road behind you all. If you would, though, help Rev with the babies. That way Tegan doesn't have to carry one of the car seats." He handed over the sat phone. "Please take this when you go in."

"You got it. Call me if you need me." Ryan pulled Jax in for a hug, clapped him on the back, and returned to the house. Jackson took off through the woods, wanting to get to Tegan's place and on the road home as quickly as possible. He removed the bases for the car seats and placed them on the ground beside Rev's vehicle before getting into his own.

The drive to where Tegan's place was only took twenty minutes. She wasn't kidding when she said it was off the grid. It took Jax a few tries before finding the driveway. How she'd gotten her car back there without bottoming out was a mystery. Jax parked and got out of his SUV and headed toward the sound of running water. He walked beside a creek about fifty yards, and when he got to the clearing, Jax turned in a circle. There was no way the dilapidated shack was where she'd been planning on living. A strong wind could blow it over. Still, he gingerly climbed the rickety steps, and when he tried the doorknob, the door wasn't latched. Jax pushed it open, and his heart sank.

There was no electricity. No running water. The glass in the windows was broken, and there were no curtains. There was no furniture, only piles of blankets and pillows. Boxes lined one wall, and upon inspection, he found several packs of diapers, all size newborn. There were wipes, butt cream, and powder, plus a few gowns, all in neutral colors. Other boxes held canned foods. She'd bought a propane stove but less than a dozen small bottles of fuel. Tears filled his eyes, thinking about Tegan and the babies out here alone. Not wanting to spend one more second there, he started hauling her things to his truck. The sooner he left, the sooner he could get home and begin showing her how good life with him could be.

# Tegan

RYAN HELPED REV WITH the babies and their things, while Tegan and Bethany followed them through the woods to their SUV. She didn't want to go to Providence House. She wanted to go home with Jackson and let him help her with the boys, but that wasn't fair to him. She'd already caused the male enough trouble by breaking into the cabin and disrupting his life by needing rescuing. Her Lion railed at her for not agreeing to stay with him.

*He wouldn't have offered if he didn't want us there. We need him.*

Tegan agreed they needed someone. If she only had one child, maybe she could handle things alone, but with two of them? Goddess, she was tired. She didn't know how human women handled childbirth without the luxury of shifting and letting their animal side heal them. Then again, human females had doctors and modern medicine.

Bethany asked Tegan about her life, how she'd chosen her sons' names, told Tegan about her own children, and kept Tegan's mind off Jackson for the first hour of the ride. But then the female asked how Tegan felt about Jackson.

"Bethany," Zareck chided.

"What? I saw the way he looked at her, and that male is smitten."

Smitten? With the cubs maybe, but who would honestly want to be saddled with a female who made such bad decisions?

"He's been incredible, and I appreciate everything he did."

"But?" Bethany hedged.

"But I've been enough trouble already, and I don't want to put him out. He has a life, the MC, and I'm assuming a job he'll need to get back to."

Zareck glanced at Bethany, and some unspoken conversation happened. He sighed. "Sultan's job is more of a freelance type of deal. He works his own hours. As for the MC, it's not your typical club. The members are Gryphons, and that means family comes first. Always. If you would rather stay with him, I know for a fact he would welcome you. He would prefer that. Gryphons don't have fated mates, but when they meet someone they want in their life, they don't hesitate to make it happen. I moved Bethany in with me two days after meeting."

"Did you know he was a Gryphon?" Tegan asked Bethany.

Bethany turned sideways so she could more easily see Tegan. "He told me the night we met. Showed me both his Lion and Eagle. He couldn't shift into his Gryphon because there wasn't enough room without him tearing apart my apartment. But after seeing his other forms, I had no reason to doubt he was being truthful. And I'll say this then drop the subject. If you have any feelings for Jackson, you might as well start living with him now instead of moving your things into Providence House. That male is going to court you until you give in, and you'll end up with him anyway."

Tegan wanted to say that Jackson wouldn't have things they needed at his house like a crib or bassinet, but she'd not had those items either. She'd had the barest of essentials at the shack, so that argument wouldn't hold water. "Maybe I should stay at Providence House a few days and give Jackson time to get the boys a room ready. I can buy them a crib, but he'll have to put it together."

Bethany grinned. "I can make one phone call, and by the time we're in New Troy, the cubs will have a room set up with everything they need. One thing you'll learn about the Hounds is when someone wants something done, it happens. Quickly. You already have Judge, Zareck, and me, but you're also going to have a host of new friends and family whether you stay with Lynette or Jackson. Rory is the matriarch of the Hounds, and she's one fierce momma Gryphon. Since Jackson's parents are no longer with him, Rory and Sutton basically adopted him much like they have others whose parents are either across the country or have passed away."

Tegan would love to have a family. She considered Rosie, Marcus, and Bobby her family, but she couldn't share her secret with them. The Hounds had their own secret, and Tegan wouldn't have to hide her true nature. Hope wasn't something she'd had in a long time, but with each word Bethany spoke, it bloomed in her chest. "Don't you need to ask Jackson first?" What was she saying? Was she agreeing to move in with the male less than twenty-four hours after meeting him? Her Lion said yes, and hadn't Tegan agreed to listen to her beast?

"No. Sultan already offered, and he wouldn't have if he didn't want the three of you with him. Judge has a key to Sultan's house," Zareck said, looking at his wife.

"Should I make a call?" Bethany asked.

Tegan gazed at her sleeping sons, remembering how Jackson tended to both with such care and affection. He had given her so much already, and maybe by living with him, she could ease some of the pain and guilt from losing his baby girl. With her heart in her throat and tears in her eyes, Tegan said yes.

Zareck called Jackson and told him Tegan had changed her mind. His excited, "Yes!" came through loud and clear, and had Bethany laughing and Tegan's heart beating faster. She'd made the right decision.

When they arrived a few hours later, Jackson was already there waiting. He must have flown to get there before them, but they had stopped to feed the boys, and that took a while.

Jackson opened the left passenger door, unbuckling Ollie's harness instead of removing the car seat. "Hello, Ollie. Bet you and Theo need a diaper change, huh?" He always knew which baby was which. Tegan climbed over his car seat, and Jackson held out a hand to help her down. When she was on her feet, Jax snaked his free arm around her waist and pulled her in for a mind-blowing kiss.

Voices reminded Tegan they weren't alone, so she patted his chest, and Jax let her come up for air. "We had to stop so I could feed them, but I didn't change their diapers."

Bethany rounded the SUV with Theo, and Zareck strolled to the back where all her things were. "Is everything in place?" Bethany asked Jackson.

His eyes were shining with happiness. "Yes. Let's go look." He led them up the front steps and into a large living room that was obviously used. Much like the cabin, there was a sofa facing a fireplace with a large TV mounted over it. Instead of one recliner, two were situated on either side of the room, also facing the side wall. The kitchen was at the back of the house, but it was an open concept, and the dining table sat across from the kitchen in front of French doors that led to the backyard. Tegan followed Jackson down the hallway to the left, and he gestured to the first door on the right. "Here we are."

"Oh, Jackson." Tegan covered her mouth with her hand as she took in the nursery. There were two cribs as well as a dresser, changing table, and rocking chair. Stuffed toys littered the cribs, which had bedding decorated with woodland creatures. "But how? You didn't have much time."

"Most of this is Ryan's doing. He went shopping for the furniture as soon as he hit town. He asked Rory to help him with the other things."

"But I hadn't said yes." Tegan wiped the tears from her cheeks. "Where is he? I'd like to thank him," she whispered.

"He wanted to let you get settled." Jackson took Ollie to the changing table and placed him on the pad. Stacks of diapers, wipes, baby powder, and diaper cream, along with various other items were lined up on the shelf below. When Ollie was dry, Jackson moved so Bethany could change Theo.

"Where do you want Tegan's things?" Zareck asked.

"I cleaned out the spare bedroom. Put them there for now."

For now. Tegan liked the sound of that. As much as she wanted to stay in his room, Jackson was being a gentleman, and she appreciated it. Zareck handed Tegan her purse before continuing to the room next to the nursery. She dug around for her phone charger, but it wasn't there. Her phone had died at some point, and even though she didn't expect anyone to call except maybe Johnny, she still wanted to be able to use it. She followed Zareck to what would be her bedroom. It was nicer than any she'd ever had. As the male placed her things on the bed, Tegan began sorting through them and placing the few clothes she'd taken to the shack in the dresser. She then started on the things in her suitcase. She didn't have anything nice that needed to be hung in the closet.

When Jackson joined her, he was alone. "Where's Ollie?"

"Bethany put them down for a nap." Jackson leaned against the doorframe. "What made you change your mind?"

"Zareck did," she answered honestly as she folded a T-shirt and placed it in a drawer. "He said you wouldn't have offered to let us stay here unless you meant it."

"He's right. I do want you here for as long as you want to stay. I'll take care of you and the boys. And if you decide being with me is something you can see long-term, we'll look for a house with more property so we'll have privacy. I don't know when the cubs will shift, but I'd hate for them to be in the backyard and have one of the neighbors see a toddler take to his fur. And speaking of houses, we need to go see how much damage Freddie did. We can get it cleaned up so you get your deposit back. If it's too much, I'll pay to have it restored so the landlord doesn't sue you for damages."

Tegan held the next shirt to her chest and gave him her full attention. "I hope the destruction is minor. I need every penny I can get in case one of the boys needs medical attention."

"I'll take care of the rental for you, but Tegan, when I said I was here for you, I meant in every way. I'm not wealthy, but Zeus forbid one of the babies gets sick, you don't need to worry about that either."

Tegan sat on the edge of the bed. "Why? You don't know me. Not really. I let a loser into my life who knocked me up. I don't regret Ollie and Theo. But I'm not—"

"Stop." Jackson walked closer and knelt at her feet. Placing his palms on her knees, he squeezed gently. "We all make bad decisions when we're young." Jackson swallowed hard, and Tegan wondered if he was referring to his decision to let Crystal go. "Nobody is perfect. We all do the best we can and move forward. I don't want you worrying about your past. You have me and the Hounds and their mates now. We're here for you in whatever way you need."

Tegan placed her hand over his. He turned his

palm over, lifting her hand to his lips, and brushed a kiss across her knuckles. When he returned her hand to her lap, Jackson stood. "I'm going to help Zareck with the rest of your things so they can get home or to the park."

"The park?" Tegan clasped her hands together and rubbed her thumb across the skin he'd kissed.

"Yes. There's a big Fourth of July celebration at the local park that runs both days if the fourth is on Saturday, and a lot of the Hounds take their kids. I would offer to take you, but I'm not sure how the boys would react to the fireworks."

Tegan hadn't considered what the date was. In all the excitement of the last thirty-six or so hours, she'd not thought of anything other than escaping. And now, here she was, with two babies, a new home, and friends. *Thank you, goddess.* "No, I agree, especially since I'm breastfeeding. I'm sure other mothers feel comfortable doing so in public, but I'm not there yet."

Jackson leaned over and pressed his lips to her forehead. "You're doing great."

Tegan eyed his strong body as he left the room. Her skin tingled from where his lips touched her skin, and her Lion purred. *Silly cat.* She abandoned her clothes to talk to Bethany. The female stood in the kitchen, looking out the back door.

Tegan nudged Bethany's shoulder with her own. "Thank you for everything." Bethany turned and pulled Tegan into a hug. Goddess, how long had it been since she'd felt another's arms around her? Not since the last time she visited Rosie and Marcus, and that had been over a year. Johnny had never offered affection out of the bedroom that wasn't a slap on her ass. He'd never held her hand. Never hugged her. He kissed her plenty, or he tried to, but it was in seduction not affection. He surely had never kissed her knuckles. Tegan leaned into the other female's embrace. She didn't think Bethany was that old, but she was a mother of teens, and she knew how to give a good hug.

Bethany leaned back and placed her palm on Tegan's cheek. "I'm proud of you. There's a strength in you that few possess. And before you argue, you did what you had to do for your children. There's no greater love than that of a mother for her children unless you're blessed to be mated to a Gryphon. That type of love is different, but it's all-encompassing. I'm not saying that will be you and Jax, but it could be. Please allow him to take care of you and the babies. I promise you won't regret it."

"I will," Tegan whispered.

Zareck joined them, wrapping his arm around his wife. "I'd like to do a more thorough examination of Ollie and Theo tomorrow at my clinic. If you need us before then, Sultan has our number."

"Thank you both."

"You don't have to thank us. It's what family does. Now, we're going to go so Zoe will stop blowing up my phone. She's ready to go to the park, and her brother doesn't want her tagging along with him and his friends. Oh, I told Sultan, but I put some of your things in the garage, like the extra diapers. He'll help you sort it out later." Zareck reached out and squeezed Tegan's shoulder, then Bethany hugged her again. They said their goodbyes to Jackson when he walked them to the door.

Now that they were finally alone, Tegan was nervous. She was hopeful for the first time in forever. That is until he said, "We need to talk."

# CHAPTER FOURTEEN

## Sultan

WHEN TEGAN'S FACE FELL, Jax realized what he'd said. "No, not like that. We need to discuss the boys' birth certificates. Since you didn't go to a hospital, I'll have Bishop, our hacker, create their documentation. Rev will give us the necessary medical information at tomorrow's visit, but I need you to give me their full names. Here, why don't you have a seat, and I'll get you something to drink." Jackson led Tegan to the island and pulled out one of the stools. Once she was seated, he said, "I have orange juice and milk. I don't drink sodas, but I do have beer, although you probably shouldn't have alcohol while nursing. What do you normally drink? I'll start a grocery list."

Tegan propped her arms on the countertop. "Water's fine for now. I usually drink flavored green tea. It was the only thing that didn't make the babies do jumping jacks."

Jax smiled, thinking about the brothers moving around in her tummy. As he retrieved a glass and poured her water, she said, "About their names. I... Well, I didn't think that far ahead. I chose first names after my parents. As for their last name, there's no way in hell I'm listing John Cashel as the father."

"And you don't have to. You can leave that blank or put unknown."

"And that makes me sound like a slut. *Who's the father? Oh I don't know. It could be any number of men, I slept with so many.* No thank you."

Jackson couldn't help grinning. "Blank it is. You don't have to decide middle names today. Just think about it and let me know. They'll have your last name. How's unpacking coming along? Do you need help with anything?"

"I don't have that much left, but I do need to get another charging cord for my phone. I must have left mine when I rushed out of the house."

"What type of phone do you have? I might have a cord that works."

Tegan twirled the glass between her hands. "It's a Nebulus. I've had it a while, but it works fine."

Jax hated that Tegan felt the need to defend her phone. While it was an older model, it was still the most popular smart phone available. He already knew she didn't have a lot by the clothes she'd been unpacking and the store-brand toiletries he had put in her suitcase. "That's an excellent phone. If you need it today, I'll run out and get a cord. If not, I'll order one and have it delivered tomorrow."

"Tomorrow should be fine. It's not like anyone is looking for me. Well, John might be, but I never want to talk to him again."

"If you were human, and he wasn't a criminal, I might disagree, but you aren't, and he is, so no. You

146

don't ever have to talk to him." Jax planned to have Bishop investigate John Cashel's life and see exactly how bad the man was. With Tegan far enough away, he shouldn't bring trouble to their door, but Jax wasn't going to take any risks. "Since your rental is paid up through the end of the month, we can wait a week or so before we worry about assessing the damages." Jackson grabbed his own phone from his back pocket. "Let me order a cord, then we'll see about sorting through more of the boys' things." Jax did order a cord, but he also texted Bishop. The sooner he had information on Cashel the better.

One of the babies started fussing, which woke his brother. Theo was angry, his little face scrunched as though the world had pissed him off. Jax took Ollie into the living room to give Tegan privacy to feed her firstborn. Since it was their first official day together in their new home, Jax fixed sandwiches for lunch, then ordered dinner to be delivered later so neither one had to cook. They spent the day playing with the babies, watching movies between naps and feedings, and asking random getting-to-know-you questions. They talked about their tattoos, and Tegan mentioned the shop where she worked.

"I should probably call Onyx and let him know I'm alive. I overheard Bucco and Freddie arguing. When I didn't show up for work, Onyx came by the house and called the cops, and Bucco was pissed because those cops aren't on his payroll."

"Fucking Mafia. What are you going to tell Onyx?" Jax hated to drink in front of Tegan, but he could really use a beer. "Will it bother you if I have a cold one?"

"Not at all. I've never been much of a drinker. Before I got pregnant, I might have a fruity drink, but that's about it. As for Onyx, I'll probably tell him my parents needed me. He's probably already found someone to replace me. People were coming in almost daily looking to work there. Still, he was good to me, and I'd rather call him than leave him wondering. Can I borrow your phone?"

Jax had put his on the charger on his nightstand. "Yes. It's in my bedroom. I'll look in on the boys while I go get it." He downed his beer and tossed the bottle in the recycling bin before heading down the hallway. He checked on the cubs first. He already knew they were still sleeping since his Gryphon had been keeping an ear out for them. When he had his phone, Jax returned to the kitchen and handed it over.

When Tegan tapped the screen, she frowned. Jax didn't have it set to need facial recognition since he was never without the device. Tegan opened the phone app and dialed the number by heart. When the answering machine picked up, Tegan's shoulders slumped. "Hey Onyx, it's Tegan. Sorry I didn't show up for my shift, but I had a family emergency. I hate to do this over the phone, but I won't be back in anytime soon. Sorry to leave you in a bind. And uh, just keep my last paycheck to make up for not giving notice. I appreciate everything you did for me."

Tegan slid the phone across the island. "I guess that's that. Maybe he hasn't found a replacement? The shop should be open today."

Jax had so many questions, but the doorbell rang before he could ask them. He went to the door and

148

retrieved their hibachi steak dinner. He returned to the kitchen and unpacked the bags. "How long did you work for Onyx?"

Tegan began searching for plates, and Jax pointed to the right cabinet. Instead of using the plastic utensils the restaurant sent with their order, he got out forks and placed them on the island. As they dished out their food, Tegan said, "Four years. It was the first job I got when I moved to Coopersville. Before that, when I still lived in Mining Falls, I waited tables. I like customer service, but having a steady paycheck was better than working for tips. Marcus offered to pay for me to go to college, but I had no idea what I would've studied, and I didn't want to waste his money."

"Why did you move away from Mining Falls?" Jax asked as he got another beer.

Tegan opened a container of yum yum sauce and poured it over her fried rice. "Other than Rosie and Marcus, there was nothing there. It's such a small town, and I wanted something other than a shoebox apartment. My rental was nothing special, but it was a two-bedroom house with a yard, even if said yard was the size of a postage stamp. I could at least go outside and sit on the back porch and enjoy the fresh air. Have you always lived in New Troy?"

"No. I grew up in Arizona. My father's family was from New York, but he met my mom when he was on a business trip and moved there for her. With the cabin being here, Dad would bring me to New York for a guy's trip, just the two of us." Jax rubbed his chest, thinking about his parents. "After my folks passed away, I wanted a change of scenery. I got on my bike

149

and rode all over the country. I met Crystal when I was staying at the cabin and decided to stay in New York."

Tegan reached across the island and took Jackson's hand. "I'm sorry you lost your parents too. I should have said that before."

"Thank you. I was a late-life baby, and that's saying something for Gryphons. My mom was probably too old to have a kid, but for the twenty years I had her, she was the best. When she passed, my pop quickly followed. One day, he told me he loved me, but he missed his mate too much to care about living."

"That's as sad as it is sweet. To love someone so much you follow them in death. Did you get to bury them somewhere?"

"I did. It isn't in a public cemetery. I bought a five-acre tract of land and buried them there. What about your family? Are they interred somewhere?"

"No. They were cremated. When I was seventeen, I drove out to the shack and spread all their ashes in the little creek." Tegan focused on her food, and Jax allowed her the silence even though he hated her sadness. She set down her fork and tapped the table. "Zareck said Gryphons don't have fated mates, but I bet your parents came close to what that would be like."

"I have no doubt. What about you? Do lion shifters have fated mates?"

Tegan removed her hand and stood. She took her plate to the sink and rinsed it before putting it and her water glass in the dishwasher. "My Lion says yes. I'm going to check on the boys." Tegan left Jackson feeling like he'd been punched in the gut. What did that mean? Yes, she did, and he was hers? Or yes, she did, and he wasn't?

Jax set his fork down, his appetite gone. He walked to the door and looked out over his yard. He could imagine two little lions running and roughhousing. He let his mind also imagine a third child, another boy, chasing after his big brothers. Jax never thought he'd get that, a son of his own, but with Tegan here, it was what he wanted almost more than anything. What he wanted most was to claim the lioness. To love her and her children. Give them his last name. Gryphons might not have fated mates, but his was convinced Tegan belonged to them, and Jax agreed.

His phone rang, and seeing Judge's name, Jax welcomed the distraction.

"Hey, Brother. Thanks again for helping get the house ready."

"It was no problem. How's it going? Tegan getting settled?"

Jax opened the back door and stepped outside. "She seems to be, but we haven't been home long."

"I have a good feeling about her. Well, as far as the two of you are concerned. Something's bothering me about Bucco taking Tegan to work off the ex's debt."

"It is me too. I sent his name to Bishop. I want to know everything about the male just in case he's worse than I believe him to be."

"Truth. Speaking of, Ryot is sending me out on a job. It won't take long, but I thought since I have to drive toward your cabin, I could pick up the bike and bring it back. You still want to do that?"

"I mentioned it to Tegan, but she never gave me a

151

solid answer. Let me ask again, and I'll text you back with a yes or no. When do you leave?"

"I'm headed out in a couple hours. I'm taking my truck, so either way, you have time to let me know."

"Sounds good. Be safe out there." As good natured as his best friend was, Judge lived for the mercenary jobs.

"You know it."

As Judge clicked off, random fireworks exploded in the neighborhood. Not everyone went to the park for the big show, and that included Jax. Normally, he would sit on his front porch and enjoy the smaller ones the neighbor kids shot off. He was friendly with those in the houses surrounding his, and he knew every kid on the street by name. He'd even given some of the older ones a ride on his Harley. Jax knew Ollie and Theo wouldn't grow up with these kids. They couldn't being lions. At least they would have each other and the other Hounds' kids to play with when they were old enough. Jax opened his shifter senses to listen for sounds from inside the house. One of the boys was crying, and Tegan was doing her best to calm him down.

*"I'm sorry, Ollie. I can only feed one of you at a time. Please, baby,"* she begged, sounding close to tears herself. Jax didn't hesitate to go help. When he was outside the nursery, he called out to her so she could cover up if needed.

"I'm decent," she responded.

Jax still kept his gaze averted and padded to Ollie's crib. He lifted the baby against his shoulder, patting his little back and swaying. "Come on, Little Man. Let's

152

find you a num num."

Ollie bobbed his little head and shoved his fist in his mouth. Jax searched the shelf under the changing table and found a pacifier. When he offered it to Ollie, the baby latched on, and his tears lessened.

Tegan giggled. "Num num?"

Jackson smiled, thinking where the term came from. "Yeah. Little Patrick loves his paci, and Tank swears he makes a 'num num' sound when he's sucking on it."

"That's the cutest thing I've ever heard."

Jax gazed at Ollie's face, those shiny eyes staring back. He loved the little one already. Jax loved his brother too, and it would tear him apart if Tegan decided to leave. Jax sang softly as he rocked the infant in his arms. He'd never had the chance to hold Coral, and before he met these babies, the hurt had eased over the years. Now though? It brought back all the missed moments that could have been his had he not rejected Crystal. Had he not, Jax wouldn't be the male he was today. The biker. The mercenary. He would be a shell of himself. He thought of Warryck Lazlo and how he turned his back on the Hounds at the behest of his mate, giving his own daughter to her mother's family to raise while War went away and lived a solitary life away from the Hounds and his brothers. His twin. War was in a better place, having found his way back. Maybe Jax would have eventually found his way back as well. The "what ifs" didn't matter. Regrets had no place in his life now. Jax had to focus on what was in front of him, and according to his Gryphon, that was his mate. His beast never insisted Crystal was theirs, so maybe it knew what it was talking about.

Needing to focus on the future, he broached the subject of the bike. "So, Ryan is headed out on a job, and it's going to take him close to the cabin. He's offered to bring back the bike."

"What about the title?"

"Bishop can hack into the county clerk's database and change it. He can put a fake name on the title so it doesn't come back to you. Or we can take the bike to John."

"No. I don't want you anywhere near him. He's not dangerous, but he is bad news."

Jax glanced over, no longer worried about Tegan being covered. "Another reason I'm glad you're here with me and not back in Coopersville."

Tegan had Theo on her shoulder, patting his back. When he let out a gurgling burp, she praised him. "Ooh, that was a nice one. Such a good baby." Tegan kissed him on the temple before laying him on her lap to wipe his mouth with the burp cloth. She hadn't bothered to lower her T-shirt, and her breast was visible. Instead of it turning Jax on, it amazed him. Nature was a wondrous thing. He averted his eyes, not wanting her to think he was being a perv.

Tegan pulled her shirt down, then said, "I'm ready." She kept Theo on her lap while Jax passed Ollie over. He then took Theo and put the baby on his chest, inhaling his scent.

"This might make me a bad person, but if you think I can get more for the bike than it'll cost to repair it, then tell Ryan to please stop and get it. John took from me all those months we lived together, so I look at this as payback."

"It doesn't make you bad. I would say it makes you human, but…" Jax grinned. "One of Rory's sons, Havyk, is a god when it comes to motorcycles. When he finds out the story behind its condition, he'll probably repair it for free. That's what family does."

"Yeah, but I'm not his family," Tegan protested.

"You are, in a roundabout way. I've committed to taking care of you. Bethany has claimed you as well, and Ryan considers himself the boys' uncle already. You have a family here if you want it." Jackson walked to the rocking chair, lifted Tegan's face with his fingertips, and kissed her forehead. He left her alone to think about what he said and took Theo to the living room. He placed the baby on the sofa, knowing he was too young to roll off. Jackson couldn't believe the brothers were only a day old. He went to the spare bedroom and grabbed a couple of quilts that he folded and placed on the floor in front of the sofa. He knelt beside Theo and stared at the little wonder. Eyes a little darker than his brother's stared back. Jax didn't know how well Theo could see yet, but he wanted his face to be as familiar as his voice. Wanted the brothers to count on Jax to be their father figure.

Once Ollie was fed, Tegan joined Jax. He picked Theo up and sat with the baby on his lap.

"Oh, that's the tummy time Bethany mentioned." Tegan sat next to him, placing Ollie on his stomach too. It was supposed to help strengthen their neck muscles. After a few minutes, they settled the brothers on the pallet Jax had made from quilts. Someone, probably Rory, had purchased a baby gym that was large

155

enough for both boys to fit under. Jax placed it over them, then sat back down beside Tegan, not leaving any room between them. Tegan leaned her head against his shoulder, and Jax wanted to pump his fist. He placed his hand on her thigh, and after a few seconds, Tegan slid her hand beneath his, threading her fingers through his.

Instead of pulling her onto his lap and kissing her passionately like he wanted, Jax kissed Tegan's hair, then set his temple against her crown. It was sweet and domestic. Just the two of them enjoying the moment with their – her – babies. He wouldn't allow himself to consider the cubs his. Not yet.

"You asked about fated mates," Tegan whispered, and Jax closed his eyes. "My Lion says you're ours, but I'm scared, Jax. I'm afraid to get my hopes up."

"Can you tell me why?"

"You had a female in your life for ten years, and you didn't claim her. I can't go through that. I can't live with you, fall in love with you, let you raise my sons, only to have you decide a few years down the road I'm not worth it. If it even takes that long."

"Would you ask me to give up the club? To give up my job as a mercenary and sit behind a desk doing a job I hated?"

Tegan scooted away from him, her eyes wide. "You're a mercenary?"

Well, fuck.

# CHAPTER FIFTEEN

## Tegan

"A MERCENARY, AS IN you kill people for a living?" That should have made Tegan grab the boys and run for the door. Instead, it instilled a sense of safety. A mercenary could protect her from people like John Cashel and his mafia boss. He and his Hound friends rescuing her now made more sense. "You mentioned you took out the leaders of The Ministry, but killing is your job?"

Jax scrubbed his hands down his face before looking at her with worried eyes. "I probably should have told you that before bringing you here. If you want me to call Rory and have her take you to Providence House, I'll understand."

Tegan scooted closer and took his larger hand between her smaller ones. "Explain your job to me. Do you kill anyone if the price is right?"

"No. We only take out the worst sorts of scum. The killers, the rapists, the human traffickers, insane cult leaders, drug lords. And mafia dons."

*Yes!* "That's exciting. Do you carry a gun? Or do you *Gryphon out* on their asses and claw their eyes

157

out?"

"Wait. You think my job is exciting?" Jackson looked gobsmacked.

"Well, yes. I don't know you that well, but I cannot see you sitting behind a desk. You're a Gryphon. A biker. Your job should be as thrilling as your lifestyle. I mean..." Tegan ran out of steam. "Wow."

Jackson grinned at her, his lush lips parting to show his perfect white teeth. Tegan licked her own, slightly crooked teeth. "Did you have braces, or is your mouth as perfect as the rest of you because you're you?"

"What?"

"Sorry. I'm getting off the subject. To answer your question, no, I'd never ask you to give up your club or your job, but that doesn't mean you won't get tired of me." Tegan slumped against the back of the sofa.

Jackson grabbed Tegan around the waist and maneuvered her onto his lap. "Is this okay?"

No, it wasn't. The closer she was to him, the more she wanted to give in and say "fuck it." Her Lion purred, and Jackson's eyes widened. Then he smiled. *Then* he cupped the back of her head and lowered his mouth to hers. Tegan wrapped her arms around his neck as he deepened the kiss, his tongue tangling with hers slowly. It was a revelation. She'd been kissed before. Not often, but it had never been good. John kissed the same way he licked her clit, flicking his tongue up and down quickly. It was why she never let him kiss her. She hated it. But this? Jackson Lynch could *kiss*. And if his kisses could melt her panties, she couldn't wait to see how he was in bed. And yes, she was thinking about sex with her Gryphon.

Jax reclined on the sofa with Tegan on top of him, his erection pressing against her core. It was all she could do not to grind against it. Sexual chemistry didn't mean he would keep her. And that was the crux of her indecision. Her Lion said they were mates. Could she trust her animal to know he wouldn't toss her aside after a few years? Then again, he had stayed with Crystal for ten years. He hadn't left her; she left him. Tegan would never leave Jax. This she knew as well as she knew her own name. When Jax slid his hands up her back beneath her T-shirt, her skin tingled beneath his fingertips. She pressed her chest against his so she could kiss him again, but...

"Ow, ow, ow." Tegan pushed against his chest and slid to the floor.

Jackson sat up just as quickly, reaching out for her but pulling his hands back at the last second. "What's wrong?"

Tegan ducked her head. "Sorry. My boobs hurt. Like seriously tender."

Jax twirled one of her waves around his finger. "Nothing to apologize for. You want me to call Bethany and ask if that's normal?"

Tegan leaned her forehead against his knee. "It is. I read about it when I was trying to learn about pregnancy and how to take care of the babies. It's not very sexy," she muttered. She'd not bought nursing bras, thinking she had time. Her breasts hadn't leaked yet, so that was a plus since she didn't have the absorbent pads either. As soon as her phone was charged, she would order both. She could ask Jax to use his phone, but her bank card was already stored in hers, and she could wear her regular bra in the meantime.

Jax grabbed her beneath her arms and easily lifted Tegan off the floor, once again placing her on his lap. "It is sexy. You feeding the boys? Taking care of them the way nature intended? Definitely a turn-on. We'll have to be careful so we don't smush 'em again."

"Yeah?" Tegan husked.

"Oh, yeah." Jax brushed her hair off her face. Theo began to fuss, which caused Ollie to complain.

"Hold that thought." Tegan crawled across the floor and picked up Ollie, handing him to Jax. She then took Theo in her lap, holding him so he was on his back with his feet pressed against her stomach. While they played with the cubs, Tegan and Jax talked about their likes and dislikes. Favorite foods and music. They kept the conversation light, getting to know one another better. After a couple hours, she said, "We should probably think about getting them fed and then down for the night. Well, not night, but their next nap."

"And we should think about doing the same," Jax suggested.

Tegan wanted to ask if they could sleep together, but she had a feeling if she got in bed with Jax, sleeping wouldn't happen. Still…

While Jax walked around, singing to Ollie, Tegan took Theo to the nursery for his feeding. Neither baby had a problem latching on, and for that Tegan was grateful. She'd noticed a breast pump on the shelf below the changing table, but she didn't know how to use it. It was probably a good idea to pump some milk in case of an emergency. That was a tomorrow Tegan's problem. Tonight, all she could think about was curling up next to Jax as they napped. If that was something he wanted.

*Of course he does. He's our mate.*

This time, Tegan didn't argue. She wanted Jax. Wanted to say yes to being mates. To raising the cubs together. She would just have to make sure he didn't get tired of her or regret taking a chance on someone so young. Lion shifters were long-lived according to her mother, and Tegan wondered if Gryphons were also. She had no idea how old Jax was. He looked to be in his thirties or forties. She was bad at gauging how old someone was. He'd been with Crystal ten years, and that was fifteen years ago. He said he was twenty when his mom passed away so... Tegan did the math, and that would put Jax around forty-five, depending on when his birthday was. It was another piece of information she needed to find out.

It took almost an hour to get the babies fed and bathed, and fatigue had set in. She wanted another shower. Since her hair was clean, she could make it a quick in and out. Tegan stopped at the door to the guest room, looking up into Jax's gorgeous green eyes. "Do you mind if I take a shower?"

Jax lifted one of Tegan's hands and kissed her knuckles. It was a sweet move she adored. "Not at all. The boys will be fine, and if not, I'll take care of them. If you want, use the shower in my bathroom. It's more luxurious than the one in the hall. As a matter of fact, why don't I move all your toiletries in there so you can consider it your bathroom too?"

Tegan placed her hands on his hard chest. "I'd like that."

Jax pressed a quick kiss to her lips. "Then consider it done."

"Okay." Before they got carried away, Tegan stepped into the guest room to grab a change of clothes. Jax had an armful of toiletries and was headed to his bedroom. Even though she didn't need to wash her hair again, she got a blow dryer from where she'd seen it earlier in the hall bathroom cabinet, then padded into Jax's bedroom. Since Jax didn't have hair, Tegan figured Rory bought that too. Either that or he kept one for guests, and Tegan didn't want to think about who that would be.

Jax opened the door and showed her all the different settings for the shower. He kissed her again before leaving her to it. Tegan placed her pajamas and underwear on the counter before removing her clothes. She piled her hair on top of her head so she wouldn't get it wet. Tegan grabbed her shampoo, conditioner, and razor before stepping into the enclosure. Once beneath the steady spray, Tegan sighed as the hot water eased her muscles. Knowing Jax was out there to look after the boys, Tegan didn't rush. She relished being able to shave her legs without her babies in the way. She'd shaved her pubic hair when she was younger, but she hated having to maintain it, so she let it go. Waxing had never appealed, so she remained au naturale. She prayed Jax didn't mind it. Tegan did strip off the hair that stuck out from her panties, but that's as far as she took it.

When she finished rinsing, she remained under the

spray a few extra minutes before turning the water off. Two fluffy towels were on hooks beside the enclosure, and Tegan stepped onto the bathmat to dry off. She felt a million times better, but she was still ready for some shut-eye. Tegan put on her underwear and redid her hair so it was a cuter messy knot. She brushed her teeth, put on deodorant, then after contemplating going to bed naked, she decided pajamas were probably a better option since she didn't know Jackson's intentions. She slipped into her pajamas, which consisted of shorts and a cropped tee. So far, her nipples hadn't leaked, so she didn't bother with a bra. She opened the door and flipped off the light. Sultan reclined on the far side of the bed with one arm behind his head. The sheet was pulled up over his legs, and he'd foregone a shirt. Tegan took a moment to drink in the ink on his muscular arms and chest.

"See something you like?" he asked.

Instead of answering, Tegan crawled onto the bed and straddled his waist. She trailed her blunt fingernails over his chest and stomach. Jackson's abs tightened, and his cock filled beneath her spread legs. Being a shifter had its advantages, and one of those was quick healing. She wiggled against his erection, and Jax placed his free hand on her thigh, squeezing.

"What do you want, Tee?"

"Everything. I want you, us, our sons," she admitted. Tegan had decided to trust her Lion, and now she was trusting Jax not to break her heart. "I want to be your mate."

"Are you sure this is a good idea?" he asked, raising his hips so his hardness pressed more firmly against her. "You just gave birth, Sweetheart."

"I'm sure. I shifted, and that took care of the healing." Tegan pressed her palms to his chest and ground against him, sliding back and forth. Before she could protest, Jackson's claws elongated and ripped her shorts down the sides.

"Raise up," he demanded. She did, and Jax used his human hands to toss her shredded shorts to the side. He pushed the sheet down his legs, and Tegan was thrilled to see he'd gone to bed with no underwear. She reached down and grabbed his length, placing it at her opening. She was wet from grinding against him, so the glide was easy. Tegan adjusted to his girth before riding his dick. Jackson's eyes were no longer mossy green. They weren't the amber of his Lion either. They were the inky darkness of a moonless night in the forest.

"Fuck, Tee. You're perfect," he husked as he gripped her waist. He thrust up each time she bottomed out, hitting something deep inside that heated her core. Before, sex had been something to scratch an itch. If John didn't lick her clit, Tegan didn't get off. With Jax? It was so much more. So much better.

*Because he's our mate.*

Tegan agreed. This was what she'd been missing. The connection. The raw intensity. The feral male whose fangs had dropped. Hers popped out in response.

"Tee," Jax husked. "Mine."

"Yours," she responded as his thrusts got harder and faster. Her insides burned hotter, bringing the tell-tale spark when she was close to coming. "Please, Jax."

164

Jackson managed to roll them over with his cock still buried in her core. "Are you sure?"

"Yes. Claim me, Jax."

Jackson didn't make her wait. He struck quickly, his fangs sinking into her shoulder. The intensity of their coupling tripled. When he removed his fangs, Jax tilted his head to the side, and Tegan gave him a return bite. At the taste of his blood, her orgasm caught and exploded, rippling through her body. It could have been the mate bond settling between them. Jax pumped harder and found his own release. He buried his head in her neck and growled low as his cum spilled inside her already wet channel. His erection pulsed, and Tegan squeezed her inner walls, eliciting another growl.

Jax raised his head, leaning on his forearms, keeping his chest away from hers. The feral eyes were gone, replaced briefly with amber before settling back into their stunning green. Green that was glistening. "You have given me the most amazing gift, and I will cherish it and you for as long as we both live."

Tegan placed her hands on his cheeks, rubbing her thumbs under his eyes, before pulling him down for a kiss. He lowered his head, careful of her breasts, but Tegan needed to feel his skin against hers, so she pulled her short tee over her breasts, then closed the distance. Yes, it was painful, but having her mate close was more important. She could deal with the ache. She couldn't deal with him being so far away. Not that they weren't connected from the waist down, but she needed more.

Jax kissed her with such tenderness, such love,

Tegan knew she'd made the right decision for once. He trailed his lips across her cheek, down her neck, and nuzzled her shoulder where her mate mark had formed. "Perfect," he whispered.

When he raised up to look at her, her Lion offered the words that would complete the mating. Tegan flashed her beast's eyes and vowed, "From now until the goddess calls us to the next journey, we offer our love, our allegiance, and our bond."

Jax kissed her softly as no further words were needed. He rolled her to her side and pressed his chest to her back. With his face nestled against her neck, Tegan closed her eyes and thanked her goddess for the incredible male holding her close.

As wonderful as their mating had been, the rest of the night was filled with fussy babies and little sleep. Ollie, who was normally content with Jax while Tegan nursed Theo, was inconsolable until it was his turn. Tegan eyed the breast pump and told Jax she needed to figure it out so the boys had milk available in instances like this. She hadn't bought bottles, thinking she wouldn't need them, but now they were top of her list. Then again, she didn't know if she'd have enough to pump, then still be able to satisfy both babies. When they were settled for their morning nap, Tegan escaped to Jackson's bedroom and fell face-first onto the bed. Her breasts protested, so Tegan turned onto her side and pulled Jackson's pillow to her face. She was out within seconds.

Tegan's sleep was riddled with nightmares, and when she woke, she couldn't shake the fog. Even her Lion was restless. Tegan squinted against the sun shining through the blinds. She sat up, knuckling her eyes, then glanced at the clock. Three hours of sleep would have been glorious, but the bad dreams left her groggy and out of sorts. The scent of bacon floated from the kitchen, and she had a desperate need to see her mate. Tegan had a mate. That helped her push down the funkiness from her dreams. She padded to the bathroom and took care of her morning needs. After brushing her teeth, she let her hair down and fluffed it out. Tegan checked on the babies who were cuddled up together in one crib, both sleeping soundly.

Jackson was talking quietly, and Tegan prayed it was to someone on the phone. She was hungry and in desperate need of something to drink. When she entered the kitchen, Jax was leaning against the counter. He held out his arm, and she went to him, cuddling up against his chest.

"What happened?" Jax asked whoever was on the other end of the conversation, and Tegan opened her shifter senses to listen in.

*"I'm sorry, Brother. The place is trashed. The cushions and mattress were shredded. Every drawer was pulled out and dumped. Pictures were pulled off the walls and the frames shattered. Fuck, Sultan, it looks like a damn war zone. Whoever did this was looking for something. I'll get it cleaned up while I'm here, and maybe whoever did it will come back. Oh, and the bike? It's gone."*

Jax sucked in a breath, squeezing Tegan a little too hard. He had said his cabin was his sanctuary, and now someone had defiled it. "The alarm didn't go off. Fuck, they probably messed with the system somehow. Listen, don't worry about cleaning up, but if you

167

would, call Bishop and see if he can use his voodoo to find whoever took the bike. There are only two ways into the cabin, so maybe he'll be able to see someone hauling a wrecked bike away. No doubt it was one of Bucco's men."

*"Will do."* The phone disconnected, and Jax sighed. Then he buried his face in Tegan's hair and inhaled. Instead of talking about the call, he led Tegan to the island and lifted her onto one of the stools. "How do you like your eggs?" He already had bacon laid out on a stack of paper towels.

"Scrambled is fine, but I can cook."

"I don't mind. I want you to rest as much as possible." Jax cracked several eggs into a bowl and whisked them before pouring them into a skillet. Tegan couldn't take her eyes off the broad expanse of his back, the way his muscles bunched, nor the way his ass filled out his sleep shorts. His legs were long and thick, with hair the same dark brown as his beard. She'd never enjoyed giving head, but damn if Jax didn't have her thinking about pulling his shorts down for a taste.

"Tee," Jax growled.

Her eyes darted up to his. "What? You're..." She waved her hand down his body. "You're sexy, you're mine, and I can ogle if I want."

Jax smiled, but it didn't meet his eyes. She hated that he was upset, but she didn't know how to fix it. They might be mates, but they still had so much to learn about the other. The sound of a vehicle pulling into the driveway caught their attention, and Jax said, "That's probably your charger."

"I'll get it." She climbed off the stool, and when she

got to the door, she looked out the front window to make sure it was a delivery driver and not one of Jax's friends. It was, and Tegan waited for them to leave before she opened the door to retrieve the small package. She ripped the paper envelope apart and pulled out the cord, taking it to the guest room where her purse was. She plugged the phone in, then returned to the kitchen where Jax had their plates ready.

"I can't believe the boys are still asleep," she said as she tossed the packaging into the recycling bin in the pantry before climbing on the stool she thought of as hers. Jax poured her a glass of juice, then added a cup of coffee to his place at the island.

"Don't jinx it," he said against her temple before he sat.

"Thank you." Tegan bit off a piece of bacon. After swallowing, she said, "Not only for breakfast. For everything. I can't imagine doing this alone. I mean, I planned on being alone with the babies, and now I realize how foolish I was. With one baby, maybe, but two? There's no way I could have managed."

"I think you'd have found a way if you had to, but I believe your goddess intervened on your behalf. You didn't wreck just anywhere. You landed close to my cabin, the home of another shifter instead of a human you couldn't trust. I think the goddess or maybe Zeus brought us together, and for that I'm grateful. It wouldn't be the first time it's happened."

"What do you mean?"

Jax took a bite of eggs before explaining how some of the Hounds had found their mates and the situations they'd been in when it happened. "I mean, Havyk was sent to take out a drug lord and his wife, only the wife was innocent. Someone was jealous of her relationship with the man and put a contract on her. Havyk realized she was innocent, and instead of killing her, he ended up mated to her."

Jax talked more about mates while they finished eating. They both stood to clear the table with Tegan offering to do the dishes, but Theo woke up.

Jax cupped Tegan's cheek and kissed her temple.

"Duty calls."

# CHAPTER SIXTEEN

## Sultan

TEGAN WAS ON THE living room floor with the cubs, giving them some tummy time on their quilt pallet, when Rev called and asked if they would bring them in for a checkup. Sutton had sent one of the Hounds to get the SUV during the night, so that left them with Jackson's truck and Tegan's little car. Jax got the car seats loaded in the backseat of his truck, which wasn't going to work long term. He needed to buy Tegan a smaller SUV. After both brothers were full, they worked together getting them dressed and loaded. The drive to Rev's clinic took half an hour, and when they arrived, Bethany met them at the door. She and Rev worked seamlessly to weigh and measure the brothers, then Rev examined them more thoroughly than he had the previous day. Rev asked questions about their feeding and sleeping habits as well as bowel movements. He also clipped their umbilical cords closer to their tummies after adding clamps.

Tegan chewed her bottom lip as she watched, and Sultan pulled her onto his lap. "Stop worrying," he whispered against her ear. He knew there was something bothering her, but he didn't know what. As far as he could tell, the brothers were healthy and thriving. They fussed when they were hungry or when they had a wet diaper, but other than that, they were good babies.

When Rev told Tegan as much, she still didn't relax. Bethany came and sat next to them and took Tegan's hands in hers. "You're doing a great job with them. Do you have any questions?" Tegan glanced over at Rev, and Bethany caught her look when she said, "Zareck, would you please get my purse out of the office?" Rev narrowed his eyes briefly, but he nodded and left the room. "Now, what is it?"

"Do you want me to leave too?" Jax asked.

"No. I was thinking I might need to pump some milk so there's some available for emergencies, or when Ollie won't wait his turn."

"That's an excellent idea, and I saw a pump in the nursery."

"I, uh, brought it with me. Can you...?"

"Show you how to use it?"

"Yes. I feel so stupid."

Bethany brushed Tegan's hair off her face. "Stop that. You're a first-time mother who has had no one to help you through this. Get the pump, and I'll show you."

Jax stood when Tegan did and went to where the brothers were lying together in a bassinet. Bethany walked Tegan through how to use the pump, how long to store the milk in both the refrigerator and freezer, and how to thaw it. She then took out a tablet and opened a web browser showing Tegan the best bottles for newborns. There was so much information Jackson had never considered, and he was thankful for Rev's female.

"Bethany, will you send that link to my phone? I'll need to order them online unless we can get them at Hudson's."

"Hudson's should have them, but I'll send you the link just in case." Jackson's phone pinged with the information. "What other questions do you have for me?"

"That's all for now. Thank you for helping me," Tegan whispered.

"Anytime. Like I said, you're both doing a great job. Unless you want to find a pediatrician, Zareck will want to see them again in a couple of weeks for a wellness checkup."

"I'd feel better if he continued to be their doctor, but like I told you yesterday, I don't have insurance."

"We can invoice you for future visits, but this is a follow-up to yesterday's. How does that sound?"

"I appreciate it." Tegan relaxed. Did she not realize Sultan would pay for their care? They were mates for Zeus's sake. It seemed another conversation was in order, but he would wait until they were alone.

"Zareck doesn't have any other patients today. Do you have any errands to run? If so, he and I can watch the boys for you."

Tegan looked at Jackson, and he could tell she was torn. "We do need to grab a few groceries and look for these bottles. If you aren't comfortable leaving them yet, I can run to the store while you stay here. Your call."

"Do you mind?"

"Not at all. And if you think of anything you want not on the list, give me a call, okay?"

Tegan placed her forehead against his chest. "Thank you."

Jax kissed her hair. "You don't have to thank me, Tee. This is us now." He squeezed her hip before leaving her and Bethany. Hudson's wasn't far from the clinic, and with Tegan and the boys safe there, Jax took his time. It wasn't that he wanted to be away from them, but he used the time to breathe. Two days ago, he was a lonely male, and now he had a mate and two sons. If history held true, he and Tegan would have another son to add to their little family one day. The store had the bottles Bethany recommended, and Jax walked through the baby section, adding a few outfits to the cart. He then gathered the food items and headed to the checkout. He passed by the jewelry section, but didn't stop. If he were going to get Tegan a ring, it would be from one of the more expensive stores.

He was loading everything in the truck when his phone rang. "Hey, Bishop. What's up?"

"You asked me to check on John Cashel."

"I did. What did you find out? Is he as bad as Tegan said?"

"Was. The man's dead."

"When? How?"

"That's what I'm trying to find out. The police department is being tight-lipped about the details. I only know this much because his name came through the EMS blotter. I'll keep digging."

"Thanks, Bishop." Jax thumbed the phone off and finished loading their groceries. As he drove back to Rev's clinic, he wondered how Tegan was going to take the news. When he arrived, she was standing at the door waiting.

"Everything okay here?" he asked, pressing a kiss first to her forehead, then to Theo's.

"Yes, but we need to get on the road. The cubs will be ready to eat by the time we get there."

Bethany walked over carrying Ollie in his car seat, and Rev had Theo's empty one. "Let's get you loaded," he said. It didn't take long to have the babies settled in the backseat.

"Thanks, Rev. We'll see you in a couple weeks if not sooner." Jax shook the other Hound's hand and inclined his head to Bethany. The two females hugged, then they were headed home. Jax wanted to tell Tegan the news but decided to wait until the boys were down for their naps.

Tegan was right. Both were fussing before they pulled in the driveway. Jax helped his mate get the brothers inside. She sat down in the rocker in their nursery with Theo since he was crying. "I'm going to pump milk later. It tears my heart out to make Ollie wait," she said.

Ollie was content in Jax's arms, but there were times when he didn't want to wait. "Come on, Little Man. Let's get the groceries." While at Hudson's, Jax had found a sling that held the baby against the parent's chest, leaving their hands free. He took Ollie to the truck and grabbed as many bags as he could with one hand. Once he had everything inside, he

175

placed Ollie on the sofa while opening the sling package. It didn't take long to have it fastened around his body and the baby snuggled inside with his num num. Jax had bought some ready-to-cook meals, so he got the oven preheating as he put away the cold foods first, then he worked on the dry goods. He then unpackaged the bottles and put them in the new sterilizer after reading the instructions so that the bottles would be ready for Tegan to pump milk into them. He reread the directions on the meals, popped them in the oven, then set the timer.

"That is adorable," Tegan said when he entered the nursery to swap babies.

"It's handy. Keeps the boys snuggled against my chest but allows me to do other things. I got you one too." He carefully lifted Ollie out and placed him in Tegan's free arm before taking Theo to the changing table for a dry diaper. "I have the bottles in the sterilizer. We should probably sterilize the pump pieces before you use it the first time."

"Maybe we can do that together. I need to learn how all this works," Tegan muttered.

"Of course. I'm just trying to help with as much as I can."

Tegan looked up with tired eyes. "I know, and I appreciate it. Honestly, Jax. I couldn't do this without you."

"And you will never have to." Jax put Theo in his crib and covered him with a soft, thin blanket. He gazed at the child while thinking about the boy's biological father. Would Tegan ever tell them about John, or would she lie and say she didn't know who their father was? Jax would be their dad in every way that counted, but with him being a Gryphon, they couldn't lie and say he was their biological father. Before he worried about that, he had to tell Tegan.

Jax removed the sling and placed it on the changing table, then left to check on their lunch. The timer went off right as Tegan entered the kitchen.

"I wonder if they'll ever want to sleep separately?" Jax had already moved the extra bed out into the garage since the brothers fussed until they were together.

"I'm sure they will at some point. Will you grab us some drinks? Lunch is ready." Jax removed the pans from the oven and swapped the food over to plates while Tegan did as he asked. As they ate, Jax was lost in thought as to the coming conversation.

"These are delicious," Tegan said of their chicken parmesan. He was glad to see she had eaten everything on her plate.

"Do you want more?" He had cooked two for himself, and she needed the calories to keep her strength up.

"No, I'm full, but thank you." Tegan stood and took her plate to the sink. He polished off his food, then did the same. She took his plate, rinsed it, and added it to hers in the dishwasher along with their forks. When she closed the door, she leaned her hip against the counter. "What's going on? You've been stressed since you came back from shopping."

"I have to tell you something, and I'm not sure how you're going to take it."

Tegan tensed, but Jackson didn't try to console her.

Things were about to be worse. He took her hand and led her to the living room. He sank onto the sofa and pulled her down onto his lap.

"Just spit it out, Jax."

"I have some bad news." He brushed her hair over her shoulder, then placed a kiss against her neck. His Gryphon wanted to take her to bed, but now wasn't the time.

"Tell me," she urged.

"John Cashel is dead."

Tegan sighed. "I'm not surprised."

"That doesn't bother you?"

"Not really. I told you he was a piece of shit." Tegan stood and stretched. "How did you find out?"

"I had Bishop run a check on him. I didn't want him trying to find you again."

"And now we don't have to worry about that. I'm going to take a nap while the boys are asleep." Tegan pressed a soft kiss to his lips before walking away. Jax stared after her. Was that it? John's boss caught up with him and... No, something was missing. Tegan knew more than she was saying, but if Jax pushed... He'd screwed up with one female, so he needed to tread carefully with this one. They might have exchanged bites, but that didn't mean things would be perfect no matter what. Instead of questioning her further, he would give her the benefit of the doubt. He would take a nap with his mate, and they would talk again later. Everything would be okay. His phone rang, and Jax answered before it could wake the brothers.

"Bishop?"

Things would not be okay. Bishop managed to find

out more about John's death, and it was so far from okay, Jax didn't know what to think. He thanked the Hound, shoved his phone in his pocket, and when he walked down the hall to their bedroom, he stopped at the door to the guest room where Tegan was tossing clothes into a bag.

"What's wrong?" he asked, stepping close enough to grab her arms. "What are you doing?"

"Jax, I need to use your car. I would give you the money I have, but I'll need it for a hotel," she murmured. A phone pinged, but it wasn't his. Tegan's was on the bed next to the bag she was filling. Tegan scowled at it like it was going to bite her.

Jax gripped her biceps and gently shook her. "Tegan!"

When she looked up at Jax, her eyes were dazed. "I did this."

"Did what?"

"John's dead."

"Yes. I told you that, then you said you were going to take a nap. What happened between then and now?"

She shook her head and pulled away, removing more shirts from the drawer. When her phone pinged again, he picked it up then held it in front of her face to unlock it, but it was an older model that required a passcode. She made a grab for it, but he pulled it away and stuck it in his front pocket.

Tegan shoved him. "You need to pack. We have to get out of here."

"And go where? Why are we running?"

"Listen to the voicemails. The passcode is 0738." Tegan stood and reached for more clothes, but Jax

179

stopped her. They were lucky the boys were sleeping through their loud conversation. Jax picked Tegan up and carried her out of the bedroom. She squirmed against his hold, beating him with her fists.

He didn't put her down until he was in the living room. "Listen to what? I'd rather you tell me the truth."

Tegan ran her fingers through her curls, pushing them away from her face.

"The cops are looking for me, Jax. They think I killed John."

# CHAPTER SEVENTEEN

## Tegan

*YOU'RE BEING AN IDIOT.*

*Shut up.*

**No, really. Jax is our mate. He's not going to let anything happen to us.**

*He's going to hate me if he doesn't already.*

**Again, you're being an idiot.**

"Tee, Sweetheart. We need to talk about this."

"There's nothing to talk about. I'm wanted for murder. If you don't want to run with me, I get it, but I need to go. If they lock me up, who'll take care of my sons?"

Jax sat on the sofa settling her on his lap. "Nope. It doesn't work that way. You are my mate, and I'm going to help you. I already have Bishop working on it."

"But—"

"No buts. You've told me what happened the morning Freddie showed up, and Bishop is already checking the cameras close to your house so we can prove you left right after John did. Once he has that evidence, we'll go to the cops. I'll tell them about you coming to my cabin, and I can also show them the video of Freddie taking you to Bucco. With John working for the mafia, there's no way they can pin this on you."

Tegan reached up and ran her fingers through his beard. "I'm sorry."

"There's nothing to be sorry for, Tee. Trust takes time, and maybe with enough time, you'll see you can trust me as well as the other Hounds. Is all this a convoluted mess? Yes, but Bishop is good at what he does. And if he can't handle it, there are a couple of Gargoyles in New Atlanta who are experts at this kind of thing." Jackson nudged his nose against her neck and inhaled before dropping the next bomb. "We have another issue. John's bike was taken from my cabin after it was trashed, which means Bucco might know where I live since the cabin is in my name. He has access to his own computer specialist, and with a little digging, they can find us here. I'm going to call Sutton and see if we can stay with him and Rory until this is over."

Tegan leaned back so she could see his eyes. "Why would we put them at risk too?" She didn't want anyone else brought into this mess she'd created.

"Because they're Gryphons and the next best thing I have to parents. They don't have kids at home to worry about. Rory can help you with the boys while Sutton and I stand guard."

*Trust him.*

"Okay."

Jax palmed her cheek, then kissed her softly before setting her on her feet so he could get to his phone.

182

"Why don't you go pack the cubs a bag while I call Sutton?"

Tegan threw herself against her mate and hugged him tightly. She didn't deserve his understanding, but she was glad to have it.

The doorbell rang, and Jax tilted his head away from hers. "Go to the nursery and close the door. Do your best to keep the boys quiet," he whispered against her ear.

"Jax—"

"Go, Tee. Now."

Tegan glanced toward the door, using her Lion's ears, but there was no sound indicating who it might be. She padded quietly down the hall and closed the door behind her once she entered her sons' room. She stood beside the crib, hoping her presence wouldn't wake them.

## Sultan

AS SOON AS THE nursery door closed, Jax eased open the front door to find a police officer looking around. Jax scanned the uniform because it wasn't what the Troy cops wore. The nameplate on his right chest listed the man's name as E. Cartwright, and the patch on his left indicated he was from Coopersville. The uniform appeared legit, but he could have stolen it.

"Can I help you?" Jax kept his body in the frame, taking up as much space as possible. He scanned the area. There was no one out and about, but it was Monday, and most of his neighbors would be at work and school.

"Are you Jackson Lynch?"

"What's this about?"

"Mr. Lynch, I'm looking for Tegan Rowe."

"I don't know anyone by that name. Besides, aren't you a little out of your jurisdiction? Like by a few hundred miles? I'd like to see some ID."

The cop squared his shoulders and narrowed his eyes. "Look, Mr. Lynch—"

"Who sent you?" Jax asked, calling on his Gryphon.

The cop's eyes glazed. "Phil Bucco."

Motherfucking mafia. Coopersville was a long way from Bucco's territory, but he'd still managed to get a cop on his payroll. "Who killed John Cashel?"

"Tegan Rowe."

"How did you find where I live?"

"Mr. Bucco gave me the address."

"How long have you worked for the mafia?"

"I don't. Bucco called and said Tegan Rowe killed John Cashel. Told me I could find her here."

"And you're going to arrest a young, single woman with no priors on her record for killing her drug-dealing ex-boyfriend with only the word of a mafia don as proof?"

"I'm not arresting her. I'm taking her to Mr. Bucco.

184

He wants the baby."

Jax knew this, but hearing it again had his talons springing forth. It took every bit of willpower not to gut the cop where he stood. Jax's chest heaved as he reined in his beast. When Cartwright finally noticed the sharp talons, his eyes widened, and he stumbled backward, falling off the porch. Jax leapt the few feet, landing with his legs straddling the man. With his talons retracted, Jackson pointed a finger in the man's face. "You were never here. You never received a call from Phil Bucco, and you will not speak of this day to anyone. Go back to Coopersville and be a good cop. Don't take bribes. Tegan Rowe did not kill John Cashel. She wasn't home at the time it happened. One of Bucco's capos, a man named Freddie, killed John Cashel. Do your job and find the proof. If Bucco calls you again, put him through to your chief and tell your boss you're being threatened. Go now."

The cop scrambled to his feet and walked away without looking back. As soon as Cartwright was in his vehicle, Jax returned inside and found Tegan standing in the open nursery door. "Did you hear any of that?"

"All of it."

"We need to move quickly. I'll pack our bags while you get the boys' things together." Jax kissed Tegan's forehead, then left to gather some of their clothes and toiletries. He took their bags to the garage and opened the tonneau cover on the truck bed and placed their bags inside. He went back inside to help Tegan. She was tossing diapers and wipes into one of their large duffels when her phone rang.

"It's Rosie," she said, looking at the display.

"Ignore it, Sweetheart. You can call her later."

Tegan looked torn but let the call go to voicemail and continued packing. Jax took the diaper bag to the garage and placed it in the bed before lowering and locking the cover in place. Tegan had a sleepy Ollie in her arms, and Jax took the baby and settled him in his car seat. By the time he was strapped in, Tegan had returned with a fussing Theo. "Get him strapped in, and I'll lock up the house."

Jax looked around for anything they might need. He spotted Tegan's purse and phone. He took both, then locked the house and set the alarm. When he got to the garage, Tegan was already buckled in the passenger seat. He got in, passing over her purse. After Jax started the truck, he called Judge before opening the garage door.

"Hey, Brother," his best friend answered.

"Are you home?" Jax asked, pushing the garage door button on the roof console.

"Yes, I got in a few minutes ago. What do you need?"

Jax eased out of the garage, keeping his eyes peeled. "A burner phone. Do you have a spare?"

"Yes, I have a stash."

"We're leaving my house now. I'll see you in a few." Jax disconnected without giving any information. Judge was smart enough to figure out something was going on if Jax needed a burner. It didn't take ten minutes to cover the short distance between their houses, and when Jax pulled in the driveway, Judge was waiting outside. Jax didn't shut off the motor. He put the truck in park and rolled down his window.

Judge passed over two phones, already out of their packages.

"I input several numbers. What's going on?"

Jax explained the situation succinctly, and Judge's eyes clouded with fury. "Fucking Bucco. Someone should put a bullet in his brain."

"If the four horsemen find him, they just might. I'm headed to the clubhouse to get one of the SUVs. I want one of the Hounds to drive my truck the opposite direction we're headed."

Ryan placed his hand on the door. "Do you want me to do it?"

"No. I'd rather have you on standby in case I need you to guard our backs. I'm going to ask Bishop to find us somewhere remote, but keep your phone charged, just in case."

Ryan peered into the back seat. "Take care of my nephews, and call if you need me."

"Thanks, Brother." Jax patted Ryan's hand before putting the truck in reverse. Ryan stepped away, and Jax backed out of the driveway, heading east. After rolling the window up, he handed one of the burners to Tegan. "Scroll through and find Bishop's number."

She did as asked, hit call, and handed the phone back. Bishop answered with, "Go ahead."

"It's Sultan. Fucking Bucco convinced a Coopersville cop to come to the house for Tegan. I'm taking her and the boys out of town until the four horsemen can track him down. Can you please find us a secluded rental house with at least three bedrooms, preferably south or west of here. We're already on the road."

"You got it. I'll send the location to this phone."

"Thanks, Bishop." Jax disconnected and placed the burner in one of the cup holders before taking Tegan's hand in his.

"Why are we going east?" Tegan asked.

"I have no doubt Bucco's hacker is tracking our phones. Like I told Ryan, I'm going to take them to the clubhouse and ask one of the Hounds to drive my truck and get rid of our phones separately to make it harder for him to track us."

Jackson called Havyk. The Hound didn't answer since it was an unknown number, so Jax left a voicemail telling him what was going on and what he needed. While they were driving, Tegan listened to the voicemail her mother left.

*"Tegan, it's Rosie. H-he's got Bobby. He s-says if you don't give him the baby, he's going to kill him. I... Tegan? I don't understand what's going on. What baby? And how did you get involved with the mafia?"* Rosie was crying, but her words came through clearly through the sobs. *"He said you have twenty-four hours. Pl-please call me back."*

Tegan dropped the phone as she clapped a hand over her mouth.

Jackson slapped the steering wheel, cursing Phil Bucco silently. "We'll get him back, Sweetheart. I promise."

Tegan snapped her tear-stained face toward him. "You can't promise that, Jax. He gave me twenty-four hours. I don't even know where the fuck he is!" The brothers started crying at their mother's raised voice, which made Tegan cry harder.

"I promise we'll come up with a plan. Please trust

me."

Tegan didn't say anything, and the rest of the drive to the clubhouse was filled with the three most important beings in his life upset. By the time they arrived, Havyk, Mayhem, Natalia, Ryker, Sutton, and Rory were waiting.

Rory went to Tegan's door and opened it. "Hi, Te— What's wrong?" Rory glared at Jax.

"We have bigger issues. Let's get inside where we aren't sitting targets."

Rory opened the back door and expertly got Theo's seat unbuckled. Sutton had gotten Ollie out and met his mate at the front of the truck. "Come on then."

With their boys safe with the Lazlo parents, Jax took Tegan's hand and followed. Sutton led them to the room the Hounds used for church and set Ollie's seat on the large oak table. As Jax introduced everyone, Rory placed Theo next to his brother, then unbuckled him so she could hold the baby. Tegan did the same for Ollie.

Sutton hovered close to his mate. "Hayden shared your message."

"Yes, but shit is so much worse now. Bucco has the kid living with Tegan's foster parents, demanding a trade – Tegan's baby for Bobby. When we last saw Bucco, Tee was still pregnant. I'm not sure if he somehow knows she gave birth, which I doubt since he only demanded one baby, or if he only wants Tegan back in his clutches. Regardless, he gave her twenty-four hours to make the swap."

Natalia stepped away from Mayhem, facing Jax. "I know just the person to help you."

189

Jax tilted his head at his buddy's mate. "Yeah? Who's that?"

"Tatiana Volkova."

Mayhem grabbed Natalia's arm and turned her toward him. "Are you crazy? Absolutely not."

"Princess badass rides again," Havyk sang.

Natalia grinned at her brother-in-law. "That's Princess Lollipop to you."

"Stop it, both of you." Mav shook his mate. "You are no longer that person."

Natalia removed herself from Mav's grip and crossed her arms over her chest, her playful façade slipping into that of someone lethal. "Maybe not, but I do know Phil Bucco and his organization. Who do you think killed his father?"

"Maybe, but Phil isn't his father."

"Mafiosi are predictable. The don trains his underboss to take over, and that man runs things the same as his predecessor. A zebra doesn't change its stripes, and the mafia doesn't change their tactics."

"Unless it's a zebra shark," Tegan muttered.

Natalia turned her dark eyes on Tegan. "Pardon?"

"Zebra sharks have stripes when they're young, but as they mature, the stripes turn to spots."

Natalia slashed a hand through the air. "Still a shark. The stripes morph, but their teeth remain sharp." She turned to her mate and jabbed his chest with her index finger. "No one understands the mafia better than me, and you know this. I will be safe because I will have you beside me."

Mav didn't agree, but he did grab her hand and kiss Natalia's palm. Jackson thought Natalia was the

perfect person to go after Bucco, but he'd never say
that aloud.

# CHAPTER EIGHTEEN

## Tegan

TEGAN GAPED AT THE petite, lavender-haired female. This woman was a killer?

"Enough." Sutton didn't yell, but his voice demanded obedience, which he got. "We can discuss who is going after Bucco once we get Tegan and the cubs somewhere safe. Jax, instead of taking them out of town, how about holing up at Lucy's? That way you'll have access to the Hounds for protection, and the mates will be able to help Tegan with the babies?"

Jax ran a hand over his scalp. "Are you certain Bucco's hacker can't connect Lucy's home to her and thus you? I won't bring the mafia to your family's doorstep."

"Son, this is *our* family, and I say bring it. I would rather fight that fucker on familiar territory. Even if we have to take the fight to him, having Tegan here where she and the boys can be guarded would make me feel better."

Sultan sighed, but agreed. "Fine." He gently took Ollie from Tegan and snuggled the baby to his chest, breathing in his scent. How could anyone remove an infant from his mother and sell him or her to the highest bidder? How could they shuffle teens and adults like cattle?

**Because they're evil bastards. And bitches.**

Her beast wasn't wrong. It wasn't only men who trafficked others. Tegan had seen enough late-night documentaries on the subject when she'd come home from Onyx and needed an hour or so to decompress from her day, or to give John time to fall asleep so she didn't have to have sex with him, if he were even home.

As they walked out of the meeting room, Tegan gave Natalia another glance. The woman indicated she had knowledge of mafias. Did that mean she'd been part of one? Her accent wasn't strong, but it was enough to indicate her heritage was something other than American. Russian, maybe?

Ryker, who had been silent up until that point, called out for other members of their club. Several large males, all wearing the same black vest, gathered round as their president handed out orders. Jackson's truck was pulled into a large garage, and the car seats were installed into an SUV like they'd ridden in after leaving the vineyard.

Meanwhile, Hayden asked for Tegan's phone. "I'm taking it to Bishop so he can clone it to an untraceable number. Then one of the Hounds will take your phone in Sultan's truck and drive it out of state. I'll bring the new phone to you at Lucy's."

Tegan didn't hesitate to hand it over. She knew nothing about fighting the mob or how to hide from one. That much was evident in how quickly she'd been found after leaving home. She also knew nothing about having a large family protecting her, but seeing how everyone came together with no thought to their own safety, it gave her a sense of peace. Of belonging. She had been on her own for six years. Tegan didn't count John living with her because he'd never had her best interest at heart. But these Gryphons did because it was the right thing to do. And she was Jax's mate. That still hadn't sunk in. She had a mate, and she would never be alone again.

The drive to Lucy's home wasn't a direct shot. They circled and backtracked, ensuring they had no one following. Her sons were being so good. Their little lives were in such turmoil, and they had no idea. Maybe they felt safe as well, being surrounded by so many strong shifters. Tegan often wondered what her life would have been like if her parents hadn't left their pride. If she had been among family when her parents were taken from her. But now? Having found her fated mate... Tegan wouldn't say losing her parents and brothers were worth finding Jax, but it did make up for all she'd gone through as a teen, then as an adult out on her own.

There were no graves to visit. Her family had been cremated, and when she was seventeen, only then had she been ready to spread their ashes in the creek beside her little shack. Some of the ashes had flittered on the breeze, and Tegan liked to think they were still floating along, following her around. So when she did talk to her parents, it was at night, outside where she imagined some of those ashes had somehow made it into the sky and latched onto stars, twinkling down at her, letting her know they were with her.

Tegan's thoughts were brought back to the present when the SUV pulled up at a massive gate. Maveryck, who was driving, rolled down the window and spoke into the intercom instead of pressing the keypad. The gate opened for them, and he drove the vehicle through, followed by another SUV and several bikes. When they got to the end of the drive, Tegan stared at what was probably considered a manor instead of a house. It was three stories of gray stone that was surrounded by trees.

On the drive, Tegan asked who exactly Lucy was. Mav answered, "She's my twin's daughter. It's a long story, but the short of it is when War and his pregnant mate were in their second year of college, Harlow was kidnapped. She put up a fight against the men trying to take her, but they beat her badly. She survived long enough to deliver their baby girl. Harlow was against how our family lived, being bikers, and she made War promise to raise the baby away from us. Warryck lost his mind when she died, and he couldn't bear to look at the baby, so he gave her to Harlow's aunt and uncle, Vera and Lucius, to raise. The Balls adopted Lucy, and after they passed, Lucy inherited everything. Lucius was a brilliant scientist, if not off his fucking rocker, and he passed down his knowledge of genetics to Lucy. So not only is she good with computers, she's also an amazing scientist. We were reunited with her when Vera passed away."

Tegan felt there was more to the story, as Mav indicated, but she wouldn't pry. Knowing she was family was enough. Tegan followed the others inside and took a moment to look around. As large as the house was, it felt homey. Lived in. Welcoming.

"Does Lucy live here alone?"

Maveryck, who ended up with Ollie, joined her and Jax, who was carrying Theo. "No, she's mated to a Gargoyle named Tamian St. Claire. The two of them are currently in New Atlanta working with Tamian's uncle on some project." When Ollie began fussing, Maveryck handed him over. "I don't have the necessary equipment to satisfy this little dude. Let me show you where you'll be staying so you can have some privacy." Maveryck led them upstairs to a large bedroom. "I'll bring in your things while you take care of the boys." With that, he closed the door, leaving them alone.

Tegan sat in a comfortable chair that was facing the window and raised her shirt and bra for her youngest. Theo seemed content for the moment in Jax's arms. "Are you staying with me? Or are you going after Bucco? And how are they going to keep Bobby alive if I'm not part of the swap? We've already wasted several hours."

"I wouldn't consider the time wasted since we were getting you and our sons safe. As soon as you've fed them, we'll join the others to start making a plan."

"That'll take at least thirty minutes. Lay Theo on the bed and go get busy. Please."

"What if he starts crying?"

"Then he'll cry. Please, Jax. I can't stand the thought of Bobby being in Bucco's hands, and the longer it takes for someone to decide on how to rescue him..." Tegan sucked in a breath. She'd met Bobby about a year ago. The boy was small for his age and had an androgynous look about him. Marcus didn't care about that. He was a great role model for all the teens he and Rosie fostered. They would be devastated if something happened to the boy. "Please," she begged again.

Jax placed Theo in the middle of the bed, then walked over to Tegan and kissed her softly. "Okay." He looked back at Theo before closing the door.

Tegan let the tears fall silently. She wanted to be strong, but damn. Sometimes crying was necessary. Rosie once told her tears were cleansing, washing away the sadness to make room for happiness. Tegan was happy, or she would be if they could rescue Bobby. Rosie had to be so scared. They couldn't have children of their own, but they treated their foster kids as if they were biologically theirs. Better than some parents treated their own children. She and Marcus had been together almost forty years, over half their lives. The love between them was tangible. Not once in all the time Tegan lived there did she see them fight. Oh, they argued, but it was never anything serious. Tegan prayed she and Jax got along that well. If she could learn to trust him completely...

In that moment, she realized she already did. Trusted him with her heart, with her sons, and with Bobby's life. He could have let her walk away with the boys and hide on her own, but he didn't. He insisted on going with them. He called on his family who was now her family. Tegan hadn't had many friends since she left Mining Falls. She had been friendly with the employees of Onyx Ink, and before she met John had gone to hang out with them on their off days for barbecues or to meet up for drinks at the local pub. She couldn't see her and Natalia having much in common, and if Tegan were honest, the woman scared her a little.

Now she wished she'd had asked Jax about the other mates. Trenton mentioned Ryker and his female had a new baby, Daisy. Then there was Patrick whose mom owned the Mexican restaurant. Maybe once this mess with Bucco was over, Tegan could meet up with Daisy's mom and let the kids play together. Not that there would be any actual playing, but just getting them together would be good. As they got older, then they could play. The boys would have each other, but they needed to be around others their age. At least she thought so. And if she and Daisy's mom became friends? Tegan would be thrilled.

Someone knocked on the door, and Tegan frowned. "Yes?"

"Hey, Tegan. I'm Rhiannon, Ryker's mate. Can Daisy and I come in?"

Speak of the devil, or angel, she should say. "Yes, please."

When the door opened, a beautiful, young woman with long, dark blonde hair entered with a baby bundled in her arms. Rhiannon smiled, and Tegan had it right – the woman was an angel. She had a glow about her that Tegan wanted to bask in.

"Sorry to barge in, but Ryker wanted us here with him. Since I'm not much for strategy meetings, I thought Daisy and I could keep you company." She unwrapped the blanket and placed the baby girl on the bed close to Theo. "How are you holding up?"

"Not well, to be honest."

"Yeah, I get that." Rhiannon sat on the edge of the bed and propped her bare feet on the footboard. She was dressed in shorts and a colorful, asymmetrical tunic. Her toes were painted pink, and she had several ankle bracelets on each leg. Her hair was pulled back in a low ponytail with a few tendrils framing her sweet face. "Ryker filled me in on what's happened so far, and let me tell you, I'm in awe of you. I can't imagine having one baby with no help, but two? Dang, woman." Rhiannon shook her head. "Who's that you have?"

"This is Ollie, and that's Theo behind you. Oliver after my father, and Theodore after my mom, Thea."

"I like that. Daisy is named after my mom. I lost her when I was younger. When she passed, David, my father, took me to one of The Ministry's compounds to live. It's not a good story, so I'll save it for another day, but as you can see, it does have a happy ending. Or middle, I guess I should say, since it'll be a long time 'til the end now that I'm mated to Ryker." Tegan found that little bit of information odd considering Rhiannon was human. Did being mated to a Gryphon somehow extend her lifespan?

"Yeah? How long? Jax and I haven't had a chance to talk much about the whole mating thing."

Rhiannon slid off the bed when Theo woke, fussing. She stood beside him and placed her hand on his tummy. Theo instantly calmed. Rhiannon ignored the question. "Oh, I thought you were mates."

Tegan ducked her face. "We are, but we probably

should have talked more before we bit each other."

Rhiannon blushed, and Tegan found it endearing. "How long do lion shifters live?"

"If we don't succumb to things like car wrecks or gunshot wounds, we can live about five hundred years."

"Wow. Gryphons aren't as long-lived. Ryker said their lifespans can be as long as three centuries, give or take a few decades." Rhiannon picked Theo up and sang softly to him. Tegan might have been a little jealous at how well the female sang. Tegan couldn't carry a tune if her life depended on it.

"Your voice is beautiful."

Rhiannon blushed again. "Thank you. But you should hear Glory. That woman should be on a stage somewhere. Maveryck's twins can't wait to have her sing for them."

"Is Glory another mate?" Tegan lifted Ollie to her shoulder and patted his back.

"Yes, Ripley's. He rescued her from Haven, the same compound where I lived. He took her to Providence House."

"Jax told me about it. He offered to take me there when he rescued me, but he's my fated mate. After I got my head out of my butt, I decided to go ahead and move in with him."

"Good choice. Not that Providence isn't nice. It is. Lynette and Branson are awesome, but it's kind of crowded right now. When they rescued Glory Saturday night from Haven, several of the other residents, including Glory's mom, sisters, and brother-in-law decided to leave the compound." When Ollie let out a wet burp, Rhiannon giggled. The female was too sweet for words. "Ready for Theo?"

After they swapped babies, Rhiannon placed Ollie on the bed next to Daisy. The baby girl turned her head toward him and cooed. Ollie was too young yet to know he'd made a new friend, but seeing her son with Rhiannon's child warmed Tegan's heart. When the other woman first walked into the room, Tegan doubted they would have anything in common other than being mated to Gryphons, but after hearing she'd also lost her mom at a young age, Tegan changed her mind. She felt hopeful she'd made a new friend of her own.

# CHAPTER NINETEEN

## Sultan

IT DIDN'T SURPRISE JAX when Rory showed up with Rhiannon and Daisy. Ryker would want his mate and new baby where he could keep an eye on them. He told Rhi to head upstairs and get to know Tegan while the rest of them talked downstairs. Instead of sitting at the large dining room table, they all gathered in the game room. Maveryck went behind the bar and poured drinks for everyone. Jax leaned his ass against the pool table and crossed his arms over his chest. He didn't know anything about hunting the mafia, but Natalia did, and he prayed Mav let her offer her expertise. Ryan, who Jax called on the way to Lucy's, settled next to him, offering silent comfort.

Jax took the proffered glass from Maveryck. "Do you think we should conference in the four horsemen? They're still out there looking for Bucco."

Ryker shook his head. "Not yet. If Bucco's hacker is any good, he might have their phones tapped." Turning to Natalia, Ryker asked, "Why didn't you go after Phil once you killed his father?"

Mav's pixie settled on a bar stool and leaned back

on one elbow, clasping her hands in front of her. "That happened right before I met Mav. After the hit on the elder Philip, my father reluctantly allowed me a vacation, figuring it would be chaos in their organization while Phil Junior took over as don. But Anatoly caught wind of the hit out on him, and he called me back to guard him before I could get on the plane. With my father dead, Mikael took over our family and turned me loose. I soon went to work for Nexus, and the Buccos were no longer my problem."

"But you know their organization? Where the houses are? What they're involved in?"

Natalia took the glass Mav offered, cradling it between her hands. "I do. Anatoly was arrogant thinking he could come to the East Coast and take over at least some of the territory. When he found he was small fish in big pond, he tasked me with gathering intel on the Buccos since they ran a big part of the northeast. Not only that, but they weren't as widespread as the Chens. Bucco has five houses, and if he's fleeing the vineyard, he probably won't stop at the one across Lake Champlain in Vermont. The other two properties are landlocked, so if he's smart, which he is, he is most likely headed to the one outside Boston so he can get on his boat if need be. As for what he's involved in, he deals in guns, drugs – Hive to be specific – and people." Natalia spit the last word.

"And if we take Bucco out, he'll have someone in place to take over?"

"Yes, although I don't know who. He has no siblings, so most likely his cousin, Victor."

Jackson scratched his beard, thinking. "John Cashel

owed half a million to Bucco. Could we pay him off?"

"I doubt it. Tell me what you found at the vineyard."

"There were six pregnant women being kept beneath the floor of an outbuilding. We couldn't get into the workroom before we left because the passageway is hidden behind a secret panel that had a biometric scanner, but Tegan said there were sixty women on the first shift bottling Hive. They work twelve hours on, twelve off, swapping with a second-shift crew. She said there were stacks of crates full of the drug. Bucco owns all the houses around the vineyard, and each one was set up the same. The master bedroom had twin beds, but the other rooms had several cribs."

Natalia took a sip of her drink. "If you had gotten to Tegan before she was taken to the vineyard, then maybe he would accept payment, but you have alerted the Feds to one of his operations where they will seize millions if not billions worth of Hive along with the pregnant women and over one hundred of his workers. If I had to guess, you have disrupted his main location, and a man like Bucco will not take that sitting down."

Jackson growled. "Then what do you suggest? The clock is ticking on the boy's life."

"Did the foster mother say how Tegan is supposed to get in touch with Bucco? We start there."

"Havyk took Tegan's phone for Bishop to clone. Fuck, we should have kept it."

"I'm here." Havyk jogged into the room, tossing the new phone to Jax.

Jax caught the device with his free hand. "That

didn't take long."

"Bishop's good. Her foster mother has been blowing up her phone."

Jax set his glass down on the edge of the pool table, then punched in the code to unlock the phone. He scrolled back through all the voicemails, putting it on speaker so Natalia could hear them. Each message was more frantic than the one before, but in none of them did Rosie give Tegan instructions.

"Shit. Tee is going to have to call her."

"I'll go get her and help Rhi watch after the cubs," Rory offered.

There was one more message from a different number. Jax hit play. "Miss Rowe, this is Detective Rawlings with the Coopersville Police Department. Please give me a call as soon as you get this message. It's regarding a disturbance at your home on Furman Road." He rattled off his number and disconnected.

Tegan joined them, walking to where Jax stood. "What's up?"

"We need you to call Rosie. All her messages are nothing more than what she left on the one you heard. Ask her if Bucco left instructions on where to meet or how to get in touch with him."

"And what if she asks why this is happening?"

Jax tugged on one of Tegan's curls. "Tell her your ex got caught up in some shady shit, and now you're paying the price."

Tegan held out her hand, and when Jax passed the phone over, she tapped the device against her forehead a few times, then blew out a breath and dialed the number. Instead of getting Rosie, Marcus answered,

"Tegan, what the actual fuck? What is going on?"

Tegan blanched at her father's ire. "Marcus, it's a long, depressing story, but I need to know if Bucco told you how to get in touch with him? How am I supposed to meet him for the swap?"

Rosie chimed in, "Tegan, you can't give a baby to that man. I've seen him on the news. He's bad. No, he is so much worse than that."

"Rosie, I'm not going to let anything happen to Bobby."

Rosie took a few breaths. "Whose baby is it, and how did you get involved with the mafia?"

"I dated someone who conned me. He was selling drugs for Bucco, then he went to jail. One of Bucco's men came around looking for my ex and the drugs. It's really not a good story, but suffice it to say, John, my ex, couldn't pay, and Bucco wanted me in exchange for what was owed. When he saw I was pregnant, he decided to take my child as payment. Rosie, did he tell you how to get in touch with him?"

"Y-yes. He left a number." Rosie rattled off the digits, and Ryker tapped them into his phone. "Tegan, we want Bobby back. He's fragile and special, but I don't want you to give up your baby. Why didn't you tell me you were pregnant?" The pain in Rosie's voice gutted Jax.

"It won't come to that. I have some powerful friends who are going to help. As for the baby, I..." Tegan closed her eyes. "I couldn't tell anyone, especially you and Marcus for this very reason. I didn't want John's boss coming after those I love. I tried to run, but they found me anyway. Rosie, we're going to do everything we can to get Bobby back to you and Marcus. I need to go so we can call Bucco. We're running out of time."

"Okay. Please be safe, and Tegan? When this is over, no matter what happens, I want to meet my grandchild."

"I promise. I love you both." Tegan disconnected and tossed the phone to Jax. "Now what?" Tegan asked Natalia.

"Now you call Bucco, but we get Bishop or Julian to try and trace the call and get a lock on his location. Bucco will give you a meeting place, but we need to get to him before that happens."

"She's not going," Jax said at the same time Tegan said, "I can't go. The boys need me."

"This is why we need to find out where he is first. Bucco has his own hacker. We know this, but if Bishop can get the general vicinity of where Bucco is, that will tell me which house he's hiding in. The Hounds will go in, voice the male, and find out where he's holding Bobby."

Jackson pulled Tegan to him so her back was against his chest. "But if we call from here, can't Bucco's hacker do the same thing and track our location? We don't need to put Lucy's home in his crosshairs."

"And we won't." Havyk wiggled his phone. "I've been texting with Bishop, and he can somehow patch the call through to Tegan's phone so it appears to be coming from where Erik took it."

"Erik Andino?" Jax had met the male a few times. His dad, Zander, owned a private security firm, and

Erik worked for him. They had helped Spyder when his female, Charlie, was in trouble.

"Yes. He was visiting with Bishop when I stopped by, and he offered to drive your truck."

"If Bishop is certain this location won't be compromised, then let's do it. The clock is ticking." Sutton was protective of all the Hounds, but Lucy was his granddaughter. Even if she was a Gryphon mated to a Gargoyle, he wouldn't bring any more trouble to her home than it had already seen.

Havyk got Bishop on the phone. "Havyk, I'm ready to forward the call, but we have another problem."

"What now?"

"The Coopersville police have an APB out for Tegan. They're looking at her for John's murder."

"We knew they wanted to question her. One of the detectives left her a voicemail."

"Tegan, are you right or left-handed?" Bishop asked.

"Left. What does that matter?"

"Not to be gruesome, but whoever killed John was right-handed. That helps your situation. Plus, I've been accessing the CCTV cameras from the time you left on John's bike as well as when John and Freddie returned to the house. Don't worry about all that right now. We need to get this call placed so I can get a lock on Bucco's vicinity. All I need is Bucco's number. Are you ready?"

Tegan relaxed against Jackson, but her hands on his arms tightened. "I... Yes. Do I need to keep him on the phone a specific length of time?"

"As long as you can, but this isn't like the movies. I have Henry helping, and he's keeping Bucco's hacker busy chasing his tail so I can do what I need to. Give me his number, and I'll patch it through to your phone."

"I've got the number." Ryker relayed the sequence.

"Thanks. Let me get Erik patched through." Everyone waited silently while Bishop worked.

Jax turned Tegan and pressed his forehead to hers. "You've got this, Tee. Don't worry about sounding strong. Bucco's going to expect you to be upset and nervous, but try to remain calm no matter what he says to goad you."

Tegan leaned back and nodded. "I'll do my best." Tegan shook out her hands. "I have a question. Can't you voice Bucco?"

"I can, but we need to know his location. More than likely, he has his second-in-command on standby."

Bishop came back on the line. "Okay, Tegan. I need you to call me back from the cloned phone so we aren't using Havyk's. Once I answer, I'll dial Bucco's phone."

"Okay, I'll do that now." Havyk disconnected, then redialed the hacker from the cloned phone and handed it over. Tegan took a deep breath.

It only took two rings before the call was answered. "Took you long enough, Miss Rowe. It's like you don't care about this sweet boy at all."

"My phone was dead, and I had to get a new charger. I didn't expect anyone to be calling me."

Bucco chuckled. "No? You thought I would forget all about the debt you owe?"

"It was John's debt, not mine."

The sound of flesh hitting something was loud. "You think I'm talking about thirty bottles? That was child's play. Between the pallets of Hive, all the workers, and the pregnant women, bringing in that motorcycle club has cost me billions, Miss Rowe. Bobby is a pretty little thing. He'll fetch good money on the dark web, as will both your children." Tegan sucked in a breath, and Bucco laughed. "You thought I didn't know you had two babies, but I know more than you and your biker think. I didn't get this far on dumb luck. I know your hacker is trying to keep mine busy while yours traces my location. Don't bother. I'll tell you where I am. Why? Because if you don't turn yourself and those babies over to me, I'll send my army after Rosie and Marcus. I'll send them after all those club members' wives and their children. So what will it be, Miss Rowe? You and your two children? Or will you selfishly watch as hundreds of lives are destroyed? I'll text you the address, and if you aren't here in eight hours, I'll release my own hounds." The line went dead, and Tegan dropped the phone, running out of the room.

Bucco hung up before Jax could voice him. "Fuck!"

"Motherfucker!" Mav yelled, while Ryker cursed Bucco's mother. Even Natalia got in a *mudak* in Russian. Everyone in the room was either cursing or yelling, some both at the same time. Jax didn't know whether to go after his mate or stay and see what the plan was.

Sutton stuck his fingers in his mouth and whistled, silencing the room. "It's obvious Bucco's hacker is good at what he does. Ryot, get Rosie's address and send a crew after her and Marcus. We need every Hound not out on assignment. Call Rafael and see if there are Gargoyles in the area available to help. Once that's done, Mav will take over so you can get Rhi and Daisy out of here. Havyk, get Bishop on the line. We need that address. Natalia, once we know where Bucco is, I want you to tell us everything you know about the location."

"Bishop has Rosie's address," Jax told Ryot.

Ryot looked at the ceiling, his brows dipped low. "Havyk, get that for me. I'm going to call Rafael. Jax, please go get the females and have them bring the kids down here. Tell Tegan she needs to call her parents back. Have them pack a bag and to expect some Hounds to pick them up."

Jackson didn't hesitate. He rushed up the stairs to find Rory trying to calm Tegan. "You need the Hounds, Tegan. I promise we'll get you out of this mess, but you cannot give yourself over to Bucco."

"She's right, Tee." Jax took Tegan from Rory's arms. "There's no way I'll let you and our sons go to him. Sutton and the others are downstairs making a plan of attack. You need to call Rosie and prepare her for a pickup."

"I won't put all the Hounds at risk."

"We're already at risk, and we've been on The Ministry's radar for years. We'll handle this like we do everything else. Rhi, Ryker needs you and Daisy downstairs. Rory, help us get the cubs. We need to move quickly."

Tegan didn't argue, but she wasn't happy. Neither

211

was Jax. The Hounds had gone up against some tough opponents over the years but never one as nasty as Bucco. He had an army at his disposal. The Hounds were badasses, but they weren't impervious to bullets the way the Gargoyles were.

Once downstairs, Ryker took Daisy from his mate. "Mom, you're with us." Rory passed Theo to Jackson, then walked over to Sutton and kissed him. No words were spoken between the two. Jax figured when he and Tegan had been together for a century, they wouldn't need words either.

Tegan handed Ollie to his uncle Ryan. "What exactly am I telling Rosie?"

Ryker handed her phone over. "For her and Marcus to pack their bags, and that three bikers will pick them up in a dark SUV within the hour. They won't be wearing our colors, so when they knock, they'll identify themselves with the names Rooster, Gunner, and Crow. They'll know it's them because Rooster has a blond mohawk, Gunner has huge biceps, and Crow will have his long, black hair in two braids."

Tegan dialed Rosie's number and relayed that information to Marcus when he answered. "I need both of you safe, and this is the only way that'll happen. Please don't argue. It'll only be until we get this mess resolved. I don't know where they're taking you, but the Hounds are good people, I promise." Marcus finally relented, and Tegan thumbed off the phone, handing it to Jax before walking over to the patio doors and staring outside. Rhi joined her, giving Tegan a hug and promising they'd get the babies together soon.

Mav and Natalia were off to the side quietly in a

heated discussion. Ryker shouted his brother's name, and the couple stopped arguing long enough to look his way. "I spoke to Rafael. There's a Gargoyle named Solomon Crenshaw in the Boston area. He and his sons will help once the Hounds get there. Sultan, Bishop will send the address to your phone via encrypted message. Mayhem, I'm taking the twins with me when I pick up Sadie and Mateo."

"Thanks, Ryot," Jax said.

"Thanks, Brother," Mayhem muttered before returning to his argument with Natalia. After a few words, Natalia cut her hand through the air like she often did when she was determined to get her point across. Mav growled, then kissed her hard. The lavender-haired pixie stormed away from him, and when she stopped in front of Sutton, he arched an eyebrow.

"Yes, Lolly?"

"You need somewhere safe for the Thompsons that is away from New Troy, and I have the perfect place. One that is not linked to the Hounds." Natalia crossed her arms over her chest and raised her chin. "When we took out my cousins, I was new to your world. Having been raised in the mafia, keeping secrets was vital to staying alive. I may have kept a few secrets of my own, like not selling my family's home."

"But you gave me nine million dollars when you *sold* it." Sutton crooked his fingers in air quotes.

"I may have fudged a bit about that. You didn't want the house since it was almost four hours away, but I kept it in case we one day needed somewhere away from here as a safehouse. Now we need one. It's only about an hour away from where Rosie lives." Looking over at Mav, Natalia said, "Daddo, call Rooster and give him the address please," using the twin's name for their father.

Sutton glanced over at Maveryck who was drinking straight from a bottle of whiskey. Maveryck's eyes softened, and he put the bottle down and pulled out his phone.

Sutton ran a hand through his dark hair. "And the nine million?"

"Is money my cousin, Mikael, didn't know about in an offshore account. Now, on to Bucco. He keeps his industries separate. Drugs at the vineyard. Trafficking out of his house across the river. It's easier to move people near the water. He runs guns at his place near Woodstock."

"But he had pregnant women at the vineyard," Tegan said.

"Like I said before, I haven't investigated Bucco since my father was killed. Maybe his house in Vermont was compromised, or maybe he changed things up. He did have those houses near the vineyard set up to care for babies."

"I thought traffickers' operations were closer to big bodies of water," Jax said.

Natalia held out her hand for Mav when he crossed the room after calling Rooster. Once he took it and threaded their fingers, she explained, "Lake Champlain connects to the Richelieu River, which feeds into Lake St. Pierre that connects to the St. Lawerence River. The St. Lawrence feeds into the bay that feeds into the Atlantic. Yes, it is a long journey

214

through Canada, but it also covers much territory."

Maveryck whistled. "Damn, Princess. You did study that family's movements."

Instead of smirking, Natalia's mood shifted to sad. Before Jax could ponder why, his phone pinged, and all eyes turned his way. With the address Bishop got from Bucco, he told Maveryck, "Looks like we're going to Boston."

Maveryck wiggled his phone. "All right, Princess. Let's get the four horsemen on the line so you can tell them all about Bucco's setup."

# CHAPTER TWENTY

## Tegan

AFTER MEETING RHI, TEGAN thought it best to get out of town. If something were to happen to the female or Daisy, Tegan would never be able to live with herself. It was bad enough Bobby had been taken, and Rosie and Marcus had to leave their home. Tegan listened in as Natalia rattled off information to the Hounds on the other end of the call. The female was amazing, in a scary way. But then Tegan thought about why Natalia knew all about one of the biggest mafia bosses in the US, and she felt sorry for the woman. Tegan couldn't imagine being trained as a killer, especially by her own father. Once the call was complete and the four horsemen were on their way to do recon, Tegan grabbed Jackson's arm, getting his attention.

"While you go to Boston, I want to take the cubs to Natalia's house. I know the Hounds can handle themselves, but I want to be as far away from New Troy as possible. There are too many mates and children here for Bucco to target."

Jax narrowed his eyes. "I'm not leaving you and the boys, Wildcat."

Tegan gripped his forearm and squeezed. "Jax, please. I need you to bring Bobby home."

"I'll go with her." Ryan had remained close to Tegan, swaying Ollie. "You know I'll protect them with my life, Brother."

"See? I'll have Ryan and the three males who went to get Rosie and Marcus guarding us."

Jax sighed. "Natalia?"

The female strode to their little group. "What's up?"

"Are you one hundred percent sure Bucco can't trace your house back to you?"

"Absolutely. The deed belongs to a shell company that is hidden in three more companies. Each one is owned by a different alias."

"And no one knows about it? No rental company or little old couple who airs it out once a week?"

"Nope. Mav and I drive up there and air it out ourselves."

"You knew about the house and the money?" Sutton huffed at Maveryck.

"Of course. Lolly and I don't have secrets between us." When Sutton growled, Mav held up his hands. "Come on, Pop. You can't tell me you and Mom don't keep some secrets from all of your kids. Well, except for the girls. Mom's thick as thieves with all of them. But there has to be some things you haven't shared with us males."

Sutton sighed. "You're right. So when you, Lolly, and the twins head out on the bike for a 'family ride', that's where you're going?"

"Most of the time. The twins love romping through

217

the woods and exploring the house."

Jax pinched his nose. "And you're sure the twins haven't let it slip about where you go and who owns the place?"

"Who the fuck are they gonna tell? Other five-year-olds at their playdates?"

"Those kids have moms, Mayhem."

"Moms who are usually getting sloshed on Sangria and not paying attention to the kids running around the playground. Sultan, I wouldn't send Rosie there if I didn't think it was safe, and I sure as fuck wouldn't take my mate and kids there either. Look, I know this whole mate and kids business is new to you. I get it. But I vow on all that's holy, Tegan and your boys couldn't have a better place to hide out. We've bought all new furniture, and the kitchen is stocked with the basics. Plus, Lucy has eyes on the security feed whenever we go there. I'll call her and tell her what's going on." Mav held up a hand when Jax opened his mouth. "On an encrypted line."

Mav was right. Sort of. Jax was new to the whole mate and kids thing, but in the short time they'd been a little family, he had proven himself. Not only to Tegan but the babies too. He got up for middle-of-the-night feedings, taking care of Ollie while Tegan nursed Theo. He changed diapers and helped bathe them. They weren't biologically his, but he treated them as if they were. But Tegan needed him to end this, and whenever Jax talked about his friend, she knew he trusted no one more than Ryan to keep them safe.

"Okay." Jax pulled out his wallet and handed over all the cash he had. "It's too dangerous to go back to the house, so stop and get anything you need once you're in New Woodland. Hopefully, we'll get in, take down Bucco, and get back quickly, but we won't know until we get there how heavily guarded he is."

Ryan shoved the bills in his back pocket since his hands were full of baby. "I'll keep them safe," he vowed again.

"Fine, but I want someone following you. It's a four-hour drive, and Tee will need to stop and feed the boys at some point." Jax turned to Maveryck. "Who's available?"

"I'll call Hawk. Wynter is off to Canada on some type of quest, and he's feeling restless."

"What about Dominion?"

"Family takes precedence. Silas knows that."

Tegan didn't know who or what Silas and Dominion were, but that was a question for another day. As Maveryck placed the call, Jackson took Theo from Tegan. Her heart stuttered at the love shining from her mate for her son. *Their* son. He wasn't their biological father, but Jax had already claimed them. Tegan thanked the goddess for this amazing male. She couldn't believe how much had changed in such a short time. Three days ago, she was alone and pregnant. Now, she had two healthy sons and a mate, as well as a fierce group of shifters who already considered her family. The only way her life could be better was if her parents and brothers were alive to witness it. She needed to get back to her rental and pack up her things, especially the picture album she'd been able to take from their home before it was auctioned. She didn't have anything else belonging to her parents. Only the pictures, and those she hadn't looked at in years. They were on the shelf in her closet. Maybe once this mess with Bucco was over, she and Jax could frame a few of them so the brothers would grow up knowing their grandparents were watching over them.

Maveryck rejoined them. "Hawk is on his way. He'll be here in ten."

Tegan wrapped her arms around Jackson's waist, needing to feel close to him before she left. It was her idea for Jax to go after Bucco, but that didn't mean she wouldn't miss him. Strangely, her beast had been quiet. Tegan figured it would fuss about Jax leaving them, but when Tegan reached out, her Lion sent her a comforting purr.

Jax kissed her temple. "What was that?"

"What was what?"

"You're purring."

Tegan pressed her hand to his beard. "Oh, that was my Lion reassuring me it's okay with you going after Bucco. I know this is my idea, but promise you'll be safe."

Jackson turned his head and kissed her palm. "I promise. I have too much to live for." He passed Theo to Tegan, then took Ollie from Ryan and inhaled his scent.

Sutton joined them. "May I hold him?" he asked. She passed her son over with a smile.

"I have another grandson named Theo," he cooed. "But he's grown now, so getting to hold you is bringing back memories." Sutton hummed, and Theo waved his arms, batting the older Hound on his face.

220

Tegan's eyes watered hearing Sutton claim her son. She'd never get to hear her own father do the same, but if things went well, Marcus would. Tegan wanted to talk to Jax about telling her parents the truth. She knew it was risky, but they were the only family she had left, and she wanted them in the boys' lives.

While they waited on Hawk, Jackson filled her in on all she'd missed while waiting upstairs. They agreed it was best to keep communication to a minimum while separated. "I promise to call you the second we rescue Bobby. I'll bring him to you and the Thompsons and leave Bucco to everyone else."

Someone knocked on the door, and everyone ceased talking. "It's Hawk," Maveryck said, looking at his phone. He went to let the Hound in, and Tegan wondered why Hawk hadn't waltzed in the way everyone else seemed to.

When they entered the game room, the newcomer strode over to Jax, gripping his shoulder while checking out Ollie. "Hello, Little One. Welcome to the family." When he noticed Tegan, he inclined his head. "Roman Hayes, at your service." The male's eyes were darker than any Tegan had ever encountered, and he was model gorgeous. A low growl came from Jax, and Tegan rolled her eyes.

"It's a pleasure to meet you. Thank you for agreeing to come with us. While I would rather my mate be the one guarding us, I'm trusting him to rescue my foster brother."

"Havyk told me what's going on. If you change your mind about Sultan going with you, I'd love a shot at Bucco. I fucking hate the mafia." When Natalia snorted, Roman held up his hands. "Present company excluded."

"I'm not mafia, so no offense taken. But we do need to get a move on."

"*We* are not going anywhere," Mav said, grabbing Tegan's and the boys' bags he'd brought in earlier, "Except to load Tegan's stuff in the car."

Natalia huffed. "We are going to our sons, so move your fine ass. Jackson, if you have questions once you get to Boston, give me a call."

"Thank you, Natalia." Jackson kissed Ollie before handing him off to Tegan. He then took Theo from Sutton and snuggled him too. Tegan rubbed circles on her mate's back when she noticed his misty eyes. Maybe she was asking too much from him, letting someone else watch over his family. Jax cleared his throat. "Let's get them loaded." When they got to the SUV, Jackson placed each boy in his car seat, doublechecking the straps were secure. He whispered to each boy how much he loved them, and it both warmed her heart as well as gutted her. When it was time to say goodbye to one another, Tegan didn't try to stop the tears. She kissed him hard, not caring who was watching.

"Come back to me. To us."

"I promise," he said against her lips. He then helped Tegan climb into the seat between the babies. Once she had her seatbelt on, he winked at her, then closed the door. Jax clasped both Ryan's and Roman's hands, begging them to keep his family safe. Ryan climbed into the driver's seat and started the motor while Roman got into his own vehicle. With a wave at her mate, they were off.

## *Sultan*

JAX DIDN'T MOVE AS he watched his whole world disappear down the driveway. His Gryphon was close to the surface, ready to shift and go after them. Jax got it. He wanted to be with them, but his mate specifically asked that he rescue Bobby, so that's what he would do. Natalia had given him all the intel he needed regarding Bucco's Massachusetts home.

Sutton stepped in front of Jax, blocking his view of the driveway. "I know it's not easy, but trust Judge and Hawk to keep them safe. You focus on the job at hand so you can keep your promise to your mate. Get to the Gargoyle's home in Boston, and trust their Clan and our Hounds to have your back. Listen to Maximus. There is no one better equipped to lead this mission." Sutton gripped the back of Jax's neck and pressed their foreheads together. "You've got this, Son."

A vehicle made its way up the driveway and stopped a few feet away. Jamison "Jackal" Porter rolled down the passenger window. "You ready?"

Jax hugged Sutton, needing his mentor's strength. When he turned loose, Jax got in the vehicle and acknowledged the three bikers along for the adventure. Yes, their mission was dangerous, but those riding with him were notorious for causing as much chaos as possible. Sultan welcomed their brand of crazy.

"Let's do this." Jackal gave Sutton a two-fingered salute before rolling down the driveway.

Jax turned in his seat to address Rebel and Ghost. "Thank you all for coming with me."

"No thanks needed, Brother. We live for this shit." Rebel reached out a fist, and Jax dapped it.

Ghost clapped him on the shoulder. "Nitro and the others will meet us in Boston, but they need the specifics." Jax pulled up the address for Solomon Crenshaw, the Gargoyle who was allowing them to use his home as base. He passed the phone to Ghost who made a three-way call to the other two vehicles.

Cameron "Cobra" Hollis said, "Ryker gave us the basics. Mafia shithead terrorizing your mate, kidnapped mate's foster brother or something like that. How about you fill in the blanks, Sultan?"

Jax spent the next few minutes recounting everything that had happened from Tegan breaking into his cabin, her ex working for the mob, him and Judge working with the four horsemen and Trenton Shepherd to rescue Tegan, all the women forced to bottle hive in a hidden warehouse, the pregnant women in the hidden hole beneath the outbuilding, to where they were now.

"That motherfucker doesn't deserve a bullet to the brainpan. He needs to be strung up naked and have his skin flayed an inch at a time," Thunder seethed in his deep, rolling bass. His nickname suited him.

224

Nitro added, "I think we should make him swallow a handful of Hive first. Let it take effect while we remind him of all the bad decisions he's made. Then we cut off his dick, shove it down his throat, and duct tape his mouth closed around it." Sultan grinned at the specificity of Nitro's plan.

Each one on the call made their own suggestion of how to torture Bucco, and Jax let their camaraderie flow through him. He had worked with each Hound over the years in searching for and taking down The Ministry. He'd even double-teamed with a few on mercenary jobs. He didn't know them all well, but the one thing he was certain of was they had his back and would do anything to ensure he succeeded in bringing Bobby home to the Thompsons. Not all Gryphons were in the MC, but these males were. They were hardcore bikers while being gentle souls around the mates and kids. He trusted every single one of them with Tegan and the boys.

"Congratulations on finding a mate, Sultan. And a lion shifter at that." That was Turbo. Like Jax, Clay "Turbo" Tallent had once had a female in his life who didn't appreciate the MC, and he'd cut her loose after a few years.

"Thanks, Turbo. This is the real deal since lions have fated mates. And the fact that she's already given me two precious baby cubs? Nothing sweeter."

"Except maybe a biological child," Nitro said.

"Except that." Jax rubbed his chest thinking about Coral. "But if that never happens? I'm going to thank Zeus every day for Theo and Ollie."

Jackal held out a fist for Jax. "Preach, Brother."

225

# CHAPTER TWENTY-ONE

## Sultan

BY THE TIME THEY made the three-hour trip to Boston, Jax was ready to crawl out of his skin. His hand twitched to call Tegan, even though they agreed to radio silence to ensure Bucco didn't somehow catch wind of them being separated. If the man knew Tegan wasn't bringing the boys, he wouldn't hesitate to kill Bobby, and they couldn't have that. It was bad enough that the teen had been taken while going to the store. It was a sad situation when kids weren't safe in their own town, but the world was a shitty place, and Jax vowed he would never let anything bad happen to his sons. He wasn't worried about Tegan once she arrived at Natalia's former home. She would be busy introducing the cubs to their grandparents. They would all be protected by five Hounds in a place Bucco didn't know existed.

Solomon Crenshaw's home was a nice-sized house on Little Nahant Island. His twin sons, Aiden, a doctor, and Avery, a professor at UMass, lived nearby. Solomon and the twins were waiting on the front porch when the SUVs pulled into his driveway. Jax had called earlier to give the male an ETA on their arrival and requested their host place an order for pizza. They hadn't stopped to eat, wanting to get to the coast as quickly as possible.

"Solomon, thank you for having us." Jax shook the Gargoyle's hand, then those of his sons. He introduced the Hounds once they were all inside.

"Let's go to the den where we'll have room to sit." Solomon led them through the spacious home. The den was a large room at the back of the house that opened to a wide deck with a view of the bay. The sky was a stunning mix of pink, lilac, and orange as the sun set. Jax wished he could share the view with Tegan. Maybe when the brothers were a little older, he would take his family on a beach vacation.

Several large pizzas, along with plates and napkins waited on a table at one side of the room. Avery played bartender, handing out beer or soft drinks as each Hound passed by with a full plate. Jax had gone into detail regarding Bucco's demands earlier on the phone with Solomon and his sons, so the Gargoyles knew the whole story.

While they ate, Aiden spoke about the many overdose cases that had come through the emergency room. "Hive is expensive, but it only takes a few pills for most users to OD. The saddest part is most of the cases I see are teens. I know taking Bucco out of the equation won't stop the mafia, but hopefully we can get his number two as well."

"Do we know who that is?" Aiden asked.

"Natalia thinks it's a cousin." Jax wiped his hands on a napkin and took a swig of beer. "The four horsemen plan on going after the organization once we take care of Bucco and get Bobby returned to his foster parents. That's our priority tonight." Once the food was demolished, Jackson called Max, putting it on speaker.

Max didn't bother with hello when he answered. "Bucco's estate is about twenty minutes west of Boston in New Sherborn. It's situated on thirty acres. There's a small house that sits back off the road. The main house is down a long driveway and is in the middle of the acreage. It looks to be approximately ten thousand square feet. The property is heavily wooded, which works to our advantage. I called Bishop, and as with the vineyard, all the neighboring houses are owned by Bucco. Unlike the vineyard, this place is heavily guarded. We counted twenty on the outside alone. Getting in won't be a problem since we're all flyers. It's getting past the assault rifles that'll be the biggest issue."

Nitro swirled the liquid in his tumbler. "What about women?"

"None as far as we can tell. There are no outbuildings. The small house is where the guards who aren't on rotation stay. It has an attached garage where they store the lawn equipment. There could be a trap door, but one wasn't visible from our vantagepoint. Still, we didn't detect more heartbeats than we counted men. Bishop and Henry are ready whenever we are."

"Send the coordinates to where we should meet you, then we'll all head that way." Bucco had given Tegan eight hours, so they still had time, but Jax had already witnessed the heavy Boston traffic, and he didn't want to miss the deadline because of an unforeseen wreck. It took over an hour to reach the rendezvous point. It was an abandoned farm, two miles from Bucco's estate. Max directed them to park in the barn. Jax eyed the old building, praying it didn't collapse on their vehicles.

After introductions were made, Solomon spoke up. "Since we're impervious to bullets, the twins and I can act as a distraction. We can get their attention while you take them out."

Max shook his head. "The only problem with that is Bucco will hear gunfire. If he feels threatened, he's likely to kill the teen. Here's what I was thinking." After Max laid out his crazy proposal, Jackson had to admit it might work and without any bloodshed.

## *Tegan*

HER PARENTS WERE WAITING outside with their three Hound guardians when Ryan wove along the long driveway leading to the former Russian mafia home. Tears were cried when Rosie and Marcus embraced Tegan, and more were shed when they got their hands on the boys. Hawk parked beside them, and Tegan introduced her parents to the two bikers. Rooster,

Gunner, and Crow clasped hands with their fellow Hounds, giving Tegan a nod.

Marcus gave all the males a side-eye. "Let's get these little ones inside. I'll get your bags." He handed Ollie to Tegan and retrieved their few belongings from the back of the SUV.

Ryan stepped away from the others. "I'll grab their pack 'n play." They had stopped an hour prior so Tegan could nurse the brothers. While she waited in the vehicle, Ryan went inside a Hudson's and came back loaded down with things for the boys, including the playpen. When she questioned him, he said the cubs would need somewhere to sleep when they stayed with "Uncle Ryan." Tegan just grinned at him.

Hawk remained outside with the others as Rosie led the way carrying Theo. Ryan set up the playpen in the enormous parlor where Rosie took a seat on the sofa, doting over her grandchild. Marcus placed their bags on a side chair, then joined his wife and held out his hands for Ollie.

"Rosie, you're holding Theo, and Marcus, you have Ollie. Theodore after my mom, and Oliver is named for my dad."

"Oh, Tegan. That's lovely." Rosie brushed a finger down Theo's cheek.

Marcus eyed Tegan warily, and she couldn't blame him. She had brought this mess to their lives. Bobby had been kidnapped, and now they were holed up far away from their home. "Start talking," he demanded gruffly.

Ryan returned from wherever he'd gone and posted up in the doorframe, arms crossed over his chest.

"I'm okay, Ryan."

"And I promised Jackson I'd keep you that way."

Marcus narrowed his eyes at the Hound who glared right back. When Ryan didn't budge, Marcus returned his gaze to Tegan. "What happened?"

Tegan sat on the loveseat opposite, kicked off her sneakers, and curled her legs on the cushions. "I met a guy named John Cashel. He ended up being bad news." Tegan told the story from how they met up until where they were currently, leaving nothing out except for the supernatural aspect. When she finished, Marcus was furious, and Rosie had tears running down her cheeks.

"And this Jackson? He rescued you, why?"

Ryan pushed off the doorframe and walked over to sit close to Tegan. "Because that's what we do. Yes, we're a motorcycle club but the good kind. We aren't one-percenters. We have families. We *are* a family."

Rosie swiped at the tears. "Why didn't you tell us you were pregnant? Why not come to us instead of running away?" Tegan glanced at Ryan, her eyebrows raised. He nodded. They had talked about this moment on the drive. He said it was her decision whether to tell them the whole truth. If they didn't take it well, he would voice them.

"About that. There's something I need to tell you. It's going to seem fantastical and unbelievable, but I can prove it. I'm not human. I'm a lion shifter." Tegan held her hands out in front of her and called forth her claws. Rosie gasped, and Marcus flinched. She retracted them and clasped her hands in her lap. "My parents left our pride when my dad got a job in New York. Both sets of grandparents were dead, and my parents weren't close to their siblings. They never said why, but I never met any aunts or uncles or cousins. Before my family… My parents drilled it into our heads that we had to keep what we were a secret because if humans knew about us, they would hunt us. Or worse. I didn't know any other shifters, so as soon as I found out I was pregnant, I began saving money. I took a few supplies to this little cabin close to where my old house was. I was on my way there when I wrecked."

"But he knows," Marcus said, jabbing a finger toward Ryan.

"I know because I'm also a shifter, just not a lion. There's a whole supernatural world out there that's hidden from humans. Like Tegan said, if we were to be discovered, it would be chaos. But Tegan's not alone now. She has Jackson and our Hounds family to help her raise the cubs."

"Tegan…" Rosie shook her head. "I think I'm dreaming. You can really turn into a lion? I mean I saw your claws, but a lion?"

"Do you want more proof?"

"I-I don't know. You were right. This is unbelievable. The boys? You call them cubs. Will they be shifters too? I'm assuming John was their father, and he was human."

Tegan shrugged. "As far as I know." She turned to Ryan. "What do you think?"

"I don't know either. With our kind, more often than not, the kids with one shifter parent are shifters since that gene is dominant. With the boys, we'll have to wait and see."

"And this Jackson, he's whatever you are?" Rosie asked Ryan.

"He is."

Theo began fussing, so Marcus stood to walk him around the room. "I know he rescued you, but you just met him, Tegan. How do you know you can trust him? You thought you knew this John character."

"Because he's my fated mate. The one being chosen by the universe to be my perfect partner."

"You can't be serious, Tegan. We taught you better than to believe in fairy tales."

Tegan stood and strode to where Marcus was glaring at her, taking a fussing Theo out of his hands. "So you can agree I'm able to shift into a lion but not that I have a fated mate?" Theo started crying at his momma's raised voice. "Shh, I'm sorry, Theo. Momma's sorry."

Ryan rose and went to the diaper bag, digging around until he came out with the snuggy and a pacifier. He strapped the holder across his chest, then held out his hands. "Let me take him outside. He likes the sunshine." Tegan handed her son over, and Ryan placed him in the sac against his chest. Theo waved his arms around, still fussing. "Here you go, Little Man. Here's your num num." As soon as Theo latched on, he stopped crying. Tegan had no idea Ryan knew about the snuggy or the num num. He and Jax must have talked at some point about both. Ryan disappeared through the door, and Tegan turned on Marcus.

"Look. I know I sprung all this on you, but if you

want to be part of my sons' lives, you'll have to accept all aspects of it. Jax included. If you'll point me to the bathroom, I'll give you two time to talk."

"It's down the hallway, first door on the right." Marcus sat down beside Rosie and slid his arm across the sofa, leaning close. He took Ollie's hand in his and wiggled, cooing at her son.

Tegan found the bathroom and closed herself in. She needed a moment. After she peed and washed her hands, she decided to let her parents have their own moment, so she began walking around the large house, trying to envision a young Natalia living there surrounded by her own mafia father and mobster cousins, or whatever they were called. Tegan found herself in the kitchen, and she wasn't alone. Crow was stirring something on the stove. He was tall like Jax, but instead of being broad, Crow was on the thinner side. He didn't look native, so maybe his biker moniker came from his hair being so dark it was almost blue.

He glanced over his shoulder when she entered the room. "Are you okay?" Having shifter hearing, he would have heard her conversation.

"Not really." Tegan closed the distance to see what he was cooking.

"Beef stew. It's not really a summer food, but it can feed a big group. Cornbread's in the oven."

"Thank you for cooking."

Crow placed the wooden spoon on a saucer and leaned his butt against the counter, crossing his feet. "Do you want me to talk to him?"

"No, but thank you. That's Rosie's job. He's the logical of the two. She's the romantic. If anyone would believe in fated mates, it'd be her."

Speaking of, Rosie entered the kitchen without Ollie. She held out her hand. "Let's walk."

Tegan clasped Rosie's hand and followed the woman outside. "This place is beautiful." Tegan was about to mention the estate's history, but Rosie kept talking. "You know Marcus. It'll take him a while to mull things over. Look at them from all angles, then he'll come to the conclusion you want. What we both want. It's a shock knowing you're something other than human, but we don't love you any less for it. And you must know we want to be in the boys' lives. They might be the only grandchildren we ever have." Rosie's voice was barely audible.

Tegan wrapped her arm around Rosie's shoulder. "Jackson will bring Bobby home."

"How do you know? Marcus was right when he said you haven't known this man long."

"How did you know Marcus was the one for you?"

"Because he punched my date in the nose when he kept grabbing my ass in front of his friends. Here I am in a biker bar with a guy I barely knew. I always had a thing for the bad boy, you see. When Devil asked me out on a date, I expected to go out to dinner. Maybe for a ride on his motorcycle. Should've known by his nickname he wasn't the type of bad boy I could handle. Anyway, we end up in this seedy little joint. Here I am in my cute jeans and off-the-shoulder sweater, while all the other women were dressed in booty shorts and cropped T-shirts. I saw more ass cheeks that night than I ever had in my life." Rosie chuckled. "Devil kept palming my butt, and I kept wiggling away. To him it was a game. To me? I was mortified. Then here comes this tall drink of water who grabs Devil's hand and tells him to lay off. When Devil told him to get fucked, Marcus knocked him on his ass, grabbed my hand, and hauled me out of there. We ended up at an all-night diner, and the rest is history."

Tegan grinned. She could see Marcus defending Rosie's honor. "Sounds like you have your own fated mate."

"At least a white knight. If you tell me this man is a good one, I'll believe you."

"He is, Rosie. I made a mistake with John, but I was so freakin' lonely. He was so charming in the beginning, and I let my loneliness override my sensibilities. With Jax, I don't have to worry about that. John wanted a handout. Jax wants my love, nothing more. We have a nice house in a good neighborhood. Granted, we'll have to move before the cubs get much bigger. Can you imagine a neighbor looking out the back window and seeing a little boy turn into a lion cub? Talk about chaos."

"If humans aren't supposed to know, why did you tell us?"

"Because I trust you, and I want you in our lives. Sultan's parents died many years ago, and an older shifter couple have adopted him, thus the babies, but they need another set of grandparents."

Rosie squeezed Tegan's hand. "I'd like that." She was quiet for a bit, then asked, "Do you really think he'll get Bobby back to us?"

"If anyone can, it's the Hounds."

"Hounds?"

Tegan had trusted Rosie this far, and Ryan had already agreed Tegan could be honest. "Jax and the others are Gryphon shifters created by Zeus. Zeus called the Gryphons his hounds, so their motorcycle club is called The Hounds of Zeus."

"Wait. I thought Gryphons were those mythical beasts that were half eagle, half lion."

"That's exactly what they are, except they're real. They can shift into their Gryphon, but they can also choose their eagle or lion separately. I've only seen Jackson's eagle, and it was extraordinary."

Rosie stopped walking. "And you can really change into a lion?"

"Yes, ma'am. I'll show you when we get inside. Just remember, I'll still be me, and I would never hurt you." Tegan opened her senses, and Theo's cries were angry, so she got them walking again. "My boy is hungry. Guess I need to feed him."

"How do you know?"

"I can hear him. I have enhanced senses. Come on, I need to rescue Ryan."

While Tegan fed the boys, Marcus and Rosie enjoyed some of the beef stew Crow cooked. When she was finished, Tegan handed them over to her parents so she could eat. All the Hounds gave them privacy except for Ryan. He remained close by, and Tegan appreciated having Jackson's best friend watching over her. As promised, she shifted into her Lion while the cubs slept in their playpen. Tegan had reiterated the fact that it was still her in her fur before leaving the room to strip and shift. Rosie had dropped to her knees and held her arms open while Marcus remained frozen on the sofa. Tegan padded slowly to her mother and sat a few feet away. Rosie grinned and asked, "Can I pet you?"

Tegan rolled to her back. Presenting her belly was the biggest show of trust she could offer. It took Marcus a few minutes, but he slid to the floor. Tegan rolled over and crawled to her father, settling her weight across his legs. When he scratched behind her ears, Tegan licked a stripe up his cheek.

Ryan's phone beeped, and Tegan scooted off Marcus's lap, sitting on her haunches. "It's time."

Tegan nodded and trotted out of the parlor to change back. When she returned to the parlor, Ryan handed the phone over. "Here's what they have planned." After the Hound explained, he turned to her parents. "We're going to step outside in case the boys start crying."

Marcus stood and hugged Tegan. "We'll take care of them. Go do what you have to do."

Tegan took a few seconds to relish in his love before stepping back. She gave Rosie what she hoped was a positive smile, then followed Ryan out of the house.

# CHAPTER TWENTY-TWO

## Sultan

THE GRYPHONS STRAPPED ON weapons and grabbed the duffels containing the needed supplies. Once they were ready, the group headed out on foot, jogging through the woods on a path Legend had scouted earlier. When they were a hundred yards from the estate, Jax texted Bishop. The Gargoyles removed their shirts so they wouldn't get shredded when they called forth their wings. The nine Gryphons who had arrived with Jackson stripped down so they could shift into their eagles, all except for Ghost. He changed out of his black fatigues into a pair of shorts and donned a blonde, curly wig. He was the smallest of the Hounds, and from a distance, would look enough like Tegan to fool the guards and Bucco.

Solomon released his wings, the Hounds shifted, and they took flight with four of them headed to the smaller house to voice the guards hanging out there. The horsemen gathered all the weapons and strode closer to the edge of the trees with Jax and Ghost following. The twins stood at the edge of the woods, ready to act as a barrier should any of the guards shoot Jax's way. The four horsemen spread out, each taking a cardinal point, rifles at the ready. Jax held his breath as each eagle and Solomon landed on the roof of the house. The Hounds shifted back to human and leaned over the rooftop. As planned, Turbo, Jackyl, Rebel, and Cobra voiced the guards below in unison.

"You will not shoot. You will not obey Bucco."

They didn't instruct them to put their weapons on the ground in case Bucco was looking out the window. That took care of the guards outside, but there were still those inside to worry about. Jax texted Bishop, telling him what they needed from Tegan. It took a few minutes while Bishop relayed the information to Tegan. When the call connected, Tegan whispered, "Jax."

"You ready, Wildcat?" He wanted to ask how she was, but they needed to keep chatter to a minimum.

"Yes." Her voice was strong, and Jax couldn't wait to hold her and tell her how proud he was.

Bishop called Bucco's number. The asshole answered with, "Miss Rowe, you are cutting it close to running out of time."

"I'm here. Send Bobby out, then I'll come to you."

"Do you take me for a fool?" Bucco snarled. "There is no one outside. The guards would have alerted me to your presence."

Jax took over since Tegan didn't know Ghost was pretending to be her. "We are at the edge of the woods, ten o'clock from the front door."

"Go look out the window," Bucco instructed

240

someone.

"They're out there, Sir."

"I want to see Bobby," Tegan said. "Until we have proof that he's alive, you don't get me."

"The deal was you and your two babies. I don't see them."

"They're here," Jax said. "Behind us in their car seats. I didn't want them in the line of fire."

"Prove it," Bucco demanded.

Jackson turned and walked a few yards into the woods. When he returned, he was holding one of two life-like dolls bundled in a blanket. The realness of the doll unnerved Jax, but it served its purpose. He handed the doll to Ghost who placed the toy on his shoulder and patted its back. Ghost hit a button, and the doll began crying. The Hound swayed the "baby" back and forth, hitting the button again to silence it.

"There's your proof, now we want ours," Jax said.

Bucco chuckled. "Fine, but don't even think of trying to pull a fast one. As you can see, I have twenty guards ready to put a bullet in your head if you make one wrong move. Let's go."

They must have been at the back of the house because it was almost thirty seconds before the front door opened. Bucco walked out with his hand around a young man's arm. Bobby couldn't be more than five-foot-six. He was rail-thin, and his brown hair hung past his shoulders. If Jackson didn't know the teen was a boy, he might have mistaken him for a female. From the roof, Turbo said, "Turn the boy loose and drop to your knees." Bucco did as instructed. Jackson held his breath as Solomon launched off the roof, swooping

241

down to grab Bobby. The kid screamed, and four guards ran from inside, surrounding their boss.

"Drop your weapons," Rebel commanded, and the guards complied. The Hounds remained where they were until Avery and Aiden could get inside and ensure there were no more guards.

"Shoot them!" Bucco yelled. The guards who had dropped their guns didn't have the chance to reach for their weapons. Legend fired off several shots from his hiding spot, and the guards danced back. Ghost placed the doll on the ground, yanked the wig off, and picked up a rifle. Before Jax could grab his own, pain ripped through his shoulder a few seconds before he heard the shot.

"Upstairs," Ghost yelled, firing at the window the shot came from. "How bad is it?" he asked, as he and Jax retreated into the woods.

"I'll live." Thank Zeus it was his left shoulder.

Ghost inspected the wound. "Through and through. I'll guard you if you want to shift."

Jax tried to get his shirt off one-handed, but the wound made it difficult. He pointed to his chest. "Please rip my shirt off."

Ghost smirked. "That's what she said." Jax barked out a laugh, then groaned at the pain. Ghost wiggled his eyebrows. "Need help with your pants too?"

"You're not right." Jackson shook his head, grinning at the Hound. He struggled with his boots, and Ghost huffed, kneeling to help. He then tugged Jackson's pants down his legs, taking his underwear with them. The male averted his gaze as he stood. Jax called on his Gryphon, needing the full force of his healing capabilities. Shifting wouldn't completely heal his shoulder, but it would stop the blood loss and begin the process of knitting muscle, tendons, tissue, and skin back together. It had been months since he'd let the beast loose, and when it came time to shift back, his animal fought him.

*Just a few more minutes.*

*We need to get this shit done so we can get back to Tegan and the boys.*

With that, the Gryphon retreated whether Jax was ready or not. He pulled his clothes back on, including the bloody shirt, and he and Ghost joined the others. All Bucco's guards were seated with their hands zip-tied behind their backs. Their weapons were in a pile, well away from the men. Avery had a pissed-off male on his stomach with a boot to his back and a rifle pointed at his head. Jax strode over. "This the fucker who shot me?"

"Yep."

Jackson swung his leg back and kicked the bastard in the ribs. "Asshole." The man curled in on himself, but Jackson didn't inflict any further damage as much as he'd like to.

Solomon was sitting on the ground holding Bobby on his lap. The boy looked to be unconscious.

"He okay?" Jax asked.

"He will be. Passed out when he saw my wings. Aiden's already checked his vitals."

Max stood in front of Bucco with a pistol pointed at the don's head. "Did you harm the teen in any way?"

"No. Buyers prefer their merchandise pristine."

Jax couldn't hold back his Gryphon. His talons

243

erupted, and his beast sliced across the man's cheek. "You motherfucker!"

Bucco screamed, grabbing his face. Blood poured between his fingers as he stared at Jax. "What the fuck are you?"

Max stepped closer, but not too close. "Sultan, I'm pissed too, but we need answers."

Jackson's chest heaved, but he backed away and gestured for Max to get on with his questions.

"Who's your underboss?"

"My cousin, Victor."

"Where is Victor?"

"On a boat in the middle of the Pacific."

"Have you spoken to him lately?"

"Not since this morning."

"And does he know of your plan to swap Bobby for Tegan and the boys?"

"Of course."

"You will call him and say the swap was successful. Then you will tell him you need him to come here and retrieve the babies for the next step in selling them." Max listed out explicit instructions for Bucco. From the sound of it, he and the other horsemen were going to wait around for Victor to show up. To Legend, Max said, "Go to the small house and gather the other guards. I want them all in one place."

Legend shifted into his eagle and took flight. Max used his Gryphon voice to make the men forget about seeing eagles and Gargoyles. Jackson wanted to leave it to the Hound so he could get on the road to his mate and sons.

With the shooter under Max's control, Aiden

244

strode over and asked, "You need me to look at that?" indicating his shoulder.

"Nah. I shifted. I'll be all right in a few days."

"I figured, but you are the first Gryphons I've met, so I wanted to be sure." He turned to the sounds of grunts and demands. Legend demanding the second-shift guards get a move on and the guards huffing their discontent.

Legend told them to halt in front of Max, who settled the rifle on his shoulder, then pulled a cigar out of one of his cargo pockets. After biting off the end and spitting it to the ground, he pointed it at the newcomers. "Welcome to the party, motherfuckers. My name is Maximus, and I'll be your host here on Mafia Island. Sit your asses down and get comfortable. You're gonna be here a while."

The guards did as they were told, but they looked at Bucco like he was going to save them. He wasn't. With all the humans under Max's command, Jax was ready to leave. While the twins waited with their father, the Hounds gathered around Max.

"What now?" Jax asked,

"Now you're going back to your mate and sons, taking Bobby to his foster parents. As for the rest of you, if you don't have merc jobs on the books, you're welcome to stay with the horsemen. The FBI has the vineyard under control, but Bucco's operation needs to be shut down."

While Max spoke, Jackson stepped away to call Tegan. He asked Bishop to patch him through, and when she answered, Jax exhaled deeply. "Hey, Wildcat. It's done. We have Bobby, and I'm bringing him to you."

"Oh, Jax. Thank you. He's got him. Jax has Bobby, and he's bringing him here." Jax waited while Tegan and her parents cheered and cried. "How is he? Did Bucco hurt him?"

"He's passed out right now. Seeing Gargoyle wings was a little much, but as soon as he comes around, the doctor with us will check him out to be sure. If he doesn't need medical treatment, we'll voice him to make him forget seeing shifters. If all goes well, we should be on the road in the next half hour, putting us there around one or so. If that changes, I'll let you know. Now, how are you? How are our sons?"

"I'm good, and the boys are being spoiled rotten."

"That's wonderful. I can't wait to see you, Wildcat. I need my mate."

Tegan hummed. "Then get your fine ass on the road. We'll be waiting."

"See you soon, Sweetheart."

Jax disconnected, then walked over to where the Gargoyles were talking to a now awake teen. They must have voiced him already considering the boy wasn't running for his life. Jax waited while Aiden did a cursory examination, asking him about his treatment since being kidnapped. Bobby was soft-spoken, but his answers had them all relieved. Once Aiden gave Jax the okay, he knelt beside the teen.

"Hi, Bobby. I'm Jackson, Tegan's boyfriend. You ready to go home?"

"Yeah. Do my parents know I'm okay?" he asked as soon as Jax helped him to his feet.

"They do. I just got off the phone with Tegan, and

they're all waiting to see you. It'll take a few hours to get there, but you can call them if you want to."

"I'd like that. And uh…" Bobby ducked his head.

Jax raised the teen's chin with a bent knuckle. "Bobby, you and I are family now. Tegan claims to be your big sister, so that makes me an older brother. You can ask me anything."

Bobby's eyes filled with tears. "I've always wanted a big brother," he said softly.

Jax placed his hand on Bobby's neck. "Now you have one. What were you going to say?"

"Can we please stop by a drive-thru? I'm starving."

Jax shook him gently. "Absolutely."

While Jackson was thanking the Gargoyles for all their help, a few of the Hounds had gone to retrieve the vehicles. Most of the Gryphons chose to remain with the four horsemen, but Turbo, Lead, and Cobra had to get back to New Troy. Jax thanked them as well before he and Bobby climbed into one of the SUVs and headed out.

While Jax drove, Bobby called Marcus and Rosie, assuring them he was okay. As promised, Jax stopped at the first fast food place they came to. Jax then pulled into the parking lot of a Hudson's, and while Bobby ate, Jax ran in and bought a T-shirt. He had to voice some of the associates who noticed the blood-soaked shirt. Bobby hadn't asked about the wound on his shoulder. Either he didn't notice it, which was kind of hard to miss, or Max had made it invisible to the teen.

As soon as Bobby finished eating, he leaned his head against the window and fell asleep. Jax smiled when soft snores filled the air. Instead of turning on the radio, he relished those chuffs, reminding him he and the Hounds, along with their new Gargoyle friends, had done their job. Gryphons had been created to watch over humans who couldn't do it themselves. Those like the trafficking victims Bucco stole. The ones who were inside The Ministry compounds against their wishes. Women like Tegan whose only crime had been trusting the wrong man. Being a mercenary paid well, but it was just a job. It was times like these when he saved someone that meant the world to Jax.

It was closer to two that next morning when they pulled down the long, winding driveway leading to Natalia's house. Lights were on downstairs, and the three Hounds who'd picked up the Thompsons were guarding the perimeter of the home. He'd no sooner shut the car off than Bobby was jumping out and running toward an older couple who stepped outside. Tegan and Ryan were right behind the Thompsons, each carrying one of his boys. Jax made a beeline for his mate, wrapping her and Ollie in his arms and kissing his mate passionately, not giving one fuck about who was watching.

The Thompsons had Bobby squished between them, but the teen was laughing. Ryan cleared his throat, grinning when Jax finally let his mate up for air. "Welcome back, Brother."

Jax reached out to take Theo from his best friend. "It's good to be back. Hello, Little One. Were you good for your grandparents?"

Bobby untangled himself from the Thompsons and walked over to Jax, smiling up at him. "Who do you have here?"

"This is Theo, and Tegan has Ollie."

"How can you tell them apart?" Bobby reached out, and Theo grabbed his finger, making Bobby giggle.

"Theo's hair is a little darker, plus he's always the first to cry when it's time to eat."

"Hi there, Theo. I'm your Uncle Bobby. I can't teach you to toss a football, but I'll show you how to make the best cupcakes in the world and tell you the best music to listen to." Theo cooed at his new uncle, and Bobby giggled again. It was a glorious sound.

Rosie snaked her arm around Jackson's side, and he glanced down at her. "Hi, Rosie." She didn't respond. Instead, she shook her head, tears belying her big smile.

A strong hand gripped Jax's shoulder. "Both my grandsons were perfect. I can't thank you enough for getting Bobby back to us safely. How did you manage going up against someone like Phil Bucco? Was anyone hurt?"

Jax barely held his growl inside. "No thanks are needed, really. It's late, and I'm wiped. How about we all get some sleep? Then in the morning, I'll tell you all about it."

"Oh, yes. Of course. I'm just… Thank you."

"You're welcome. Ry, you got this?" Jax made a twirling motion with his finger.

"I do. Go be with your family, and we'll keep watch."

A squawk came from a nearby tree. Since Hawk was the only Hound missing, Jax assumed it was him. Jackson inclined his head, silently thanking the Hound for watching over his family. Once inside, Rosie offered to watch the boys while he and Tegan rested, but she reminded her mother that she was the only one who could feed her sons.

"Come on. Ryan put the pack 'n play in one of the bedrooms." Tegan turned toward the stairs, but Bobby ran up to Jax and threw his arms around him, careful not to disturb the baby. Jax cupped the teen's head and pressed his cheek against Bobby's hair. No words were needed.

# CHAPTER TWENTY-THREE

## Tegan

WHEN THEY GOT TO the bedroom, instead of putting the boys in the playpen, Jax placed them in the middle of the bed and laid down beside them. Tegan settled on the other side, staring at her mate while he doted on the babies. Jax didn't talk about Bucco or the rescue. He asked about how things went with her parents. Tegan was honest about Marcus's initial outburst. She told him about her walk with Rosie. When she replayed shifting for her parents, Jax grinned. Goddess, she loved his smile. She nursed Theo while Jax cuddled Ollie against his bare chest, laughing when the baby grabbed a tiny handful of chest hair. After feeding Ollie, they changed the boys' diapers and put them in the pack 'n play, covering them with a soft blanket.

Tegan fussed over Jax's wound, but he assured her he was healing fine. Tegan wasn't one to cry often, but knowing her mate could have been killed... If the house hadn't been massive, and her parents sleeping in the other wing, Tegan would have balked at having sex where they could hear. Jax distracted her when he turned out the lights and made slow, sweet love to her, taking care not to mash her still tender breasts. Tegan had expected hard and fast, but her mate was in a loving mood. She didn't object. In between feeding the babies and making love, Jax told her about the rescue and taking Bucco down. Needless to say, they didn't get much sleep.

Later that morning, they entered the kitchen to the smell of bacon frying. Crow stood in front of the stove, and Bobby was at the counter making biscuits, casting what he probably thought were sly glances at the long-haired Hound. His earbuds were in place, and he was bopping his head to the song playing. Rosie and Marcus sat at the table, sipping coffee.

"There's my grandsons." Rosie rose from the table and held out her hands.

Tegan passed Ollie over. "Good morning, Tegan. How are you, Tegan?" she muttered in a falsetto.

Rosie chuckled. "Good morning, Tegan. Good morning, Jackson."

Jax grinned at the woman as he took Theo to Marcus. "Morning, Sir." Jax went to the refrigerator and pulled out some orange juice. He poured Tegan a tall glass before fixing his own coffee.

The back door flew open, and Hawk strode in. "Mmm, biscuits." He kept moving until he stood behind Bobby, looking over the teen's shoulder. A low growl came from Crow, and Hawk stepped back, his hands in the air. Tegan frowned at the male. Bobby was only seventeen.

*"Crow's an honorable male, Wildcat. If there is a connection between him and Bobby, he won't act on it until Bobby is of age."*

That was something else that happened during the night. They figured out they could speak to one another silently.

*"Is Crow even gay?"*

*"I'm not sure. I've never seen him with a man or a woman. He could be pan or ace or somewhere else on the spectrum."*

When it was time to put the biscuits in the oven, Bobby hip-checked Crow who scooted over, smirking. Bobby then pulled eggs and vegetables out of the fridge and set about preparing omelets for everyone. He tapped his phone which was sitting on the counter, then removed his earbuds and shoved them in the pocket of his shorts. "Anyone allergic to anything?" he asked, rubbing the side of his neck. When everyone gave a negative response, he began by whipping a cartonful of eggs. He and Crow danced around each other as though they'd been cooking together for years. Rosie and Marcus were too caught up in the babies to notice.

Instead of speaking of the previous day's events, they kept the conversation light, mostly chatting about the babies. Rooster, Gunner, and Judge joined them when breakfast was ready, and Jax retrieved the pack 'n play so no one had to eat one-handed. The Hounds complimented Bobby on his culinary skills, and the young man blushed.

"It's just breakfast, but thank you. And Crow helped." When everyone's plates were scraped clean, he jumped up and began gathering the dirty dishes, but Rosie stopped him.

"You know the drill. You cooked, so I'll clean."

"But—"

"Bobby," Crow cut him off. "How about we take the little ones outside for a walk?"

"Me?" Bobby's voice came out in a squeak. He cleared his throat. "Uh, yeah. A walk. Sounds good."

Crow took his plate to the sink. "How long before they'll want to be fed?"

Jax stood and leaned over the playpen, removing one of the slings. He showed Bobby how to put it on. "They should be good for at least a couple of hours." He lifted Ollie, then slid him into the carrier. Crow watched how it was done, then fitted himself with the second sling, taking Theo and easing him into it. Theo grabbed hold of one of Crow's braids, but the male didn't try to remove it. He silently waited, and once Bobby was situated, he strode to the door and held it open for Bobby.

Bobby patted Ollie's back. "Come on, nephew. The adults need to talk about things not fit for little cub's ears." Crickets could be heard it was so quiet as everyone turned in unison, staring at the teen.

Crow stopped Bobby with a gentle hand on his arm. "Did you say cubs?" When Bobby nodded, Crow asked, "Something you want to share with the class?"

Bobby swallowed hard, his eyes wide. "Not really."

"Bobby." Crow must have let some of his Gryphon out in his voice because Bobby shivered. Even Tegan felt the compulsion.

"Fine." He returned to the kitchen and closed the door behind him. He stopped in front of Marcus, his eyes down. "You promise not to make me leave?"

Rosie stood and went to her foster son, grabbing his shoulders around Ollie. "There is nothing you could tell us that would make us kick you out of our home. You're our son, Bobby."

"I was *his* son, too." His voice hitched, and his eyes filled with tears. Tegan already knew Bobby's story, and it pissed her off. Yes, she was new at being a mother, but she loved her sons unconditionally. If one of them turned out to be gay, she'd love him just the same. She went to her brother and took Ollie out of the carrier, but not before she pressed a kiss to Bobby's temple and whispered that she loved him.

"Come sit down." Rosie took Bobby's hand and led him to the table.

"Do you want us to leave?" Crow asked.

Bobby shook his head without looking up. He took a couple of deep breaths. "My parents didn't only argue because they found out I'm gay. They thought I was crazy. It started when I was little. I would see things they couldn't. They chalked it up to a child's overactive imagination. When I got older, my father wanted to have me committed. Said I was an embarrassment. But my mother..." Bobby shook his head. "She fought for me. Defended me."

Marcus scooted his chair closer and wrapped his arm around Bobby's shoulder. "What are you saying, Son?"

Bobby looked up at Jackson. "I didn't pass out because of Solomon's wings. It was the gunfire. My mom didn't die in a home invasion. My father did it. He got drunk one night and tried to kill me, but mom put herself between us."

"Oh, Bobby." Rosie reached out and grabbed his hand. "What happened then?"

"My father was so shocked he dropped the gun and ran. I called 911, and a couple of my father's buddies showed up. See, they all knew my father thought I was crazy, so they took the gun and made up the story about it being a random attack so he wouldn't lose his badge or go to jail."

"What about him dying in a wreck? Was that part true?" Marcus asked.

"Yeah. He didn't make it a mile from the house when he wrapped his car around a light pole. The story his friends told was he was coming home at the time the crime happened, but if anyone had been paying attention, they would have noticed the direction he was driving – away from our house."

"Those sons of bitches," Marcus seethed. "They gave him a hero's burial."

Tegan couldn't believe it. "Why, though? If he died in a car crash?"

"The story they told was that he was chasing a wanted drug dealer even though he was off duty." Marcus leaned away from Bobby but grabbed his free hand. "Son, what made them think you were crazy? What exactly is it you can see?"

"Monsters. At least that's what I thought when I was younger. I guess what I really see are parahumans."

Jax arched a brow. "Parahumans?"

"Yes. Humans who are also paranormal, like Tegan's lion, and all you guys'... what are you exactly?" he asked Jax. "You look like an eagle and lion mixed."

"That's right; we're Gryphons. So you've been able to see shifters your whole life?"

"Shifters? Right because you can change into what I see beneath the surface. That makes so much sense. Like I said, my parents thought it was my imagination, but we'd be in public, and I'd see a wolf staring back at me from inside a human's face. I was just a little kid, and it freaked me out. I tried to hide my fear if my father was with us, but some monsters are freakin' scary. Sorry. Not that you all are monsters, but…"

Jax frowned. "Max voiced you. You should have forgotten everything you saw, and you didn't mention the hole in my shirt."

"So that's what he was doing. It didn't work on me. It felt like a cool breeze."

"But Crow said your name earlier, and you came back inside."

"*You* try ignoring that sexy, Daddy voice," he muttered. Jackson barked out a laugh, and Bobby groaned. "Crap, I said that out loud, didn't I? Someone kill me now." Bobby thunked his head on the table.

A phone pinged, disrupting their conversation, and Bobby sat up but kept his eyes down. Tegan glanced at Crow to see how he was taking Bobby's comment, and the male looked to be zero point five seconds away from exploding. Like Bobby's mother, Tegan was ready to jump between her brother and Crow, until he pointed at Bobby. "I want the name of every one of those cops."

Judge wiggled his phone. "That'll need to be put on the back burner. Bishop is patching Max through on an encrypted line."

A few seconds later, the phone rang. Judge connected the call, and after a funky clicking sound, a deep voice came over the line. "Sultan?"

"We're here, Max. What's going on?"

"Victor never showed."

"Bucco did say he was in the middle of the Pacific."

"Yeah, but here's the thing. That Gargoyle hacker, Henry? He was able to trace the call, and Victor wasn't on a boat. He was at your cabin."

"The fuck? I didn't get an alert on my phone. Again. Why is he there? They've already trashed the place, plus they sent a Coopersville cop to my house in New Troy, so they know where I live."

"Maybe that's it. You aren't in Troy, so it could be they're looking for you to come back to the cabin. Henry and Bishop assured me Bucco's hacker couldn't access the cameras at his place in Boston, but for Victor to not obey his don's orders? He had to know something was up even though Bucco said exactly what I told him to. Either they already had a plan in place before we showed up, or their hacker found a way to see everything that went down. If that's the case—"

"We're fucked."

"If you'll send me the address of your place, I'll have a few Hounds head that way."

"There isn't an address, but I'll text you the coordinates. Max, I think we need to move. If Bucco's hacker bypassed Bishop, we could be sitting ducks."

"How many Hounds are there?"

"Six, including me, but we don't have any weapons other than our claws and fangs. I'm not waiting around for Victor to show up with an army. Zeus, what a clusterfuck."

"Stay safe, Brother. I would say keep me posted, but I think the less communication we have between us the better."

"I agree. Good luck, and I'll see you when I see you." Jax growled, squeezing the phone. Before he crushed it, he dropped it on the table. "We need to find a new hideout."

"I have a place." Crow pulled Theo from the sling and handed him to Marcus. "It's about an eight-hour drive from here, which isn't ideal, but it's off anyone's radar. Unless Bucco has eyes on us already, we should be able to slip away no problem."

"Or," Gunner said, startling Tegan. "We could fly. My jet is in a private hangar a couple hours down the road. Think the babies will be okay on a plane?"

"They should be. Crow, are you sure you want all of us invading your home?"

"I'm sure." Crow explained where his home was in Virginia and told Gunner the closest airport was at Norfolk. Tegan hated the reason they were going, but she'd never flown before. Never been out of New York, so she was a little excited to see somewhere new. Jax had already told Tegan he had money, and if Crow had a second home on the water, it seemed mercenary work paid well.

Rosie tugged Bobby's short ponytail. "Let's get the kitchen cleaned up before we leave." Bobby opened his mouth, then closed it. Her brother seemed shell-shocked, and Tegan could understand. He had just bared his soul to not only his family but a group of strangers. So much shit was happening all at once, but the good thing was nobody addressed the fact that he could see shifters. He had called Ollie a cub. Was that because Tegan was a lion, or because he'd seen the baby's true nature? She would ask him later. For now, she needed to get their things. Tegan didn't wait on Jax to give the order. She rushed from the room and ran up the stairs.

Two and a half hours later, their vehicles were hidden in the private hangar where Gunner's plane had been, and everyone was loaded on the jet. Gunner offered for Marcus to act as co-pilot, and her father jumped at the chance. He was in his element, talking bikes and cars with the Hounds on the ride to the airport.

The boys each had their own chair with their car seats strapped in. Tegan didn't know how the air pressure would affect them, but for now, they were content not being held. Gunner had shown them the small bedroom at the back of the jet, offering for Tegan to use it when she needed privacy to nurse her sons. Rosie sat next to Tegan on one of the leather sofas as Jax sat on her other side, lacing their fingers together and settling their hands on his hard thigh.

Hawk had opted for the flight attendant's seat outside the cockpit, and Ryan and Rooster sat in open captain's chairs when Gunner announced they were clear to take off. Ryan was closest to the babies, and he reached out a hand to touch Theo. Theo grabbed Ryan's thumb and cooed, bringing a smile to the

Hound's face. It was nice to see these badass males soften in the presence of her children.

Rosie took in the furnishings of the expensive plane. "This is kind of exciting. I feel special flying on a private jet instead of in a crowded coach seat."

Bobby sauntered up to them. "My name is Roberto, and I'll be your flight attendant. If you would, direct your attention to the emergency exits." He swung his arm out with a flourish, and it smacked Crow in the stomach. When he saw who he'd smacked, Bobby let out an "eep" and sat down on the sofa opposite Tegan.

Crow sank down next to him, keeping a respectable distance between their legs. "You could have a future as a flight attendant if the bakery thing doesn't work out."

"Shut up." Bobby reached back and tugged at the elastic band in his hair, allowing it to fall around his face. He removed his earbuds from his pocket, buckled his seat belt, and clasped his hands on his lap. Tegan narrowed her eyes at Crow, but he was focused on Bobby.

"I wasn't teasing. Okay, maybe a little, but you have the perfect personality to be a flight attendant." When Bobby kept his gaze down, Crow tried again. "Tell me about some of the items you'd sell in a bakery. I love to cook, but my baking needs some work." Bobby loved talking about food, so he launched into all things baking, and Crow listened intently.

Tegan relaxed when Jax squeezed her fingers. "*I love you, Wildcat.*"

She sucked in a breath and faced her mate. "*I love you, Jax. Thank you for rescuing not only Bobby but me and*

261

*the boys. We're all lucky to have you in our lives."*

*"I'm the lucky one."* Jax kissed her temple, taking a deep inhale of her hair.

The engine roared, and Tegan tensed, looking at her sons. Soon the jet was speeding down the runway, and seconds later they were lifting off the ground. Bobby let out a "whoop," and Tegan grinned at her brother. Theo fussed a little, but Ryan was there to soothe him. Ollie was fast asleep, his num num hanging halfway out of his little mouth.

Instead of getting lost in his music as usual, Bobby pretty much commanded the entire conversation during the two-hour flight, but no one seemed to mind. Tegan and Rosie were used to it. Once they landed, it took an hour and a half to secure rental cars and drive across the bay. They passed an industrial area, then wound their way toward the southwest corner of the city. Crow's home was nestled in the middle of two wooded acres with a view of the bay. As he explained, the land around his had been expensive and thriving with lavish homes, but after the apocalypse, families had moved inland, and he'd bought up the surrounding properties so he had plenty of privacy. When things began turning around, he had many offers for those now empty houses, but he refused to sell.

"Are you just going to let them sit empty?" Bobby asked.

"Until I find somewhere better as a retreat, then yes."

"Do you have a boat?"

"I do. It's currently in storage, but depending on

how long we're holed up here, I may get it out."

Tegan had never been on a boat, and she doubted she would get to see Crow's since she had the babies. Speaking of her sons, both had slept the entirety of the flight. Neither one fussed when they landed nor when they were transferred to one of the rentals. Tegan worried they would want to eat on the drive, but both had been content until the vehicle stopped in Crow's driveway. As she and Jax got the brothers out, Bobby was still peppering Crow with questions.

"What's your name? And do they call you Crow because the color of your hair?"

"Sage Crowley, and I guess that might be why. I always figured Sutton just shortened my last name."

"Who's Sutton?"

Marcus grabbed Bobby's shoulder. "Bobby, let the man breathe, Son." Tegan and Rosie shared a look. If Marcus only knew how many questions Bobby had asked that he hadn't heard, he'd have come out of the cockpit and chastised him earlier. Crow seemed to take it in stride, and Tegan was grateful, especially after hearing the truth surrounding Bobby's parents' deaths. If Robert Senior were still alive, she would go all momma lion on the human.

# CHAPTER TWENTY-FOUR

## Sultan

JAX PLACED HIS HAND on Bobby's nape. "Want to help get the boys situated?" He didn't wait for a response. He handed Ollie to the teen so Jax could help Judge get their things out of the SUV. As patient as Crow had been, Jax could sense the male was ready for a break. He led them inside his gorgeous home and directed Jax and Tegan to the master suite at the back of the first floor.

"There are three bedrooms upstairs plus a bonus room with a large sofa, but I figure the other Hounds and I will rotate keeping watch."

Marcus stopped in the middle of the hallway. "You think we're still at risk?"

"Until Victor is sitting next to Phil with his hands tied behind his back? Absolutely. They didn't get to be one of the biggest mob families in the US by dumb luck."

Jax had to agree. They couldn't let their guard down. There was something they were missing. They had some of the best hackers on their side, yet it seemed Bucco's computer person was just as capable.

Bobby followed them to the bedroom, talking nonsense to Ollie. Theo was fussing, and it was past time for the babies to eat. When Rosie took Ollie from the teen, Bobby muttered he was going to check out the kitchen, sliding past Crow without looking at him. Judge came in carrying the pack 'n play, and Jax pointed to the other side of the room. He wanted the boys far away from the door.

Crow tapped the doorframe. "I'm going to run to the grocery store. I'll be back within an hour. While I'm gone, make yourselves at home."

Rosie placed Ollie on the bed. "Where's the diaper bag?"

"Here." Marcus set the bag next to the baby, and Rosie fished around for a clean diaper. "I'm going to keep an eye on Bobby while you feed the boys." He kissed Rosie on the temple, then left the room.

"Rosie, since we have a minute alone, how did Bucco's men get Bobby?"

"Bobby was working on a new recipe and didn't have one of the ingredients, so he ran to the store. The cops found our car on the side of the road and called us. We asked him last night what happened. He said a large SUV pushed his car off the road, and when he came to a stop, someone pointed a gun at him, demanding he open the door. He was so scared, but he didn't know what else to do other than comply. As soon as the door was open, they injected him with something. When he woke up, he was at the house in Boston, only he didn't know where he was at the time." Rosie took a deep breath. "He said they didn't hurt him, just locked him in a bedroom and left him there.

Whoever took him left his phone in the car."

"Did the cops follow up with you at all?"

"Yeah, they came to the house and asked a few questions, but with him being a foster kid, they mentioned he could have run away. I explained why he'd gone to the store, and that none of his things were missing from his room."

"Did you call them when Bucco got in touch with you?"

Rosie shook her head. "No. He said if we went to the police, he'd kill Bobby before Tegan could make the swap. That man is evil, so we figured he wasn't lying. What are we going to tell the police when we let them know Bobby's home safely?"

"That's a good question. With Max sitting on Phil and the men he had guarding his house, we'll have to wait and see if they take Bucco out or turn him over to the Feds."

"They'd kill him?" Rosie fastened Ollie's onesie and picked him up, cradling him to her chest.

Tegan was sitting in a cozy recliner feeding Theo. "Rosie, these men don't just peddle drugs. They kidnap people and sell them. They force women to have babies, then they sell those babies off. Why do you think he wanted Ollie and Theo? It wasn't to start a family of his own."

"Let me rephrase that." Rosie patted Ollie's padded bottom. "I hope they kill him. I hope they kill all of them."

Well, all right then. Jax wrapped an arm around the woman's shoulder and kissed her hair. "On that note, I'm going to talk to the Hounds. Get a feel for the layout of the grounds." Jax gave both his boys some love, kissed Tegan on the lips, and left the females to take care of his sons, shutting the door behind him. Marcus was listening to Bobby go on about how the kitchen was a baker's dream, so Jax left them to it and continued outside. One of the vehicles was missing from the driveway. Jax chuckled to himself. Crow hadn't wasted time leaving.

Rooster was leaning against the deck railing, smoking a cigarette. His usual blond mohawk was braided instead, making him look more like a Viking than a punk rocker. He grinned at Jax. "That kid's sweet, but he can talk the ears off an elephant."

"You're not wrong on either account."

Rooster took a deep pull off his smoke and held it in several seconds before exhaling through his nose. Leaning his arms on the railing, he flipped the ashes onto the rose bush below. "How, though? How is he this sweetheart who's still sane after what he went through?"

"Strength, Brother. And lots of love from Rosie and Marcus."

"I bet once this shit with Bucco is over, Crow's gonna track down those cops. I might help him."

"If I didn't have a brand-new mate and two new baby boys, I'd help you." Jax tapped the railing twice. "I'm going to take a look around. Stretch my legs a bit."

Rooster pointed the cigarette toward the trees. "Gunner went north, Judge went south, and Hawk went west."

Jax thanked the male and jogged down the steps.

He first circled the house before heading into the woods to the east. There were well-marked paths, so he followed one until he reached the dock. Jax didn't know anything about boating, but the platform appeared to be in good shape. He walked to the end of it and eyed the different types of crafts on the water. It was summertime, and that meant families were enjoying the sunshine. He thought about his own little family, imagining the cubs as they got older. Would they be into sports? Or would they be bookworms? Would one of them prefer to help his uncle Bobby in the kitchen? Jax remembered his own childhood. How his dad taught him how to throw a football, then a baseball. They had both enjoyed the major league teams in Arizona, going to see games together while his mom stayed home reading. There weren't many other Gryphon families around, and Jax had learned at a young age that he couldn't divulge his secret. His dad allowed him to have friends over, knowing he could voice the kids if they somehow found out Jax wasn't human, but he'd never had to. Jax and Tegan would have to teach Ollie and Theo the importance of keeping their lions hidden.

That was a worry for another day. Using his Eagle's vision, Jax studied every boat on the water and the people aboard. When he was confident none of them posed a threat, he retreated up the dock and headed into the woods. He walked each path, studying where they led, then headed back toward the house. When he reached the deck, Rooster was no longer there.

Judge stood where the other male had. "Rooster's

down by the water. There are too many trails leading to the house. We need to remain vigilant."

"I agree. I can't help but think we're missing something. Yes, Bucco's hacker is good, but so are Bishop and Henry." A car pulled in the driveway. It was Crow returning from the store. When he got out, Jax asked, "Need some help?"

"Please." Crow popped the hatch, and Jax walked his way. Crow handed over the keys. "I'm going to let you take those in while I go check the woods."

"Crow —"

"Jax, I know we don't have fated mates, but…" Crow leaned his head back, looking at the sky. "Something about him calls to my beast, but he's just a kid who's been through hell. Until Bobby's eighteen, I need to stay away from him. I probably need to stay away longer. Let him live a little."

"Everyone can see he's taken with you. He won't be seventeen forever, and maybe you're what he needs to help heal those parts that have been broken." Jax left the male to his thoughts and threaded the handles of the reusable bags over one arm before grabbing the rest of the bags in his other hand. He waved his foot under the bumper where the sensor was that closed the lid.

Bobby was no longer in the kitchen. Reaching out with his senses, Jax found the teen in the next room. Faint music and humming meant Bobby had in his earbuds. He set the bags down, then went to retrieve the kid. When he got to the door, Bobby was tapping his fingers against his thighs while staring out the window. Jax didn't want to startle him, so he eased his way into Bobby's peripheral vision. When he noticed

Jax, Bobby pulled one earbud out.

"Want to help me put the groceries away?"

"Sure. I'm interested to see what he bought." Bobby smiled, but it didn't reach his eyes. Jax looked out the window in time to see Crow disappear into the woods.

Jax emptied the bags, and Bobby put the items either in the refrigerator or the cabinets. He could see the appeal of the space to someone like Bobby who spent a lot of time cooking. The teen kept some of the groceries out, and as soon as everything was unpacked, he put his earbuds in, then began pulling out pots, a cutting board, and a knife. Jax went to the window and looked out while the young man worked. Before long, a delicious blend of garlic and tomatoes permeated the room.

Jax felt his mate before he saw her. Tegan walked into his waiting arms and hugged him tightly with her head on his chest, sighing. They stood silently, letting Bobby's humming fill the silence. Jax wanted to take Tegan to the master bedroom for some alone time, but there were too many people in the house, including her parents, so instead, he let himself be content holding her. With Victor unaccounted for, Jax worried they were in another calm-before-the-storm holding pattern.

Hawk came through the back door, sniffing the air. Bobby looked over his shoulder, and after seeing who it was, went back to cooking.

When Rosie and Marcus joined them, Marcus rubbed his hands together. "Bobby's lasagna is some of the best you'll ever eat."

"It smells heavenly." Hawk started toward the

stove, but a low growl stopped him. He rolled his eyes and moved to the other side of the kitchen, sitting at the table.

Crow appeared from somewhere in the house and walked over to stand beside Bobby. The teen smiled at the Hound and pulled his earbuds out, putting them in his pocket. Crow asked, "Anything I can do to help?"

"You want to put the salad together?"

Crow nodded, but leaned over Bobby's shoulder and took a big whiff of the sauce. At least that's the way it probably appeared to Bobby and his parents. To Jax, the male was inhaling his mate's scent. Once the salad was prepared, Crow pulled down plates and bowls for everyone.

While they waited for the lasagna to cook, Marcus and Hawk chatted about motorcycles. Tegan joined Rosie on the deck for some fresh air, and Jax excused himself. His phone needed charging, so he made his way to the bedroom. The boys were down for a nap, but he enjoyed watching them sleep. He couldn't help but wonder if he and Tegan would have a child together, or if Coral had been his one shot at his own offspring, breaking the Lynch family tradition of having a male child. If so, he would accept his god's decision and be satisfied with Ollie and Theo. Theo whimpered, and Jax moved to comfort the infant, but Ollie reached his little arm out, touching his brother. Theo let out a little sigh and settled. Putting his phone on silent so it didn't wake the brothers, he plugged it in, then returned to the kitchen.

Marcus hadn't been lying about Bobby's lasagna. Italian was Jackson's favorite food, and this would

271

rival anything he'd eaten at a restaurant.

They were almost finished eating when Judge's phone rang. He wiped his mouth on a napkin before pulling the phone out of his back pocket. "It's Bishop." Instead of putting it on speaker, Ryan answered, keeping the device to his ear. For that, Jax was grateful. The shifters in the room would easily hear the conversation, while the humans would have to wait in case it was something they shouldn't know.

When Ryan pressed the accept button, the phone made a clicking noise, indicating the call was secure. "Judge here."

*"I tried calling Sultan, but he didn't answer. Victor Bucco is on the move. He boarded a private jet, but we haven't been able to find out where he's headed."*

"Maybe he got tired of waiting at the cabin and is headed to Boston. Max was sending some Hounds to check it out."

*"I just spoke with him. He said there was no one there when they arrived. He wanted me to pass along that information to keep calls to a minimum."*

"Victor shouldn't be able to find us where we are. We didn't tell anyone where we were going, and Gunner filed a false flight plan."

*"That doesn't mean you should let your guard down. We'll keep at it on our end, and if we find out any usable intel, I'll call back."*

"Ten-four."

Marcus leaned forward so he could see Ryan around Rosie. "Is everything okay?"

"Yes. That was our computer specialist keeping us updated. Victor boarded a plane earlier, but like I told

Bishop, no one knows where we are."

Jackson prayed that was the truth. They couldn't underestimate the mafia or their reach.

Rosie insisted on doing the dishes, and Hawk offered to help. Marcus snuck off to the master bedroom, and Tegan grinned at his retreating back. Jax wasn't the only one who enjoyed watching the cubs sleep. The other Hounds returned outside to stand guard. Everyone except Crow. He asked Bobby if he wanted to ride to the marina to check on the boat. The teen blushed furiously but said yes. That left Jax and Tegan to fend for themselves.

He held out his hand. "Let's take a walk." Tegan readily agreed, placing her hand in his. Once outside, he led her along the path to the dock. When they reached the end, they removed their shoes and let their feet dangle in the water. Tegan leaned her head against Jackson's shoulder.

"Do you think we'll get out of this unscathed?"

Jax squeezed his mate's hip, pulling her closer. He didn't want to lie to her. She'd be able to smell deceit anyway. "I don't know. If it were anyone other than the mafia, I'd say absolutely, but we've never gone up against someone like Bucco's organization. But I've been thinking. I have plenty of money. I could get Bishop to create new identities for us and your family. We can disappear if we have to."

Tegan ran her foot across the water. "Where would we go?"

"Anywhere you want. We could get lost in a big city. Settle in a little town in the Midwest. Hide out in a Tuscan village. Set up yurts close to the Serengeti."

"Yurts?" Tegan snorted, then slapped a hand over her mouth, giggling.

Jackson chuckled, rubbing his thumb over her bare thigh at the hem of her shorts. "You have something against yurts?"

"Can you honestly see Bobby living in the wild? How would he cook his amazing cakes and pies?"

"That kid would find a way. He's strong, just like his big sister."

"He's handling being kidnapped well."

Jax had been waiting for the adrenaline crash. "I think your parents have something to do with that. And Crow."

"What's up with him? I know you said he's honorable, but..."

"He and I talked earlier. Crow feels a connection with Bobby. Like he might be his mate, but he's worried about how young Bobby is. Said he should leave him alone and let the boy live a little before pursuing him. However, I think Crow is exactly what Bobby needs to get past all the shit he's endured with his parents and now being abducted. Crow won't take advantage of him, but he can be there for him. I promise you, Wildcat, I wouldn't suggest it if I didn't know Sage well. He's the best male I know to help Bobby achieve his dreams, whether that's going to college, attending culinary school, or opening a bakery."

Tegan raised her head, reached up, and turned Jax's face towards hers. "I trust you." Then she pressed their lips together. Jax angled his head, opened his mouth, and searched for her tongue with his. When it turned from heated to scorching, he pulled his mate onto his lap so she was straddling his legs. Tegan pressed her core against his erection. They might have gone too far if Judge hadn't called out for them to get a room.

"I think that's an excellent idea." Tegan palmed the back of his head, pressing their foreheads together. "I need you. I need to feel you inside me, but I don't want to have sex where my parents can hear us."

Jackson groaned, pressing his hard dick against his mate. "I have an idea."

# CHAPTER TWENTY-FIVE

## Tegan

AT FIRST, TEGAN BALKED at Jackson's idea. Letting her parents watch the cubs while she was close by was one thing. Leaving the house was another. Still, she wanted to be alone with her mate. Sure, they could disappear upstairs for some "quiet" time, but Tegan frowned at having sex with so many Hounds around. Shifter hearing and all that. Once Jax got his erection under control, they walked back to the house, and after feeding the cubs, Tegan asked her parents if they'd watch the babies long enough for Jax and her to go look for bathing suits. Her parents assured her the boys would be fine.

She and Jax didn't need swimwear merely because they might be going out on Crow's boat, but it was a good excuse to leave for a bit. Jax found what he thought was a secluded dead end. They laid the second-row seats down, then climbed in the back of the SUV. It wasn't the most romantic place to have sex, but Tegan wasn't complaining when he licked her to orgasm before driving his hard cock home. If they hadn't been so into each other, they might have heard the cop pull up behind them. It wasn't until he knocked on the glass with his flashlight. Tegan was afraid he was there to arrest her, but he scolded them for having public sex. Jax voiced the man, and once he was gone, Jax pushed back inside her and finished getting them off.

They cleaned up using a rogue pack of baby wipes they found on the floorboard, then Jax found a surf shop not too far away that stayed open late during the summer months. Tegan snagged the first one-piece she saw, itching to get back to her sons, and Jax grabbed several pairs of board shorts in multiple sizes. On the way to the checkout counter, Jax also picked out a bunch of beach towels and a few bottles of sunscreen in varying levels of SPF.

As they walked to the SUV, Jackson's phone pinged. He checked the message after stowing their packages in the back. "Shit." He tossed the phone to Tegan. "Get in." Once they were both seated, he pealed out of the parking lot. She read the message, and her eyes filled with tears.

Judge: *Forget the suits and get your asses back here. Theo is having a meltdown.*

"What kind of mother leaves their children to go off and fuck?"

"The kind who needs alone time with her mate, Wildcat. The cubs have been okay with their grandparents, otherwise you wouldn't have left them."

That didn't make her feel better. Ignoring her mate, Tegan stared out the side window, not focusing on the scenery. Instead, she got her anger under control as best she could. By the time Jax pulled in the driveway,

Tegan was ready to shift and claw someone's eyes out. Namely, her own. Fuck! She jumped out of the vehicle before Jax had it in park and raced into the house. The first thing she noticed was the lack of crying.

"Where is he?" she asked Rosie, who was playing on the floor with Ollie.

"He's okay, Tegan. He had gas, and once he pooped, he was fine. Bobby has him on the deck."

As soon as she was through the back door, she slowed her steps. Theo was on Bobby's legs, stretched out on his back. His arms were waving as Bobby sang to him.

When she realized the group, Tegan huffed. "Seriously? You're singing Cyanide Sweetness to my child?"

Bobby grinned over his shoulder at her. "At least it's a ballad."

Tegan sat next to her brother and ran a finger down Theo's soft cheek. "I heard you caused a ruckus?"

Bobby pretended to gag. "It was awful. How can babies poop that much? I just about tossed my lasagna."

Tegan narrowed her eyes. "*You* cleaned him up?"

"Oh, god no. If it had been me, I'd have put him in the shower and hosed him off. Rosie took care of it. She also gave Ollie a bath, so both my nephews are clean as a whistle." Bobby blew a raspberry on Theo's tummy. "Who's gross? You are, that's who."

Tegan was relieved Theo was okay, but she still felt guilty for leaving him. Bobby handed Theo over. "I'm going inside. I need to bake something."

"You okay?"

Bobby held out his hand and rocked it side to side. "Yes and no. But loud music and something smelling up the kitchen will help."

Tegan's eyes welled with tears. "I'm so sorry my shit came back on you."

"You know Rosie says everything happens for a reason. If your shit, as you call it, hadn't happened, I might never have discovered that I'm not actually nuts. Also," Bobby paused, looking around. "I'd probably never have met Sage. And since Bucco didn't hurt me, I'd go through it again for this outcome." He pressed a kiss to her cheek. When he got to the door, he said, "By the way, I have a bone to pick with you, woman."

Tegan scrunched her nose at his teasing tone. "Yeah, what's that, boy?"

"You showed Marcus and Rosie your lion. I want to see it."

"I'll show you if you make me something sweet."

"Deal."

Tegan held Theo to her chest and nuzzled his neck, inhaling his clean baby scent. A few minutes later, Jax sat down beside her, holding Ollie. "I'm sorry."

Tegan sighed. "No, I am. You didn't do anything wrong. You were trying to give me what I needed, and…" Tegan blew a strand of hair out of her eyes. "I'm so new at this, and I felt like I screwed it up again."

Jax turned Ollie so he was lying in Jax's right arm, and he placed his left hand on her nape beneath her hair. "Little Patrick is several months old now, but when he was just a few weeks old, Martina left him in

279

the car while she was putting up groceries. She then started a load of laundry, and it wasn't until she was putting one of Patrick's outfits in the washing machine that she remembered he was still in the car. The car was in the garage, and the weather was mild, so he wasn't in danger, but she still felt like the worst mother in the world. Shit happens, Sweetheart. All parents screw up at some point, but you didn't do anything wrong. The cubs were here with your family and five Hounds."

Even though the sun had gone down, movement in the trees caught Tegan's eye. Ryan was peeking at them around a tree, and she could feel his sadness even from a distance. Jax whispered, "He feels so bad about scaring us."

"I guess I'm not the only one new to this baby stuff."

"No, you're not. If we had been here, I'm sure I'd have freaked out too. I don't think there's anything worse than a child hurting and not being able to tell you why."

"Hey, Ryan?" The Hound poked his head around the tree with his eyebrows raised. "Can you please come here?" Ryan shoved his hands in his front pockets, and with shoulders hunched, made his way to them. "Can you please hold Theo for me? I want to go help Bobby in the kitchen."

"You're not mad at me?"

"For worrying about my son? Hardly. I'm grateful, is what I am." Tegan stood and passed Theo to his uncle. "Thank you."

The Hound's face brightened. "You're welcome."

Tegan pressed a kiss to Ollie, squeezed Jax's shoulder, then went inside. Bobby was bopping his head to whatever song he was listening to, so Tegan bypassed him to go pee. After doing her business, she stopped off in the living room where Marcus and Rosie were snuggled on the sofa, watching a baseball game. Rosie didn't care much about winter sports, but she enjoyed baseball. Tegan sat next to her mother and leaned against her shoulder.

"Will it ever get easier?"

"Nope. No matter how old your children are, you'll still worry about them. Want to protect them and take away their pain. Did I ever tell you why we only foster teens?"

"If you did, I don't remember."

Marcus turned the volume down on the TV as Rosie grabbed Tegan's hand between both of hers. "When Marcus and I first started fostering, we accepted kids of any age. At first, we were emergency parents, taking in the children who needed a place to stay a few days while the caseworkers searched for family members. We had teens, toddlers, tweens, and babies as young as a few days old. There was one such infant, and she was so tiny. Her mother died giving birth, but the baby was healthy. At first, she was fine, but all of a sudden, she wouldn't stop crying. It broke our heart because we didn't know what was wrong. We tried everything, even called the pediatrician. He said it was probably colic and told us several things to help reduce her pain. We changed her formula, rubbed her belly, rubbed her back. Kept the room dark. Played white noise. We gave her plenty of skin-on-skin time, but that seemed to hurt her worse. Nothing worked. We took her in to see him. He ran tests and assured us the colic would eventually run its course. Finally, he said to take her back home and just love her. We did. She would cry herself to sleep, but it would only last fifteen minutes at most, then it would start all over again. I've never been so strung out in my life." Rosie removed one of her hands to wipe her face. Marcus grabbed her hand when she lowered it.

"The caseworker came a few weeks later. The biological mother didn't have any family, but she found the biological father. He didn't want little Brianna, but his mother did. I'm ashamed to say I was relieved. Marcus and I were both drained. Never have I endured so much heartache as I did trying to help that baby, and I told Marcus I couldn't do it again. I couldn't take in someone that young, who couldn't tell me what was wrong. I know colic isn't rare, but I couldn't do it again. I told you all that to say when Theo started fussing, I didn't panic. I didn't think, 'oh no, not again.' I remembered everything we tried with Brianna, and even if nothing had worked, I knew he'd be okay because he has you for a mother."

"You're wrong. The first time I nursed Theo, I forgot to burp him. If Jax hadn't been there..." Tegan took a deep breath.

Rosie turned and gripped Tegan's hand tighter. "You listen to me. You gave birth to those boys by yourself. With no anesthesia. With no one telling you what to do, guiding you through the pain. You are the strongest person I know. You also have one of the biggest hearts I've ever seen. Of all the kids who've come through our door, I worry about you the least. Did you make the wrong choice in trusting John Cashel? Sure, but look what you got from meeting him – my beautiful grandsons."

"But if I had waited, maybe Jax would be their father."

"Jax *is* their father now. But if you had waited, you may have never met him. If you waited, Bobby might not have met Sage." When Tegan gasped, Rosie grinned. "I might not have shifter hearing, but I do pay attention."

Tegan studied Rosie's face. "And you're okay with that?"

"Why wouldn't I be? Bobby will be eighteen next month. Besides, all Marcus and I want is for our kids to be happy. You and Bobby endured so much heartache before coming into our home. Who better to watch over you both than a couple of supernatural beings who'd protect you with their lives?"

Crow entered the room from the hallway and stood between the sofa and the doorway to the kitchen. After glancing toward Bobby, he lowered his voice. "What she said. I'm sure you're worried about our age difference, but in all my forty-six years, I've never dated. Never pursued another. I always thought something in me was broken. Then I met Bobby, and for the first time, that part of me woke up. Until he's eighteen, I'll be his friend. Afterward, I'll court him properly. If he decides I'm not what he's looking for, I'll respect his wishes. But as for my beast and me, we know he's it for us." Crow approached them and placed a hand over his heart. "I vow to you now, if he chooses me, I will spend my life cherishing that young man."

Marcus stood and held out his hand to shake. "I'll hold you to that, Son." Crow inclined his head as he clasped Marcus's hand.

"Hey, Crow?" Bobby stood in the doorway, a mixing bowl cradled in his arm.

Crow tensed, taking a step back from Marcus, and turned toward the kitchen. "Yes?"

"Strawberry or cream cheese frosting?"

Crow relaxed, grinning. "Yes." Bobby returned the smile and pivoted on his toes. Crow ran a hand down his flat stomach. "I'm glad I have shifter metabolism. I have a feeling I'm going to need it."

Marcus patted his own belly. "That you are."

Jackson and Ryan brought the babies into the living room. Jax kissed Tegan's hair as he passed Theo to her. "We're going to relieve Gunner and Hawk. Save me a cupcake."

Tegan and her parents played with the boys until Bobby announced the cupcakes were ready. Hawk, Gunner, and Crow were sitting at the dining table where Bobby placed two platters in the middle, then poured tall glasses of milk that no one protested. Crow stood and retrieved dessert plates for everyone. Tegan wondered why the Hound had enough dinnerware to serve so many people if he'd never dated. Maybe he hosted parties or had lots of friends stay with him.

She took one of the seats with Ollie pressed to her chest and reached for one of the treats with strawberry icing. "Do you have a big family?"

"I do. Ours is like the Lazlos in that my parents

had four kids when they first mated. Once my brothers were out of the house, they started again, and I have three sisters close to my age. Three of my brothers and one of my sisters have mates, and they all have at least two kids each. My brothers were born in Puerto Rico where my dad is from. They moved to the States in the 1970s so my mom could be closer to her family in California where my sisters and I were born."

Gunner and Hawk then spoke about their families and where they were from as everyone enjoyed Bobby's scrumptious cupcakes. Her brother beamed when the Hounds praised his baking abilities. Tegan helped take the plates and glasses to the dishwasher while Bobby put the remaining cupcakes in containers to keep them fresh. She held out her free arm for her brother, and when he went to her, she hugged him tightly. The two of them had always been close, even if she didn't visit often.

Tegan kept her hand on his shoulder when he stepped out of the embrace. "Were you ever scared of me since you could see my Lion?"

"No. I learned a long time ago to judge others based on their actions, not what was hidden beneath the surface. And speaking of..." Bobby wiggled his eyebrows. "You promised."

"I did, didn't I? Okay, let's do this before the boys decide it's time to eat again. I'm going into the bedroom to shift. I'll be right back." Tegan tugged on his ponytail before heading out of the kitchen. It was still weird to be able to let her beast out freely. Once she was in her fur, Tegan padded down the hallway to where Bobby was waiting in the living room. She stopped several feet from him and sat.

"Oh, my god. You're beautiful, Tegan. You can understand me, right?" Tegan chuffed, and Bobby laughed. "Can I pet you, or is that weird?"

"If her Lion is anything like mine, she'd love that," Crow said.

Tegan dropped to her belly and placed her head on her paws, waiting. Bobby got down on his knees and scooted closer slowly. When his hand touched her fur, she closed her eyes and purred. Bobby chuckled as he sat next to her and stroked his hand along her back.

"This is so cool. My sister, the lion."

She was almost asleep when the air changed, and Bobby crab-crawled backward. Raising to four paws, Tegan turned and faced a much larger beast. One whose long fangs could rip her throat out if he so desired.

# CHAPTER TWENTY-SIX

## Sultan

GUNNER FOUND JACKSON NEAR the dock. "Your mate is getting ready to show Bobby her Lion. I thought you might want to join them."

"You sure? You've been out here a while."

"Yeah, Brother. I got a couple of delicious cupcakes in me. Go be with your family."

"Thank you." Jax clasped the Hound's shoulder, then took off toward the house. While Bobby was focused on Tegan, Jax slipped into the bedroom and stripped out of his clothes, then shifted to his Lion. He padded silently down the hallway, and when he stopped a few feet from Tegan, Bobby's eyes widened, and he scrambled away from her. Tegan stood and turned, her long tail swishing.

*"Hello, mate."*

*"Hello, yourself."* He shook out his massive mane and stalked toward his female. When he reached her, she butted her head against his, scenting him.

Bobby stood on shaky legs. "Uh, is that Jax?"

"It is," Ryan confirmed. "He won't hurt you if you want to go say hello." Ryan walked over and knelt by

Jax, clasping his head in both hands, and shaking it gently. "Who's the big bad lion?" he teased.

Jackson nudged his best friend in the chest, and Ryan fell on his ass, laughing. "Asshole." Jax chuffed and shook his mane again. Bobby finally got the courage to pet Jax, and when he came closer, Jax laid down next to Tegan. Crow held Ollie while keeping his eye on the young man. They trusted each other with those most precious to them.

After a while, Theo began fussing, and Tegan stood and left the room. When she returned, she was back in her skin. She'd pulled on shorts and his T-shirt, but her feet were bare.

*"Put Ollie down here with me."*

Tegan held her hands out for her youngest son, and when Crow handed him over, she placed the baby on Jax's outstretched paws. Jax lowered his massive head and inhaled. Ollie wiggled and cooed as Jax stared at the infant. Tegan disappeared to the bedroom with Theo, and her parents announced they were headed upstairs for the night. Bobby reclined on his stomach with his chin on one hand while the other traced circles on Ollie's chest. They stayed that way until Tegan returned for her youngest.

"Come on, Papa. It's time for bed." She lifted Ollie and smiled softly at Bobby who'd fallen asleep. "You'll get him upstairs?" she asked Crow who nodded. Jax stood and followed his mate down the hallway. Once inside the bedroom, she closed the door. He ambled over to the playpen and looked down at Theo who was already asleep. While Tegan fed Ollie, Jax reclined on the bed next to her in his fur. It felt natural to watch over his family in his shifted form, and Tegan pressed her bare foot into his side, rubbing back and forth. Jax chuffed, and his mate smiled. He looked forward to many more nights like this one.

The next morning while sitting around the table devouring piles of blueberry pancakes and no telling how many pounds of crispy bacon, they discussed whether it was safe to take the boat out. Tegan tensed, and Jax threaded their fingers together, lifting her hand to kiss it.

"It's up to you, Wildcat. We can stay here with the boys."

Judge leaned around Jax so Tegan could see him when he spoke. "Or you and Jax can go out with Crow and Bobby, while the rest of us stay here and watch the cubs. You don't have to stay out long or go far. That way if Theo decides to scare the crap out of me again, we can call you."

Tegan bit her bottom lip, her hands clasped in her lap. Jax reached over and squeezed her fists. He wouldn't try to sway her one way or the other, not after the scare she'd had the day before. Before she could decide, Bobby stood and wrapped his arms around Tegan's shoulders.

"The boat is huge. We could all go and take the cubs with us."

Crow chuckled. "It's not that big."

Bobby glared at the Hound. "It's a yacht."

Crow held up his thumb and pointer finger. "Yeah, but a small one."

Bobby released his hold on Tegan to cross his arms over his chest and raise his chin. "It. Is. A. Yacht."

Before they could argue further, Rosie interrupted. "That's a big fat no for me. I'll keep my feet on terra firma, thank you very much."

Bobby moved to hug his mother. "Sorry, Rosie. I forgot you don't like the water."

"I like water just fine when I can see the bottom. It's all the things beneath the surface that scare me. No matter who goes, I'll stay here and clean the kitchen."

Tegan blew out a breath. "I'll go, but I don't want to take the boys. Not sure I want to deal with two infants getting seasick." Tegan looked to Crow. "But only for a little while. Is that okay?"

"Whatever you want. We can sail about half an hour, then turn around and come back, dropping anchor close to the dock."

With that settled, the other Hounds opted to remain behind to guard the cubs, and for that Jax was grateful. Another thing he was thankful for was the underground storm shelter. The original owner of Crow's house had it built because he didn't want to evacuate during hurricanes. Even if Bucco's hacker somehow figured out where they were, the shelter wasn't included in the house plans.

Crow went to retrieve the yacht from the marina while Tegan fed the cubs. As they were nursing, Tegan promised them she wouldn't be gone long, and she was only a phone call away as though they could understand her. It was sweet.

While she was busy with the boys, Jax hooked a jet ski and trailer to the back of one of the SUVs and took it down to the dock. The water by the dock was too shallow for Crow to moor, so he dropped anchor about thirty yards out, and Rooster shuttled them to the boat on the jet ski. Instead of riding the waves, the Hound returned to the dock, and as promised, took up a position outside to guard the little ones.

Before weighing anchor, Crow gave them a tour of his craft. Bobby was correct; the boat was huge. At least by Jackson's estimation. He'd been on ferries and even a cruise ship once with Crystal for their five-year anniversary. His Gryphon had threatened to burst free and fly to land every time she insisted they swim in the miniature pools surrounded by drunk adults and unruly kids. This type of sailing, however, he could get behind. It was luxurious with three cabins, ample seating above deck and below, and a galley Bobby was raving about. There was plenty of room for some of his family to enjoy, thus the reason Crow said he'd bought a vessel so large.

Crow insisted Bobby coat himself in sunscreen before coming topside. Jackson helped Tegan with her back, and if he got a little handsy doing so? Sue him. She was his mate, and he loved touching her. When everyone was situated, Crow eased the large vessel out to open water. Jax and Tegan sat together on one of the padded benches and let the breeze wash over them. Bobby leaned over the railing close to where Crow piloted the yacht. Bobby waved to someone behind them, but Jax didn't turn to see who it was. Most people on the water were friendly, waving to one another.

A few seconds later, Jackson's phone vibrated. Frowning, he pulled it out of his back pocket and saw Judge was calling. Fuck, this couldn't be good.

"Judge?"

"Sultan! Lucy called, and they found the hacker. Victor is here."

Jax stood and looked back toward the dock, but they had rounded a bend, and he couldn't see it. "Here as in at the house?"

"No, but he's in Cape Charles and has been since yesterday. You need to get off the water."

"We'll head back now." Jackson disconnected. He didn't have to relay the conversation to Crow. The Hound was already turning the yacht around.

Jax pulled Tegan to her feet and directed her toward the stairs. "Bobby, get below deck with Tegan."

"What's going on?" The teen took a step toward Jax right as a bullet hit the side of the boat.

"Fuck! Bobby, get down!" Crow turned loose of the steering wheel and pushed Bobby down to the deck. Bobby belly crawled to where Jax was crouched, holding his hand out. Once the teen grabbed on, Jax covered his smaller body until he joined Tegan on the steps. His mate's eyes were wet.

"I'm going to end this."

Tegan wiped her face and took a deep breath. "I love you."

"And I love you, Wildcat."

Jax used his eagle vision to scan the surrounding crafts. Another shot hit the seat where he and Tegan had been sitting. The shooter had to be using a suppressor since there wasn't loud gunfire. That didn't bode well for the other boaters since they weren't aware of the danger around them. Jax caught sight of where the shooter was.

"Get my family back to safety."

Crow narrowed his eyes at Jax. "What are you going to do?"

"I'm going to kill that motherfucker." With that, he tossed the other Hound his phone, then eased his way to the sundeck on the bow, making sure there was no one around to see him shift into his Eagle. He dropped his board shorts, then launched himself into the air, flying in a low, straight line away from Victor so he could circle around behind. Keeping to the water's surface, Jax banked left, then rose higher above the craft. His element was air, and it was harder to manipulate in bird form than as a Gryphon. Harder but not impossible. When the other vessel was directly below, Jax sent a current of air into the water, forming a massive eddy in front of the boat. The pilot yelled, yanking the wheel hard to the right, but it was too late. The bow dipped forward, and the movement upended the three men aboard. Jax didn't know for sure what Victor looked like, but the third man aboard the boat resembled Bucco enough to make the connection. As the boat rocked violently, Victor and the shooter were tossed into the water, the rifle going over with them. The pilot held onto the wheel, but the impact proved to be too much, and the man slid to the deck with blood coating his forehead. The boat spun in the whirlpool until Jackson released his power over his element.

Jax didn't have much time, as other boaters were coming closer to either offer aid or try and figure out what the hell happened. Jax dove for the shooter first. Right before he reached the man, he enlarged his eagle's size and used the bulk to push the bastard

293

below the surface. Once submerged, Jax shifted to his skin and dragged the shooter farther into the water, his grip tight as the man struggled against his hold. It was no use. When Jax was certain the shooter was no longer breathing, he released the body and swam toward Victor. Jax broke the surface and inhaled before diving behind Victor and dragging him under to join the shooter. He had no doubt there would be someone waiting to take Victor's place as second to the don, but with Phil under Max's command, hopefully the Hounds could influence the mafia family's next movements.

Jax turned loose of Victor's body and headed away from the commotion, swimming underwater until he could no longer hold his breath. When he broke the surface, he turned toward the capsized boat, where several crafts had pulled close. Jax wasn't worried about the pilot. Nor was he concerned with the two bodies, which would eventually rise to the surface. It would be a mystery as to what caused the boat to lose control. If the driver happened to mention seeing a large eagle, well, Jax figured folks would chalk that up to his head wound.

He took another deep breath and once again dove beneath the surface and swam toward Crow's place. When he was far enough away from the mayhem, Jax swam with long, steady strokes atop the water. The yacht finally came into view. Standing along the railing were Crow and not surprisingly, Judge. Jax tread water, giving them a thumbs up. His friends high-fived one another, whooping. Crow called down to Tegan and Bobby, letting them know it was safe to come topside.

Tegan met Jax at the back of the yacht with a towel. He hauled himself up, sitting on the sundeck and pulled his mate onto his lap, not caring that he was naked. She gave him a kiss worthy of a hero, which Jax felt like in that moment.

"You okay?" he asked against her mouth.

Tegan leaned back. "Me? I'm not the one who went after an armed man. What happened?"

"Their boat had a little mishap. Somehow, a wind current caused a whirlpool in the water, and the boat capsized."

"Somehow, huh?" Tegan grinned. "I wish I could have seen that."

"Eh, I'm sure with all the phones around, someone got it on video."

"But that means they could have gotten you on video too."

"If they did, all they'll see is a massive bird diving into the water."

Judge climbed down to join them with a phone to his ear. "Yeah, Lucy. He's fine. You might want to set up alerts about a boating accident. Yeah, I'll tell him." Judge disconnected and pocketed his phone. "Henry was able to locate Bucco's hacker, and Lucy and Tamian went after her."

"Her?"

"Yep. And get this; Bucco had her sister to ensure the hacker did as he instructed. Constance, the hacker, was a cousin of one of Bucco's capos. She graduated MIT top of her class, so when Bucco needed a computer specialist, the capo offered his cousin up thinking that would score points with the Don. Lucy contacted Maximus to find out where the sister was being held. Constance is willing to testify against Bucco once she and her sister are reunited."

"That's good news, but how the hell did they find us here?"

Judge glanced at where Bobby was standing with Crow. "Bucco put a tracker in Bobby's earbuds while he was passed out. They always knew where he was."

"Then why go to my cabin? We were never there."

"That's been bugging me too. We should search it well to make sure they didn't leave something that could incriminate you."

Jax set Tegan on the deck so he could stand. He helped her to her feet. "We'll worry about that later."

Tegan pressed her palm to Jax's beard. "Is it really over?"

"We still have to prove to the police you didn't kill John, but Bishop assured me he had plenty of evidence to the contrary. If that doesn't work, I'll voice every fucking cop in New York State."

"Then let's go home. Crow's house is nice, but I'm ready to be back in New Troy."

Jackson was ready too. Once they dealt with the cops and cleaned out Tegan's rental, Jackson was going to take a long vacation with his mate and sons.

# CHAPTER TWENTY-SEVEN

## Tegan

WHEN THEY ARRIVED BACK at Crow's house, Jackson had to recount how he got rid of Victor and the shooter to her parents and the other Hounds. Tegan wanted to leave immediately, but that didn't happen. Gunner needed time to get the jet ready, and Bobby insisted on cooking an elaborate meal for supper, which led to Crow taking her brother to the grocery store. While they were gone, Marcus and Rosie talked things over and decided to hang around Virginia for a few days, giving Bobby more time with Crow. Rosie begged Tegan to stay as well, but Tegan explained about the Coopersville police wanting to question her and the need to clean out her rental.

"I'll come help with the rental. Or at least watch the boys while you and Jackson work." Rosie winked. Tegan had a feeling her parents were either going to ask Tegan to move closer to Mining Falls, or they were going to make their way to New Troy to be near the cubs. Tegan preferred the second option because she had a lot of mates to meet, and the boys needed to be around other shifter kids. That would also allow Bobby to be near Crow for what the Hound called their courting period.

They were able to leave the next morning after another delicious breakfast cooked by her sweet brother. Before sitting down to eat, Tegan asked about the boys.

"Did you see Ollie's inner lion, or were you making an assumption based on my nature?"

"Oh, that boy is all lion. So is Theo."

The meal was filled with love and laughter and delicious food, and Tegan was going to miss being with her family. Afterward, she thanked Crow and Rooster for everything, the latter who remained at Crow's house because he wanted to go out on the yacht. Judge traveled home with them, and by the time they arrived in New York, Bishop had sent all the evidence to the police, and they dropped the charges against Tegan. It hadn't hurt when Bucco called and confessed that one of his men was guilty of killing John. The four horsemen were staying in Boston until they were positive Bucco's organization was dissolved or at least handled by the FBI.

When it came to her rental, Jax hired a cleaning crew to come in after he and Tegan went through the house to pack up everything except the furniture to donate. Before they did that, he hired a different type of cleaners to remove the evidence of John's murder in the form of blood in the kitchen. The only thing Tegan wanted to keep was her family's photo album. While Rosie watched the boys, Tegan and Jax went through the house and loaded everything into boxes to donate or trash bags to toss. Tegan was dumping John's things from the spare bedroom closet into a bag when Jax let out a curse. Tegan stood and went to her old bedroom, finding her mate on a stepladder with the top half of his body hidden in the opening to the attic crawl space.

"Jax?"

Jackson retreated down the ladder with a duffel in his hand. "I found the money." He dropped the bag beside her feet, climbed back up, retreated, dropped another bag. He did this twice more before pulling the board over the opening. Jax dusted off his hands before setting them to his hips, staring at the bags. "We can put it in a trust for the cubs."

Tegan stepped back, not wanting to be anywhere near the reason her ex had been killed with a knife to his throat. "No. I don't want it." Tegan pointed to the bags. "That's the reason I was kidnapped. The reason..." She shook her head, not finishing the thought. It was the reason Bucco had been willing to sell her and her cubs.

Jackson crossed the room and drew Tegan into his arms, pressing his cheek to hers. "We can donate it. I'll hand it over to Sutton, and he can use it for Providence House."

"Sounds good."

Getting in and out quickly was easier said than done when her neighbors, people she'd never spoken to, came by to get the gossip. Brittany was the only one Tegan didn't mind speaking with. Tegan hadn't been kidding when she said there was nothing in the house that she wanted other than her family's photos, so packing the rest of it took a while. Once the local women's shelter came and picked up what wasn't going in the trash, Tegan fed the boys, then they took Rosie out to lunch.

Their little family of four got into a routine of sorts, especially when the boys began sleeping for longer periods of time. That meant Tegan got more sleep, but she also got more one-on-one time with her mate. For the first month, Jackson didn't take on any mercenary jobs, choosing to stay home with them for the most part. He still had his position as sergeant-at-arms with the MC, and some days he said he needed "Hound time" with Judge to go work on his cabin. Ryan had gone alone the first time to search for anything Victor might have left, and he found the security cameras had been tampered with, but now that Bucco's hacker no longer worked for him, they were easily dismantled and useless.

On those few occasions Jax rode out with his MC or visited his friend, Tegan took the boys to see Rhi and Daisy. Tegan also met the twins, Major and Marshall. She'd heard about their antics, but seeing them in person was truly something special. Natalia brought them around at least once a week, and meeting the other mates was just as wonderful as Tegan had hoped. She now had a group of females she called friends, and her life was full to bursting.

Bishop called, asking for the cubs' names for their birth certificates. She'd chosen middle names – Jackson for Ollie and King for Theo. Tegan wanted to ask Jackson to adopt the cubs so they had his last name, but the time hadn't been right. Bishop had even sent the paperwork to make that happen through Natalia so Jackson didn't see the documents.

When Jackson said he had a surprise for her and told her to get the boys ready for a road trip, Tegan thought she could surprise her mate as well and hid the documents in the bottom of their diaper bag. As they got closer to their destination, Tegan assumed they were going to the cabin, but Jax drove past the turnoff.

"Where are we going?"

Her mate gave her a soft smile. "You'll see." It didn't take much longer for Tegan to figure it out. The once rutted path leading away from the road was now a smoothly grated, gravel driveway with a gate at the entrance. Tegan knew in her heart her mate had done more than fix the ruts, but when what once was her shack came into view, Tegan couldn't help but sob. The dilapidated structure was gone, and in its place sat a cute little house. The scrub had been removed, making way for a small yard. Jax parked and shut the motor off, but Tegan couldn't move.

"I can't believe you did this."

Jax reached out, wiping her tears with his thumbs. "Come on, Wildcat. Let me show you around." He got out and removed Theo from the backseat, leaving Tegan to get Ollie. When they had the boys in hand, Jax led Tegan up the steps to a porch that spanned the front of the house. He opened the door and let her go inside first. It was different from Jackson's cabin. There was no loft, and there were two doors instead of one. She placed Ollie on the floor in front of the stone fireplace and looked around. One of the doors opened to the bathroom, and the other led to a small bedroom with a double bed. There was a portable crib in the

301

corner.

"It's not finished, but I couldn't wait any longer to show you. I found out who owns the property, and I bought it as well as the surrounding ten acres. We still need to dig a well so we have running water. The cubs can sleep in the bedroom with us for now, and when they get older, we'll get a pullout sofa for the living room. The most important thing I want to show you is outside."

Tegan lifted Ollie off the floor and followed Jackson. When he headed for the creek, she never would have guessed in a million years the surprise he had in store. Her parents, Bobby, Crow, and Judge were waiting on them. Marcus took Theo from Jackson, while Rosie commandeered Ollie. Once the babies were secure, Jackson laced his fingers through Tegan's and led her closer to the water.

"When you told me about spreading your family's ashes, it broke my heart. With Rhiannon's help, we came up with this." Jax moved aside so Tegan could see a garden with four headstones surrounded by all types of flowers in bloom. If he hadn't been holding onto her, Tegan would have fallen to her knees. Jax held on tightly as he led her closer. "I hope this is okay."

"Okay? It's perfect. Oh, Jax. Thank you." Tegan's voice broke as the tears flowed down her cheeks. The markers had their names, birth dates, and death dates, but also on each one was an engraving special to their respective person. About a week after they arrived back in New Troy, Jackson had asked a hundred and one questions about her family. Now she knew why.

302

Tegan knelt beside her mother's headstone and ran her fingers over the etched tulip.

"Would you like some privacy?" Marcus asked.

"No." Tegan held out her hand and motioned everyone closer. "When I came to live with you, I couldn't talk about my family for fear of letting it slip what we were. I think that made it so I couldn't grieve properly. If you don't mind, I'd like to now share with you who they were."

Tegan spoke of her parents. Of her brothers, Thomas and Terrance. She shared about the wonderful parents Oliver and Thea had been. How her brothers had been as close as twins. She admitted how she sometimes wished she'd been in the car that fateful day. "Now I know why I wasn't. I was left alive to be Jackson's mate. Ollie and Theo's momma. Bobby's sister, and your daughter. I know that wherever they are, they're not worried about me because I had the both of you to step in and love me like your own." Tegan stood and held out her hand to Jackson. "Loving someone else's children, that's a gift, and I couldn't ask for a better papa for my boys. When Bishop fills out the birth certificates, I want the boys to have your last name. Would you be willing to adopt them and be their papa officially?"

Jackson ducked his head, and for a few seconds, Tegan was afraid he was trying to figure out how to let her down gently. Until he raised his head. Never had his smile been so wide or his eyes shiny.

"Nothing would make me happier. I'd be honored to be their papa."

"Then let me introduce you all to our sons, Oliver

Jackson Lynch, and Theodore King Lynch." Tegan wiped Jax's cheeks before turning to her family. "The next ones, we'll name after you."

Bobby gave a fist pump. "Yes! Little Roberto, my nephew."

Tegan turned to her mate. "I guess I should have asked you first if you want more kids."

Jax wrapped his arm around Tegan and pressed a kiss to her temple. "For as long as the Lynch Gryphons have been in existence, there has been only one offspring, and those were male. I would love nothing more than to carry on that tradition with you. What would make me even happier is if we break that tradition and have as many babies as you want."

Tegan grinned. "Let's shoot for one and see how that goes. But maybe let's wait a few years."

"Deal."

Bobby bounced up to Tegan. "But you will name him Robert, right?"

"Bobby," Crow said, his voice low. Her brother shivered, and everyone laughed at the teen.

Tegan turned and wrapped her arms around her mate's neck. Looking up, she said, "Thank you. Not only for this special place, but for loving me and our boys. When I lost my family, I thought my life was over. Then Rosie and Marcus helped heal some of the cracks in my heart, but you? You have made me whole again."

Jax pressed his forehead to hers. "You did the same for me. After Coral, I thought my shot at being a father had passed. You and our sons are the light that surpassed the cloudiest of days. But there is one thing I must ask of you."

"What's that?"

Jackson went down on one knee and held out his hand. Bobby placed a box in it, and Jackson lifted the lid showing off a band of diamonds. "The boys aren't the only ones who should bear my last name. I know we're mates, but I'd love nothing more than if you'd be my Wildcat forever."

*Now* Tegan was whole.

# The End

# A Note from the Author

I'm not going to lie; this book kicked my ass, but my human writing partner, Kerstin, is my sounding board and kept me from tossing it in the trash. So thank you, my dear friend, for all the chats and positive words and suggestions. This book wouldn't have made it to *The End* without you.

The first time I contemplated Sultan's story, I knew his mate would be different. And I knew exactly how their book would begin, so that's how I wrote it. I got a third of the way in and realized I was closer to the end than where I needed to be, so I had to rewrite the beginning. Thirty thousand words I had to put aside and hopefully be able to use later in the book. Another thing that threw a wrench in my monkey was the timeline. This story takes place during the end of *The Ripley Effect*, and that meant some of the characters couldn't be in two places at once. Therefore, I introduced quite a few Hounds and brought in some Gargoyles. In the end, I love how it turned out. I hope you did as well.

I've had the cover photo forever. As soon as I saw it in RLStalkers (Randy Sewell's photo group), I knew Alfie was my Sultan. I also have the photo for the next book which will feature Ace, and as of now, it will be the last featured book. My editor, Candy, hates that I don't put epilogues in this series, so I'm planning another book after Ace's that will be a "what are they doing now" book. Speaking of Candy, she is instrumental in keeping me on track, and my books are so much better with her help.

Nikki, my BFF, my sister from another mister, is my daily cheerleader. The one who knows me best. The one I go to when I need a pick-me-up, and she never fails.

Katie, thanks for the daily memes and laughs. I treasure our chats.

As always, I have to give a shoutout to the man. He's my rock, and I love him dearly.

# ABOUT THE AUTHOR

Multi-genre author Faith Gibson began writing in high school, and through the years, penned many stories and poems. Since she was a child, her dreams (and sometimes nightmares) were vivid constructs, making her shake her head and ask, "where the hell did that come from?" Many of these nighttime escapades have led to a line, a chapter, or even a complete story.

"Love is love, and there's not enough love in the world." This belief she holds strongly, and it's the prevailing theme in her works, all of which come with a happy ending.

Faith believes her purpose in life is to entertain the masses, even if it's one person at a time. Aspirations of becoming a rock 'n' roll drummer didn't come to fruition, but she's fulfilling a different dream, and that's bringing stories to life one book at a time.

Faith lives just outside of Nashville, Tennessee, with the love of her life and her American Staffordshire pup, Luna, the writing partner. When she's not hard at work writing her next adventure, Faith can often be found reading, cooking up something in the kitchen, listening to live music, or off on an adventure of her own.